# THE SLOW ROLL

SIMON LENDRUM

# THE SLOW ROLL

upstart press

A catalogue record for this book is available from the National Library of New Zealand

ISBN 978-1-990003-57-8

An Upstart Press Book
Published in 2022 by Upstart Press Ltd
26 Greenpark Road, Penrose
Auckland 1061, New Zealand



Cover design by Nick Turzynski, redinc. Book Design
Interior design by Nick Turzynski, redinc. Book Design
Cover photo © Ekachai Sathittaweechai | Dreamstime.com
Printed by Everbest Printing Co. Ltd, China

To Claire, Jack and Chloe.
Thank you for not giggling when I said
I was going upstairs to write a book.

# ABOUT THE AUTHOR

Simon Lendrum grew up in Newcastle-upon-Tyne in the North of England, gradually moving south after leaving school. He went to Cambridge first, then progressed to London. In 2004, he took a bigger leap and moved to Auckland, the place he now calls home. Simon has had a successful career in advertising and is currently CEO of the Commercial Communications Council.

# CHAPTER ONE

The man sitting across the table has O'Malley's attention.

It's not the man's size that has O'Malley rapt, though he is impressive in all dimensions, his stomach pushing for space against the constraints of the booth's table, and his width dominating a seat intended for two. Nor is it his voice, which is deep yet soft, encouraging O'Malley to lean in to hear his words. It is Mr Tupuola's eyes. As he speaks, his large brown irises are the hooks, pulling O'Malley in. They are full of deference and humility, focusing downwards towards the table's surface, avoiding direct eye contact. This is a man accustomed to social hierarchies, to calling lesser men 'boss', and to the iniquities of the world he struggles through. O'Malley's a sucker for the type, and he knows he'll end up helping him, but he still puts up a fight. It will serve as evidence for the defence at a later date, when O'Malley is telling himself 'I told you so'.

'You can't hire me. I don't know what you've been told, but I'm not a private detective.' Firm, yet factual.

'But you've helped others — Grant gave me your name, said you're the man,' counters Mr Tupuola, applying a dose of flattery.

'That's different: I helped Grant out as a friend. A favour, that's all.' And seeing Mr Tupuola drawing breath to argue this point, continues: 'You need a professional. Someone who does it every day. I'm not that.'

O'Malley's reluctance to get involved isn't lost on Mr Tupuola. But those eyes aren't done yet. They moisten, a hint of despair creeping through.

'Please, Mr O'Malley. My daughter has disappeared, and the police aren't interested. I asked around, and my friends say I need to speak to you. I will find the money, if that's what you're worried about. I just want my Sefina back.'

'Two things. First, it's just O'Malley — no "mister". Everyone just calls me O'Malley. Second, it's not about money. As I said, I am not a professional. I have helped a few people out over the years, but this,' he says, spreading his arms wide to take in their surroundings, 'this is what I do.'

The booth the men are occupying sits in an over-priced burger joint, which itself sits within the bowels of the city's only casino. Every walkway is populated with slot machines, but the domain O'Malley is indicating is the poker room. It is where you can find O'Malley most evenings, and where Grant sent Mr Tupuola to ask for him tonight.

'I am sorry for interrupting your card game, Mr — Sorry, O'Malley,' Mr Tupuola says, correcting himself in line with O'Malley's preference for informality. But maybe it also reveals a diminishing respect for this man who cares more for gambling than for a missing girl. 'I have got the wrong end of the stick. I won't keep you any longer.'

Sometimes the best poker players are the ones who've never held a playing card. As Mr Tupuola makes to move from the booth, his despondency clear, O'Malley finds himself raising a hand in protest.

'Wait,' he says, halting the big man's exit. 'I can't promise anything, but I can ask around, and see what I can find out. You'll need to tell me more about your daughter first, though.'

Mr Tupuola shifts his weight back to face O'Malley, a small movement that only emphasises how little he'd actually moved before O'Malley folded to his bluff. Some poker player I am, O'Malley thinks.

As O'Malley reflects on his poor negotiation skills, a waitress approaches the table, offering them both a drink. O'Malley orders a beer, whatever's on tap. His new client opts for water. It doesn't take O'Malley long to get the skinny on Sefina. It's a familiar tale.

The Tupuolas were once a happy family of Samoan descent, surviving in the south of the city, attending church on Sunday morning. Loto and Natia worked four jobs between them to provide a steady life for their children, of which there were three, with Sefina the baby of the family. Life was as good as it could be, with enough money coming in to get by, and no signs of the darker influences that sometimes come when geography puts you side-by-side with those you wouldn't choose as your neighbours.

But the world had other ideas for the Tupuolas, as it seems to do too often to God-fearing people with good hearts. Sefina's older sister was killed in a car crash, when she put her faith in the unlicensed teenage boy behind the wheel. The driver survived, but Talia didn't even make it to the hospital. Things spiralled from there.

'When we lost our daughter, Natia was so strong, and I was weak.' Loto Tupuola tells it slowly, uncomfortable opening up to a stranger about matters that he has perhaps never spoken of with such clarity.

'I drank, and I lost one of my jobs when I failed the alcohol test on-site, and then I drank some more. I was angry, and sad, and … I left Natia to carry the load, and look after the kids, and I think holding all of that inside her, it's what made her sick …' His words trail off. It's O'Malley's turn to stare at the table, trying to dilute the shame and grief that Loto is sharing. There's no let-up, though, and O'Malley guesses what's coming even before Loto says it.

'Natia died eighteen months after the crash,' the grief-stricken man continues. 'She ignored the signs until she couldn't, and by then it was too late.'

O'Malley's beer is looking pretty good at this point, but when he takes a drink it tastes sour, as if the grief that has enveloped their table has already settled at the bottom of his glass. He pushes the glass to one side and tries to comfort the broken man in front of him.

'I'm sorry for your losses, Loto,' he says. It is all he can think of to say.

'Thank you, Mr O'Malley, but you understand now why I need you to find Sefina.' A statement rather than a question.

'What about your son?' O'Malley asks. Loto's face darkens, and O'Malley thinks he sees a flash of anger in those eyes that have done so much of the talking this evening.

'Paremoremo,' he states simply. A destination O'Malley is all too familiar with.

'How long?' O'Malley asks without judgment.

'He's been there eight months. Maybe another three years, if he keeps out of trouble,' Loto says. Great. Another thing for Loto to blame himself for. O'Malley doesn't probe. He can follow it up later if it becomes relevant, but pressing Mr Tupuola for details about his son's incarceration for now feels like unnecessary punishment. There are times when even the largest of men are no match for the weight on their shoulders.

'So now it's you and Sefina. And what — she's just taken off, no warning?'

'Nothing. It isn't like her. She's gone. Her bag's gone, and a few clothes, I think. But I need her back, O'Malley. She's all I've got.'

O'Malley thinks it's strange, and maybe there's something Loto is leaving out. An argument, perhaps, or words spoken that can't be taken back. But he pushes Loto and gets nothing more. The big Samoan seems sincere, and O'Malley's been looking for a project anyway. Chasing a teenage girl around town isn't quite what he had in mind, but you play the cards you're dealt. He pushes Loto for more details, somewhere to start.

'You've asked her friends, their parents?' Most kids who run don't go far. Mostly, they leave a trail of breadcrumbs so their parents can find them. But Loto has searched and drawn a blank.

Doesn't say it, but he's here with O'Malley as a last resort.

Loto gives O'Malley some names. Friends of Sefina, places she likes to hang out, but nothing that gives O'Malley a strong starting point. He isn't confident that Sefina's friends will be any more forthcoming to a stranger than to a worried father. Still, he's worked with less, and he takes the recent photograph of Sefina that Loto has brought with him, shaking his hand in confirmation that he will do what he can.

'I'll see what I can do, Loto. I can't promise I'll find her, but I'll do my best. If that's not good enough, I'll put you in touch with a cop who *will* listen.'

'I hope it doesn't come to that, O'Malley,' Loto replies, all business now he's got O'Malley on board. 'From what I've been told, you'll get the job done. Please find my daughter, O'Malley.'

Apparently, they've talked enough. Loto Tupuola thanks O'Malley for his time, and squeezes himself out of the booth, shuffling down the corridor, leaving his problem firmly in O'Malley's lap.

O'Malley's never been one to rush into a problem. He needs time to think about the challenge of finding Sefina, and he figures he may as well play some cards as he does. He returns to the poker room, taking a seat in a small-stakes cash game. He isn't looking for big action, but wants to feel the comfort of chips riffling in his hand as he contemplates where to start on his latest fool's errand.

The table is full, and the faces are familiar. O'Malley returns nods of greeting around the table, and settles back to work out a plan, wondering where a real detective would start. He plays poker for a living. The detective work is a hobby. It's one that he picked up accidentally and keeps returning to because he's a sucker for a sob story. Proven, once again, by his inability to say no to Mr Tupuola. Now he's got to work out how to find Sefina. Harder still, persuade her to come home. He's thinking about this, how he's going to build rapport with a stubborn teenage runaway, when he's drawn into the table conversation that co-exists with the game that's being played.

'Hey, O'Malley, how'd you finish up last night?' Johnny asks. Johnny's one of the regular low-limit players who's here for the company as much as the cards. He's a pretty average player, but he's good-natured, polite to the dealers and waiting staff, and avoids conflict with other players. O'Malley likes him, likes all the old fellas who come to play cards because there's no one at home and the five-dollar special is better than anything they'll make for themselves.

'Not bad, Johnny,' O'Malley says. 'Up a grand or so when I left.'

He throws some chips into the pot as he speaks, backing his pair of tens with a decent raise, which pushes most people out of the pot. Two players call the bet, and the dealer, Frank, turns over the flop, ten-five-three, with two hearts.

Both players check to O'Malley — they want to stay in the hand, but they don't want to bet. There's no point getting clever in low-limit, and though O'Malley has three tens, which is the best possible hand right now, another heart could give someone a flush, so he puts out a pot-sized bet to defend his hand. Everyone folds. O'Malley scoops the chips in, knowing he could have played it differently and made more, but he's got a case to think about, and he's not here to break the old-timers.

Johnny isn't finished talking about last night, though, because what he really wants to do is tell O'Malley how he got unlucky.

'I couldn't catch a break. Had aces cracked by five-eight, and top set got beaten by runner-runner straight,' he complains.

It's the gambler's lament, and O'Malley doesn't pay much attention to the details. At the poker table, bad beats are the equivalent of talking about the weather. Players remember the intricate detail of the hands they were unlucky to lose, but conveniently forget the times they got lucky and won. Sometimes there's someone there to keep everyone honest. Tonight, Sunny is that man.

'You're not mentioning that you misplayed both those hands, Johnny,' Sunny pipes up, from Seat Nine. 'You made the aces too cheap, and you tried to slow-play the set. No point blaming anyone else for either hand.'

Sunny's name is ironic. He's consistently dark in mood, and this can lead to storms when he drinks, which is often. He isn't drunk tonight, though, and his needling is good-natured. But he still won't let Johnny off the hook.

Johnny makes some weak attempt to reject Sunny's criticism, but really Johnny's just enjoying the chat, because the poker room is one of the only places he feels sufficiently comfortable to make conversation, and there's a captive audience. He lets it go, and the chat moves on to other familiar subjects. Who played a hand well, who played like a fish, whether to back the Celtics or the Nets, why the casino is so poorly run, and on it goes.

O'Malley drifts back into his own world for a while, checking in with his subconscious to see what progress it has made with the task he took on earlier in the evening. Not much, as it turns out. He figures he'll start the modern way, dedicating tomorrow to a search of social media.

Sefina may have disappeared from view, but if she's like every other teenage girl she'll still be online. The world could end, and she'll still be on Instagram checking out what Kylie's wearing for the apocalypse. That's where he'll start. He'll have the case cracked by the end of the day. Like a professional.

Approaching midnight, O'Malley makes his excuses, racks his chips, and leaves the table. He stops at another table where the real game — higher stakes, serious money — is in session. He says hello to a couple of the more heavy-duty players in the room. Big Tone and Chinese Steve (no creativity here, the names are strictly functional) are dominating the game, and when they see O'Malley they try to get him to join the action. There's a spare seat, and O'Malley's usually a definite.

'Not tonight, boys. I've got a few things to take care of.'

'Come on, O'Malley,' Big Tone implores, 'it's just getting started. Matt's in donation mode.'

'Nah, you'll all keep for another day.'

He's right. They'll all be there tomorrow night, and the night after that, because that's how it goes. O'Malley's no different — he can play twelve hours straight and feel short-changed, but tonight he's got Mr Tupuola in his head, and it's enough to make him walk away.

Chinese Steve gets up, steps away from the table, out of earshot.

'Hey, O'Malley, you still good for the game tomorrow?'

'Yeah, I'm good. Call me with the details,' O'Malley replies, patting Steve on the arm as he heads off.

Steve's got O'Malley an invite to a private game, where the stakes will be higher than the casino can offer, and O'Malley's definitely good for it. But their conversation is hushed, because it's better to keep those games on the down-low, because they're not strictly legal, and poker players are inscrutable at the table, but terrible gossips when they're not playing. Especially when they're not invited. O'Malley and Steve keep things between themselves, because if the game is profitable, they don't want it to come to an end because someone can't keep their mouth shut.

O'Malley makes his way out, criss-crossing his way through the banks of slots that are strategically positioned to impede a quick exit. If there's a fire, everyone's fucked. They'll discover bodies trapped in the maze of machines, hapless gamblers who found themselves disoriented, running around in circles. Some of them won't even have tried, staying fixed to their seats, chasing the jackpot that's only ever moments away. O'Malley's never seen the appeal of the slots and he navigates them on autopilot, thinking only of Sefina and Mr Tupuola, and the bad luck that's been thrown their way.

# CHAPTER TWO

O'Malley is a night dog. He prefers the rhythm of the city after dark. People who've finished their day jobs move more peacefully and with less inhibition. Predators and those with ill intent are easier to spot and, wherever possible, to avoid. He rarely sleeps before 4 am, often later. His body clock is set to this pattern, and he gets joy from the notion that he's winding down as others begin their slow trudge to office jobs, or to the many gigs that feed the daily commute. It's early now, just after midnight, and O'Malley heads off into the city streets, alert for any trouble that might come his way, but relaxed because the city he calls home isn't Vegas, or LA, but Auckland.

New Zealand doesn't come with a reputation for crime. But it's here, lurking beneath the surface, and O'Malley has found himself submerged in it too often to be carefree. He's unlikely to suffer random violence, though; his size alone is enough to send people elsewhere, looking for easier targets. He looks bigger than his six foot two, his wide shoulders an indication of the strength that lies beneath his t-shirt, and the definition in his brown forearms confirming it. He's learned how to use that strength, too, so it's probably for the best that his looks are enough to ward away any evil that is sharing the streets on this humid Auckland night.

The casino sits proudly in the centre of the city. It's a landmark now, many years after it first opened. The tower that dominates the city skyline is a permanent record of the exchange that took place between city councillors and those who wanted to bring organised gambling to this small corner of the South Pacific. Build us a monument, the council demanded, and you shall have your licence to print money. And so they did. The tower rises up some 300 hundred metres and is still to this day the only notable feature of what is, in truth, a very minimal skyline. It acts as a homing beacon, guiding people to the heart of the country's biggest city, and to the gambling den that sits beneath the tower.

O'Malley stands at the bottom of the tower now, navigating his way through the taxis that sit in wait, hoping for a decent fare to make their nightshift worthwhile. The streets that surround the casino are a little quieter now, but there are still plenty of people milling about looking for one last drink. O'Malley is heading for last orders, too, and walks down Federal Street, past barber shops and convenience stores, past the rear of the city courtrooms that by day condemn men — mostly men — to the prisoner vans that now sit empty and idle waiting for the next day's passengers. A hotel sits on the opposite side of the street, offering one last taunt to the unfortunates who are heading for a different sort of accommodation. O'Malley picks up his pace as if one of the vans might suddenly open and pull him inside; ghosts from his past telling his feet to get a move on.

He works his way through St Patrick's Square, criss-crosses down Wolfe, over Fanshawe, and down to the Viaduct Harbour, where the restaurants are now closed or closing, but the bars are still clinging on to their final customers, both parties pretending that this is a twenty-four-hour city, which is definitely not the case unless you're in the casino or McDonald's. It's a sleepy part of the world, and the population is too small to sustain around-the-clock entertainment and wouldn't have the inclination even if it were available. But for night owls like O'Malley, there's always somewhere to go, and his destination tonight is particularly welcoming.

Nestled between two large, sterile establishments catering for tourists and post-work office crowds, The Brandling is an altogether darker establishment, less inviting from the street outside. Inside, the lighting is warm, giving the place a womb-like cosy feel that is timeless. It's been this way for as long as O'Malley has been a customer, and while the neighbouring bars require constant reinvention, the formula for success that The Brandling follows is actually very simple. Good staff, good lighting, and good music at the right volume makes your drink taste better and your spirits lift.

The bartender stands imperious behind the long wooden bar that stretches the length of the room. She is as striking as when O'Malley first laid eyes on her, her long, dark hair matched by her sleeveless black blouse and black jeans. She wears no discernible make-up, but still her eyes shine bright, holding a hint of amusement, as if sharing some private joke with the customers who cluster around the bar.

There are still a couple dozen people enjoying themselves in The Brandling, and O'Malley threads his way through to the bar, narrowly avoiding the wild, gesticulating arms of a twenty-something girl who dressed for a night of glamour, but is now nearing her bedtime. She spills her drink but takes it well, and O'Malley keeps on moving towards the bar to avoid getting pulled into her vortex. She'd be too much for him to handle at this time of night.

'Well hello, O'Malley,' the bartender says softly. 'Not upsetting my customers, are you?'

'Hey, baby,' he replies. 'How's your night been?'

'Pretty slow, tonight. I was hoping you'd come by,' she says, stretching her long, ink-covered arm towards him and placing a glass down on the bar. She throws some ice in the glass and pours him a double Zacapa rum. Claire has been gently improving his palate in the year since they met. Civilising him. House-training.

'Have a drink with me. If it stays like this I should be able to finish up early, and if you're entertaining me I might let you take me home.' He accepts the challenge. In fits and bursts when she's not at the other end of the bar serving drinks, he tells her about his visitor earlier that evening, and the task he's taken on.

O'Malley passes muster, and scores the invitation back to Claire's apartment, which is a twenty-minute walk from the bar. They live apart, but part of the deal is that O'Malley does the cooking in both kitchens. He makes Claire a simple pasta, combining spaghetti with cherry tomatoes, basil, capers and a little anchovy, and opens two bottles of a local IPA while she showers. As he plates the spaghetti, Claire comes back into the kitchen, wearing some irresistible pyjama shorts and a cropped t-shirt, her damp hair leaving small traces of moisture on the thin cotton that clings to her upper body. O'Malley pushes aside an altogether different kind of hunger, and places dinner on the countertop that separates the kitchen and lounge. Claire leans back onto a bar stool and takes a long drink from her beer bottle.

'Oh, that's good,' she says. 'Well done, O'Malley.' Using his last name, like everyone does.

'I'm glad you approve. I hope the food is up to scratch.'

'Your worst efforts are better than my best attempts,' she says, twirling the pasta around her fork and taking a bite. 'And yes, it's good.' Still with her mouth full, a smile in her eyes.

As she eats, O'Malley is happy to sit in silence, appreciating the simplicity of her beauty, and how fortunate he is to have times like these, just sitting down and watching her eat. His life hasn't always been so simple, and it is moments like this that remind him of his past. He still carries demons with him, picked up in childhood and never fully shaken. His appreciation of what he has to be grateful for is significant. More so, perhaps, than if he'd had an easy life, with no darkness against which to appreciate the light. He mulls this as he watches Claire lay down her fork and turn her attentions from the food to the man in front of her. O'Malley's no philosopher, but she's one hell of a psychologist — midway through a doctorate — and can read his tells better than anyone he's encountered at the poker table.

She senses he's in an introspective mood, approaching melancholy. She opts for distraction, focusing him on the challenge of finding Sefina.

'I don't want to teach you how to suck eggs, but you need to look for the boy,' she says.

'What boy?' O'Malley says, startled from reflection to confusion.

'When a fifteen-year-old girl goes off-reservation, nine times out of ten there will be a boy — or, more creepily, a man — at the heart of it. Your case doesn't sound like someone hiding out at a girlfriend's house. The father would have chased that down already. I think you're looking for a boyfriend who's slightly left-field. If he was in her inner circle, they'd already be busted, and your client would have given you two names, not one. Look for the boy, and you'll find your girl.'

Who needs a pretend detective when you've got a wise woman to hand? O'Malley loves how she humours him with words like 'client' and 'case'. He's taken on many lost causes in recent years, but makes no pretence that he's qualified to consider himself a private eye. But once he takes on a task, he pursues the truth doggedly. In Claire's view this is reason alone to give what he does legitimacy, licensed or not. She doesn't always like where O'Malley's searches take him, but she respects his need to help others, and shows that respect in the words she uses when she talks to him about his efforts. The psychologist in her also has a very clear explanation for why he does what he does, but she leaves that unsaid.

O'Malley thinks about what she's suggesting.

'OK, I get what you're saying. I'd got as far as boy.' He's the sleuth, after all. 'And what you're saying about him coming from a different circle makes sense. But it could be simpler than that. I suspect the father is a traditional, religious man — he'd probably react badly to any hint of boyfriends — so she might have been hiding a relationship even if it's within their community.'

'Maybe. But her friends wouldn't risk their own parents' wrath to protect her. More likely, they just don't know where she's gone. Besides, with your charms you'll soon have them spilling what they know, and my bet is that they're as worried as her father.'

'Hmmm.' O'Malley's not so keen to apply his charm to a bunch of teenage girls. If Claire's theory is right, there's little point anyway. If she's right, it's going to be even harder to find the girl.

'It wouldn't be satisfying if anyone could do it,' Claire points out, standing up to clear her plate as she speaks. 'Sleep on it and see where your day takes you tomorrow. Right now, I need you to clear your mind of teenage girls and start focusing on the woman in front of you.'

O'Malley needs no encouragement to put the Tupuolas out of his mind, as Claire takes his hand and leads him to the sofa. She curls herself against him and turns the screen on. They are halfway through season two of *The Wire*. Second time around. They've both watched the whole thing in previous lives, but it's even better on second viewing, and it's the one show they agree is *their thing*.

Another reason O'Malley thinks he's different from real private eyes. Despite his tough, gambler/detective exterior, he loves the escapism of a good TV show. Unlike the paperback heroes he discovered when he began to read in earnest, O'Malley doesn't like jazz, has no faithful dog to walk on the beach, and his relationship with alcohol is loyal and uncomplicated. Like most everybody in the real world, he likes to turn on the TV and escape into someone else's world.

In truth, their progress with McNulty and Bunk has been slow. They've been on the same episode for the past couple of weeks. They get distracted. Claire's shorts have risen up as she curled into O'Malley, and he is finding far more satisfaction tracing his fingers over the smooth contours of her thigh than from the happenings in Baltimore. Soon they are messing around, and when he begins to softly kiss Claire's neck just below her earlobe, things get serious. Claire wordlessly puts the TV on pause and leads O'Malley towards the bedroom, poor old Idris Elba looking on with frozen jealousy from the living-room screen.

O'Malley gently extricates his arm from under Claire's neck, making every effort not to wake her.

'You're going home?' she mumbles, not even half-awake.

'Yes, baby. I'll call you,' he whispers as he slips into his jeans. He doesn't sleep over, nor does he let Claire sleep at his place. It's a rule he established at the outset of their relationship, and one that only a woman with Claire's empathy and understanding would accept.

He has his reasons. O'Malley suffers night terrors. When they occur, he'll scream and shout the house down, and on occasion wake to find bedside furniture strewn across the room, victim to the residual violence he carries within him. He's given up replacing lights to read by, and his bedroom is now a shrine to minimalism. The need to sleep alone is driven from a fear of harming someone else when the terrors strike. Shame plays a part, too, but mostly O'Malley just wants to avoid hurting Claire. There's another issue, too. He can't fall asleep in company. He tried, early in the relationship with Claire, and found himself staring at the ceiling, counting the hours, her presence more caffeinating than calming. If he's to get any sleep at all, O'Malley needs isolation.

Claire accepts the baggage that O'Malley carries with him because she knows its source, and she's patient enough to let him deal with it in his own time. But it's getting worse, not better, and the longer he leaves it, the harder it's going to be to fix. But she won't fight with him on this, not now, so she lets him go, spreading out across the bed to fill the void.

The last person O'Malley shared a room with suffered ample regret when they disturbed him in the night. It was a cack-handed attempt to assert dominance in a world that still prizes strength ahead of smarts. O'Malley was in jail, on remand, still hopeful that he'd soon be free, and he was sharing a cell, because they reckon the threat from other inmates isn't as high when there's still a hope of getting out. Nobody told Luke, a dumb kid left holding the bag in a robbery gone wrong. Someone gave him bad advice, told him act quickly when you arrive, find the biggest guy you can and take him down. You'll get left alone after that.

The biggest guy Luke could find was O'Malley, and he was sharing a cell with him. Luke, who was not the sharpest tool in the box, decided to make his move once they were locked up for the night. When no one was there to see it, which pretty much defeated the point, but he didn't realise that. What to say? Not the sharpest tool.

O'Malley woke to find a pillow covering his face and blows raining down on his body. Whatever advantage Luke thought he would gain through stealth was removed when he decided to cover O'Malley's head and attack his body, not the other way around.

O'Malley moved his head rapidly from side to side, which meant Luke had to focus on keeping the pillow in place and took his attention away from the primary task of breaking O'Malley's ribs. O'Malley didn't need much of an invitation to take control of the situation. He felt his way up Luke's body and looped an arm around the back of his head. Then it was just a matter of doing some very fast sit-ups, bringing his knees up to his arm which had Luke's head locked in place to receive the knee. Hard to tell when Luke began to regret his plan, but O'Malley didn't stop to ask. He ripped the pillow aside and threw Luke to the floor.

The cellmates' roles were reversed now. O'Malley was in control — both of the situation and his own actions. He had no interest in causing irreparable damage to the idiot beneath him, but prison etiquette dictated that provocation be met with greater force. If he pushed Luke off and tried to reason with him, Luke would be obliged to continue in his efforts. It would also signal that O'Malley was weak, attracting future trouble. So he struck him just enough to put him to sleep, taking care to go no further. Even then he felt guilty, because Luke was just misguided and stupid, and he wasn't going to last long when he finally made it to

Paremoremo or Rimutaka, where there'd be no one pulling their punches. O'Malley hoped Luke had the capacity to learn from his mistakes, but doubted it. Prison wouldn't help. For men like Luke, it was like smacking a dog for being noisy an hour after he's barked.

Luke knew better than to say anything the next morning when his injuries were apparent to all. But it got O'Malley a cell he could call his own, along with a fourteen-day loss of the privileges he'd had. It also left him with the mental scars that he carries to this day. When his own time in Paremoremo came, on the few occasions he found himself sharing a cell, he didn't sleep when the door was locked. He'd sneak naps through the day, but even then he slept like a dolphin, half his brain alert to potential threat. Luke, inept though he was, had succeeded in hurting the biggest man he could find. But in a way that no one else could appreciate.

The night terrors came later. It doesn't take Claire's clutch of degrees to connect them to the events that O'Malley experienced when he was a young man. But his insistence that he'll beat them on his own means that here he is, more than a decade later, sneaking out of his girlfriend's bed for the lonely walk home. He knows counselling *could* help, but he experienced his fair share of state-enforced talking before they let him back out into the world, and those are not fond memories. So, once again, he quietly lets himself out of Claire's apartment, and walks across town to his own sanctuary, enjoying the temporary tranquillity of a city that has no problems sleeping.

# CHAPTER THREE

It is approaching midday when he wakes. O'Malley had promised Mr Tupuola that he would try to find his daughter but he'd made no promises that he would keep to office hours. The blackout blinds in his bedroom are ruthlessly efficient, and he's had no unwanted visitors in his dreams, so now he's refreshed and ready for some detecting. With coffee brewing, he arranges himself for business, opening the lounge doors to let the breeze and sounds flow in from the small balcony that overlooks the marina below. He starts by clearing his phone messages — replying to a text from Claire that suggests he is handsome and has missed out on some morning exercise, and noting that Chinese Steve has sent an address for the poker game, as promised. Now he has no distractions, just a pen and a pad of blank paper, and an empty computer screen. He pours himself coffee and gets to work.

There wasn't much access to computers when O'Malley was growing up, but he's picked up some pretty good skills in later life. His formal qualifications can be written on a postage stamp, but he discovered a certain affinity for the internet upon his release from prison. He spent several months living with a crew who dedicated themselves to the world of online poker, and a couple of them had a sideline as explorers — and exploiters — of the dark side of the internet. They were good tour guides. O'Malley picked up the basics pretty quickly — finding back doors into websites, installing tracking software, breaking passwords. At the beginning, it was in pursuit of knowledge, rather than malfeasance. It soon took on a practical application, taking the legwork out of his budding detective endeavours.

One of O'Malley's first successful cases involved his friend's father, Grant. Grant had built a successful family building business, and had a kind heart that resulted in many waifs and strays coming and going through his household. In every box of apples there's one with a rotten core, and Grant's generosity to those in need was interpreted as weakness by a young man called Gabriel Kwon.

Gabriel had more reason than most to be thankful for Grant's pastoral inclinations. He'd been fending for himself in his adopted homeland ever since his mum and dad went back to South Korea to look after a sick parent. At sixteen, with Korean now a second language, Gabriel chose to stay behind, and soon realised that the art of self-sufficiency was hard to master and found himself homeless, and without income. Grant's son had recounted his friend's predicament at the dinner table, and Grant had a bed made up before he'd cleared the dishes. Like most small-business owners, Grant worked hard during the day, and most evenings were taken up with staying on top of paperwork. He'd sit in the kitchen at his laptop, making the numbers add up amid the chaos of a home that encouraged boisterous sociability. In this open environment, where trust was a given, Gabriel slowly observed Grant at his work, and before long he had the keys to Grant's kingdom, modest though it was.

Grant woke one morning to discover that his newest house guest had left without a goodbye, and later that day, when he checked his bank accounts, he discovered that his business was in jeopardy. The accounts were empty, with a large transfer having been made the previous evening. Several calls to his bank confirmed there was no mistake. The money was gone, and it had been sent legitimately. Every other scenario went through Grant's mind before he was willing to accept that he'd been robbed by someone he'd provided for. Once he reached this conclusion, he called O'Malley.

O'Malley owed this man a debt. When he was released back into society, he wasn't welcomed with open arms. Few people want to take a gamble on a convicted man. Grant saw the world differently. He saw O'Malley as a man who'd made a mistake, but one that shouldn't condemn him forever. He gave O'Malley a job labouring on his building sites and helped him get used to the world again. He was indebted to Grant for the job alone, but the guidance that accompanied the work could never be repaid. Answering Grant's call gave O'Malley the opportunity to at least make a contribution.

Grant went to O'Malley and not the police because, whatever harm Gabriel had done him, he couldn't bring himself to be the reason another person went to jail. He needed his money back, but O'Malley knew he wanted no further repercussions. Grant had learned of O'Malley's new skillset during one of their many evening sessions, when they had a beer and O'Malley took the older man's counsel. He'd warned O'Malley that his new associates would bring him trouble, but it was the sort of trouble he now needed to get his money back.

O'Malley set about finding Gabriel with low expectations. He had no track record to take comfort in, and the fate of Grant's livelihood lay heavily on his shoulders. He tried to follow the money, like they say in the movies, but realised quickly that his skills didn't reach that far. So he'd called in favours from those who had taught him, and they quickly concluded that following the boy was easier than following the money. Gabriel's crime was an unsophisticated one, and he hadn't thought too much about where he would go or what he would do once he'd taken the cash. His footprints were large. They pretty quickly tracked him down south to Wellington, and when O'Malley turned up at his side in a shabby bar in a shitty part of town, the wannabe thief looked more relieved than concerned. O'Malley towered over Gabriel's slight frame, and it took no more than implied threats to recover the majority of Grant's money.

O'Malley's threats were not idle, though — he took the crime personally, stealing from a man who would have given Gabriel everything he had if he'd been asked. But part of the deal with Grant was to recover the money and leave the boy unharmed. O'Malley had also made a pact with himself to avoid violence becoming anything more than one chapter in his life. He left Gabriel unharmed, but in no doubt that his previous home was now out of bounds, and he was on his own. Grant, for his part, was back in business, and in his mind forever in O'Malley's debt. Sending Loto Tupuola his way turned out to be a funny way to return the favour.

O'Malley doesn't think he'll need to open any back doors to find Sefina. If she's smart, she'll have stopped dropping breadcrumbs; she certainly won't be advertising her location. But unless she's deleted her life history, there's usually plenty to be found from a teenager's everyday use of the internet. Out of diligence, O'Malley has a brief hunt around Facebook, but he knows that this long ago became unfashionable for the smartphone generation. Instagram is his best hope, and he begins digging. He makes some progress before his phone rings, a Hendrix riff letting him know that it is Claire calling.

'Hey, how's your morning?' O'Malley asks, turning his attentions away from his work.

'I'm good. How are you doing? Have you made any progress?'

'Some. Do you want the exciting details?' Suggesting the opposite.

'Yep, all of them. Tell me how clever you've been,' she says, teasing. But, you know, any opportunity to show off. He tells her from the beginning.

'Right, well, no one has told her about privacy settings, so I'm off to a good start. I'm following on from my hunch yesterday and looking for the anomalies beyond her immediate circle of friends.'

'Umm-hmmm.' *Her* hunch. Claire lets him have that one.

'So I'm basically creating a big Venn diagram. Who she's following, who's following her, who they follow, and on like that. Then it's a process of elimination. Take the celebrities away — that's a big circle, by the way, and got quite distracting for a while — put the close friends to one side, map the smaller circles together, and see what's left. If I'm lucky, our boy will be there somewhere, and part of a different circle.'

'Must be some sheet of paper you've got in front of you,' she says, amusement in her voice.

'Yeah, well, the Venn diagram is figurative — it's all in a spreadsheet. Each column is a circle, and wherever there's duplication, I'm putting a line through it. It's riveting.'

'I bet it is. I'd come and watch you at work, but I've got a tutorial in half an hour.'

O'Malley finds his manners. 'I'm sorry, baby, tell me about your plans for the day.'

'Don't be silly. I called you, remember? I just wanted to hear your voice before I have to listen to undergrads tell me how the world works. I'm at uni until four, then at The Brandling from seven. Want to grab something to eat before I start tonight?'

'Definitely. Call me when you're ready. I may need a massage by then: I don't think this work is doing my back any favours.'

'Well, go see one of your other girlfriends for that. If there's anyone using their hands this evening, it's you, not me.' That statement is going to play havoc with O'Malley's concentration. Which is just what she wants.

'That will have to do, I suppose,' O'Malley says. 'Call me, OK?'

'OK, Mr Venn. Get to it. Love you.' She hangs up before O'Malley has a chance to choose a response.

The approach he has chosen is hard work.

Every thread he pulls leads to four more.

But the world he is stepping into is a relatively small one. Sefina's online connections are modest: eighty-nine real people, once he ignores the accounts that are written from foreign shores. He narrows this down by ignoring anyone who she follows but who doesn't follow back. Real friends reciprocate.

That leaves him with forty-six names, so he's got forty-six columns. Then he repeats the exercise for each name. Then he de-dupes — seeing where the overlaps are strong. This gives him a clearer picture of Sefina's social life. Once he gets this far, he does draw a picture in his little detective's notepad: a strong central circle of friends, with smaller satellites falling off from the centre.

After several hours, four coffees and a hastily made omelette, O'Malley's got four names that look like outliers — they lead to completely new groups that have no obvious correlation to the rest of the page. Now he's confident enough to switch from words to pictures. Looking at the posts of each of the four names gives him some context beyond the data.

The first account doesn't fit the profile Claire has built. The girl who goes by the name sinead_shoregirl appears older than Sefina. O'Malley *hopes* she is older, because he can't help noticing that she also has a very nice ass, which is the focus of many of the pictures posted. If she keeps this up for another few decades it will become a fine study in gravity. Her most recent post is from this morning, so she is certainly not hiding from the world as Sefina is. She isn't hiding very much at all.

It occurs to O'Malley that he and Claire have been presumptuous in assuming Sefina has orthodox love interests, and, God knows, Sinead has charms. But she is older than Sefina, and her obvious love of self makes her an unlikely runaway. For professionalism's sake, O'Malley examines the account a little longer before concluding that Sefina will not be found by pursuing Sinead any further. He moves on.

The next two accounts are similar dead-ends.

One belongs to a girl of Sefina's age, but not from the same group of friends that dominates Sefina's account. It doesn't take long to figure out their connection. They've both done some part-time weekend work at a local retail store — and O'Malley has the photo of them together in their work polo shirts to prove it. There isn't much to suggest a deep relationship beyond this, so he puts a line through the account.

The other dead-end is male, at least. But it is a clerical error on O'Malley's part. The account belongs to a television actor from the UK. Admittedly, it's a bit creepy that he followed back a teenage girl, but O'Malley doubts he'd go as far as getting on a plane to elope with her. He scratches a line through it.

One lead left before he'll have to hit the streets and go old-school detecting.

He opens the account with low expectations.

What are the chances that the last place he looks will contain the lead he is looking for?

Still twenty-five per cent if he sticks to maths rather than fate.

The account is in the name of jesse.browning11. It's everything O'Malley hates about social media — an artificial world of boats, bourbon and booty. Teenage boys living a life of excess and showing off about it to the world. The boy's feed is pretty much one long party, with recurring faces and shirtless torsos in different locations. There's a hint of wannabe gangster in the poses of the guys, borrowed no doubt from other lives they both mimic and aspire to. Girls are props in these tableaux, adding aesthetics and street cred to the scene, but revealing no personality. It appears that in this life every girl wears a bikini and is there as background to the male ego.

Jesse is, at first glance, a grade-A asshole. O'Malley finds it difficult to reconcile this world, which reeks of rich white boys flashing their parents' wealth, with the picture he's been given of Sefina, a church-going Samoan girl who has known only hardship. If it is Jesse to whom Sefina has turned to pull her from her wretched life, she'll just be trading one form of misery for another. But there is nothing in his first pass that suggests any connection. And yet they were connected on Instagram, and he conforms to

Claire's initial assessment: a guy outside Sefina's immediate circle, who might have some appeal to a messed-up teenage girl who is looking for a way up and out.

O'Malley gives the account another scan, and in among the bling and bravado that Jesse wants to project to the world are two photographs that on closer inspection feel a little different. Posted a couple of months ago, the images are selfies, taken by Jesse as he sits on a clifftop, the fading sun casting a beautiful hue on the blue skies behind him. In the first, he sits side-by-side with a girl in obligatory bikini, but she's facing away from the camera, her dark hair falling down over her shoulders, her head leaning towards Jesse's right shoulder. Her back is athletic, dark and glowing in the evening light. Promising.

The second photograph is of the same ilk; Jesse looking at the camera, and his companion now standing a couple of yards behind him, hands on hips and looking to the horizon. Her face is again concealed, but it is angled towards Jesse, and when O'Malley looks closely, there is enough of a profile for him to persuade himself that he's found his girl. O'Malley has to work hard to match this young woman to the picture of a prim girl in school uniform that Mr Tupuola presented. The girl a father wants her to be versus the woman who is growing her own sense of self, perhaps. But this is the same girl, O'Malley is sure. Jesse is his most likely lead.

He takes another look at the boy in the photographs. Late teens, tanned, dark-haired and handsome. Still a dick until proven innocent, but in these images he looks a little different. Maybe less cocksure, a touch more wistful — as if he's inadvertently let his guard down and lowered his façade without his boys around to play up to. Or maybe O'Malley is just giving him the benefit of the doubt, for Sefina's sake. Either way, now he's got a lead, so he starts to put some meat on the bones he's dug up.

With a little know-how, it's not very hard to pull the threads of identity from the online world. With a name, everything else pretty much falls into your lap if you've got the basic skills to get beyond a firewall. O'Malley goes from Instagram to Facebook, and from there to a school website, and then conducts a brief though legally questionable search inside the school's database. Now he's got an address. It is rural, and from the satellite images looks impressive. And if you were designing a place to hide out in from your father in the city, it would look just like the property O'Malley is staring at on-screen. He'll have this wrapped up by tomorrow evening. Buoyed by his own brilliance, he calls it a day. He's got a hot date with a beautiful woman, and a poker game to look forward to. O'Malley is on a roll.

# CHAPTER FOUR

'Jesse Browning, eighteen, in his last year of high school, lives on Whitehills Road, up past Silverdale.'

O'Malley's pleased with his progress and gets Claire up to speed as they order drinks. They're in the mood for seafood, and they're sitting on the patio of Jeremy's, a waterfront restaurant famous for its shellfish. It's the tail-end of summer, but the evenings still have some heat in them, and the low sun reflects sharply off the water, adding further shine to Claire's long hair. She looks like a shampoo commercial, if you airbrush out the grinning idiot reflected in her sunglasses.

'Good work, honey. So what's next?' Claire's not letting O'Malley rest on his laurels.

'Footwork. I'll head out there tomorrow, put eyes on the property, see if she shows her face.'

'What I mean is: what's your plan if you find her? Is that job done? Are you going to give the address to the father and walk away, or are you intending on bringing her home?'

O'Malley hasn't got that far.

'I don't know. If I can talk to her, then I guess I should let her know her dad's going crazy.'

'Maybe.' Claire pauses, thinking it through. 'But you might just spook her, and if you're right that she's staying with this kid, at least you know she's not on the streets. How far did you promise the father you'd go?'

It's a good question. O'Malley hasn't thought it through. Finding Sefina is one thing, but getting her home is another.

Maybe he's over-promised. What can he really do? Bundle her into the back of his car and forcibly drive her back to her father? Basically, that's kidnapping.

'Hmmm. I'll play it as it comes. I don't know what I'm dealing with yet. For all I know this kid's running a porn empire from a farm, and Sefina is there against her will.'

'Come on, O'Malley, I think you've been spending too much time on your own. You hear "missing girl" and the first thing you think of is porn? I may need to confiscate your laptop.' She has a point. He's prone to overthinking.

'OK, probably not that. But still, I don't even know for sure I'm on the right track. The photographs are inconclusive. I'll get out there, see the lay of the land, and go from there.'

'Good enough, Poirot. Do that. Now let's eat, I'm starving. And if I'm going to be on my feet for the next seven hours I need sustenance — especially if you're not going to be coming around later.' She lets that hang for a while. She isn't mad that O'Malley's going to play cards, but she wants him to know that she won't be taken for granted either. It's a tough call. Poker is, effectively, O'Malley's job. It's where he makes his money, and it funds his hobby playing private eye, but it demands antisocial hours — time when he should be keeping the bed warm.

'Sorry, babe, tonight will be a late one. But I'll be around tomorrow when you get off work, if I'm wanted.' He attempts a puppy-dog face. It's not pretty.

'You're always wanted, O'Malley, so don't pull that face,' she replies. 'It's not sexy,' she continues, 'which I guess is a good thing, because you wouldn't want me to go to work all hot and bothered and with no one to come home to.'

It had better be a good game tonight.

'Anyway, what are you having? I might go for some oysters,' she says, really testing his resolve now.

'Stop. Sashimi, then the snapper,' he suggests.

'All right, all right, order for both of us. Share the sashimi?'

'Works for me,' he agrees, and beckons the waiter, ordering the food and a couple of glasses of Pinot Gris to go with it. O'Malley settles back, feeling the warmth of the waning sun on his face, taking in the boaties mooring up for the evening, and the couples walking up and down the boardwalk, wondering where to eat. He has one up on them all. Sitting here with the most beautiful woman he's ever met, anticipating the food that is still to come, on this late summer's evening: he doesn't have a care in the world.

They are well fed, and the wine has taken the edge off the day as they walk arm-in-arm towards The Brandling. Claire's arrival causes a few turned heads, guys thinking their nights are looking up. She'll keep them thinking that, without giving any overt signals that would turn interest into drama. But they'll stay for a few more drinks than they intended, and Claire will come away with the lion's share of the tips.

'OK, baby. Have a good night — call me if you need me to come and get you home safely. Don't take any chances, OK?' O'Malley the gentleman.

'I know you want me to be a damsel in distress, but I can look after myself.'

She's right. O'Malley has seen her in action. She can handle herself.

'That's one of the many reasons I love you, baby,' he says.

'Good. If I get a break, I'll call you, and you can take a break from your game and tell me a few of the other reasons.' She leans towards him and, with a small lift of her heels, gently kisses him. He kisses back, but her hand prevents O'Malley from getting ahead of himself. If he isn't going to be home later, he is on rations. He reluctantly unwraps himself from her little finger, and walks backwards towards the bar's entrance, stealing a last glance at her like a sailor looking to shore before setting off into a storm.

The address O'Malley's been given by Chinese Steve is in Parnell, an upscale suburb east of the city. He swings by his apartment, picking up a combination of cash and casino chips; both are legal tender at this sort of private game. He gets in his truck — a recent-model Ford Ranger Double Cab — and heads east. He finds the location easily enough, but parking is a tougher proposition. Most of the neighbours are now home for the evening and settling in for their Netflix dinners, unaware of the makeshift casino in their midst. He tucks the truck in a side street, joining a couple of town cars nestling tight against the rear walls of the properties that stretch back from the main street. One of the cars is still occupied: a husband making one last check for messages before he plays happy families, is O'Malley's guess.

Steve has put O'Malley's name down for the game, so he's not expecting any difficulty getting in. He walks up the stone porch steps of a grand townhouse and rings the bell. O'Malley's aware of the security camera bearing down above the door, but security is not uncommon in this part of town. O'Malley is left to his own devices for a couple of minutes, and wonders if he should give the camera a side profile to ease identification. He settles for a wide, friendly smile to let them know he's spotted the camera. It does the trick, and the door is opened by a young Chinese man who introduces himself as William.

William is mid-twenties, O'Malley thinks, sharply dressed in a dark navy suit matched with an expensive-looking pale blue shirt. He plays the part of concierge very well. He would blend in at any of the five-star hotels around town. William has two notable features. The first, a two-inch faded scar that begins alongside his right eye and travels down across his cheekbone, suggesting a less than five-star past. O'Malley suspects it attracts the girls, allowing William to spin stories that talk to his bravery and cunning. He probably got it falling off a swing. The other notable feature is a thick tuft of white hair that offsets his otherwise perfectly black hair. It looks like William has been painting a ceiling.

'You're O'Malley, right?' William asks.

'That's me.'

'Come in, come in. We are upstairs,' he says, ushering O'Malley through a small, sparsely furnished hallway towards a staircase on the left. O'Malley takes a quick look around, noticing a further set of stairs down the hall, leading to what he presumes is the basement. He likes to know where the exits are. As he reaches the stairs he also catches a glimpse of a pretty, young Chinese girl darting across the hallway, emerging from one room and swiftly disappearing behind another door. She is wearing a white towel and pink bunny slippers. He doesn't ask after her. He's learned that curiosity is often misinterpreted. William fills the silence.

'The poker is on the second floor,' he explains, as they reach the top of the first flight of stairs. It's clear that there are other options available.

'Some of our guests like to play Sic Bo — in that room there,' he says, pointing to an open door. Beyond the door there's a plush, high-ceilinged room, with a small bar in one corner. The room is dominated by a gaming table surrounded by high-backed leather chairs. The table has a raised leather surround and is covered with an elaborate felt featuring the many betting options that Sic Bo requires. It's impressive, and suggests the visitors to this house expect a certain level of service. And *that* indicates that the stakes will be significant.

'You like Sic Bo, O'Malley?' William asks.

He doesn't. It looks complicated and sophisticated, but it's essentially a game of pure chance. There's no edge for a player like O'Malley, who doesn't believe in fate nor relies on luck alone. No need to offend the host, though.

'I've played it a little. It's fun.' A little white lie that harms no one.

'Well, maybe a game happens later. We can be dealer if that is wanted, but some of our players like to take turns as dealer. Maybe you would like that?'

He certainly would not. The pay-outs for many of the bets were far higher than even money. In the short-term, playing house requires a strong stomach. It's a fast track to loss and ruin.

O'Malley mumbles a vague response as they go up the second set of stairs. He can hear the excited chatter of at least two languages as he arrives on the upper floor of the house-cum-casino. There are only two rooms on this floor: a palatial lounge that takes up the majority of the floor plan, and a bathroom that comes off the lounge. The lounge is vast and consists of three distinct areas.

The poker table sits pride of place at one end of the room, facing a large fireplace over which three television screens sit, currently beaming various sports from around the world. To the left of the fireplace there's a well-stocked bar, with reassuringly heavy glasses and a good selection of whiskies and other spirits, and two ice buckets bookending the counter. William invites O'Malley to help himself. The middle of the room is taken up with four sofas, surrounding a large, low coffee table, on which a number of oversized books about birds sit incongruously. Perhaps the owner is a twitcher in their spare time. The third part of the room is taken up with a very modern kitchenette, where another pretty Chinese girl is preparing a variety of small finger-food. William doesn't introduce her.

The game is already underway. William ushers O'Malley to Seat Seven, the only empty chair at the table. O'Malley nods to the other players as he sits, but most of them are mid-hand, and their cards take priority. O'Malley settles down in his seat, taking the opportunity to assess the size of chip stacks in front of each player. There's no gain to be had trying to join a game with too much or too little ammunition. He settles on an amount that is closer to the low stacks than it is to the chip leader, and discreetly extracts the right amount from his pockets, handing it over to the dealer who gives O'Malley a nod of recognition and exchanges his money for chips. It's time to go to work.

# CHAPTER FIVE

The game is in full swing. O'Malley is taking his time, sizing up his competition before getting too involved in the action. He recognises a few of the players at the table from games gone by. Sarah, the only female at the table, is a formidable opponent with a successful record in Macau and Australia. She's probably the biggest threat, and O'Malley makes a mental note to avoid her where possible. Danny Cain, who's sitting to O'Malley's right, is a regular fixture wherever there's money to be made, but, as ever, his appearance is deceiving. He's forty-something, and out of shape. Always a coffee or food stain on his shirt. Looks like a down-at-heel accountant, which is what he was before he ran into trouble with one of his client's trust accounts.

But the player O'Malley is most interested in is sitting to his left. Bobby Q is why everyone is here. His reputation precedes him. He's a renowned gambler, volatile, and he's had some high-profile legal issues. Despite gaining citizenship in New Zealand, he was wanted back in China for crimes unspecified. He was forcibly returned to face the music, but after paying a hefty fine allowed to return to his new home. He must have some good dirt on people in high places. Those troubles haven't dampened his search for action, and O'Malley senses this game was built around Bobby Q. He has the funds and the gamble to attract a crowd.

The rest of the players are Chinese; some familiar to O'Malley, others new. He settles into his seat, and joins the conversation while James, the dealer, silently deals the cards. Jack, an older player, who could be in his sixties but might just as easily be in his eighties, holds the table in conversation, telling everyone about his recent journeys in the South Island and how stunned he was when he visited Milford Sound. It's odd to hear such appreciation of Nature from someone who's casually throwing a thousand dollars into a pot, but O'Malley reminds himself that how people present themselves in a poker game is rarely aligned to who they are away from the table. The glint in Jack's eyes suggests a deep intelligence that O'Malley is drawn to, and he's about to ask him more about his travels when the calm at the table is interrupted violently by Bobby Q.

'You fucking slow-rolled me!' Bobby shouts, throwing the two cards in his hand in Danny's direction. The cards don't reach that far, and instead land on O'Malley's arms as they rest on the table. Bobby stands up aggressively, and his chair falls back loudly on the floor. Danny has a look of innocence on his face, like he's got no idea what Bobby's talking about. But this just gets Bobby more worked-up, and he begins pacing back and forth in small bursts, away from the table then back towards it, like he's contemplating a serious attack on Danny Cain.

O'Malley is alert to the very real threat that now pervades the room. There's a lot of money in the middle of the table, the result of the hand that Bobby Q has just lost. The offence that he's accusing Danny of is one of poor etiquette. The way the hand was played gave Bobby every reason to believe he had the stronger hand. But when Danny eventually showed his cards, it was clear that he's had the best cards throughout the hand. Taking his time to reveal those cards was tantamount to rubbing salt in the wound. And O'Malley knows it was deliberate. Danny wanted to tease Bobby into thinking he'd won and waited until Bobby reached for the chips in the middle of the table before showing him he'd lost. It's the sort of thing that starts fights, and Bobby looks very much like he's about to launch himself at Danny. He's muttering in Mandarin or Cantonese, and when he looks up at Danny and sees a smirk on his face, it's too much for his pride to take, and he throws his whisky glass to the floor, shattering it and causing Sarah to yelp.

A couple of the other players at the table appeal to Bobby in Mandarin, and O'Malley turns his attention to Danny, knowing that how he responds now will dictate what happens next.

'Jesus, Danny. There's a time and a place. Why the slow roll?'

Danny's still thinking that denial is the best policy, and protests to O'Malley, 'I didn't do anything. I thought I was beat.'

'Bullshit, Danny. Your straight was the best hand possible — don't make it worse. You need to apologise.' O'Malley doesn't know what Bobby Q is capable of, but he's pretty sure Danny's out of his depth. 'Apologise, before this goes any further.'

Danny is a mess of a man, but he's not stupid. He considers O'Malley's words, and looks across to Bobby, who's now deep in counsel with a younger player who introduced himself as Michael, and who appears to be trying to calm Bobby down, without obvious success.

'OK, OK,' Danny says to O'Malley, and then louder to Bobby he says: 'Bobby, I'm sorry.' He stands up to give his words more credibility, holding his hands out in front of him in a conciliatory way. 'I am sorry. I meant no disrespect. I misread my hand. I didn't realise I was that strong.'

Bobby considers this. He's looking intently at Danny, and O'Malley's hoping like hell that Danny's face doesn't betray him. He's given a plausible reason for his late reveal that excuses it as a mistake. If Bobby senses a lie now, it's liable to get ugly. There's a long pause while the two men look at each other. O'Malley is watching both men, preparing to move quickly if the situation goes south. He looks across at the dealer, who's staring down at the table, wishing he is somewhere else. But he's stacking the chips that sit in front of him into neat piles, and discreetly moving them closer to Danny, so Bobby doesn't have to watch his opponent gather the pot. Sarah is holding her breath, waiting for the testosterone to dissipate.

Bobby Q finally speaks, softly this time, not in English. He's obviously addressing Alfred, one of the other players, who has been quietly observing the drama, sipping from the tea flask that he's brought with him. O'Malley picks up the gist of it. Bobby's asking if this *gweilo* is on the level. Alfred might as well have been asked the time, for all the effort he puts into his response. Yes, yes, it's fine, Bobby, let's play, is what he seems to be saying. It's enough for Bobby, who returns to the table, to a collective sigh of relief from those still seated.

'Go on, take your money,' Bobby instructs Danny, who's smart enough now to do what he is told without commentary. Bobby Q turns to O'Malley and pats him on the forearm, apologises for throwing his cards at him, and O'Malley waves it away, no problem. Bobby makes an effort to lighten the mood, speaking to the table as he makes a joke of it all.

'No slow roll, huh? He didn't know what cards he had. I am lucky, I could have lost more if he knew. But I will win it back now — against the man who doesn't look at his hand properly.' He laughs as he says it, and it gives permission for everyone to relax. Not Danny, though. He's finally realising how badly he misjudged the situation, and he excuses himself, asking William where he can go for a smoke. He's directed downstairs and leaves the rest of the players to get on with the game. The pretty girl who is serving refreshments silently and efficiently clears up the broken glass and spilt whisky that lies behind Bobby's chair.

The game gets back to normal. After returning, Danny gets back in the action, and gets into a couple of hands with Bobby that he has no intention of winning. He dumps some of his previous winnings back to Bobby, a show of contrition. It is enough to restore balance around the table. Soon enough, O'Malley wins a decent pot against Michael, the young player who has been juggling two phones all night, and now can't keep track of all the messaging he's engaged in *and* the game in front of him. Losing to

O'Malley is a sign to call it a night, and Michael thanks everyone for the game, stopping to talk to William before he leaves.

O'Malley still hasn't worked out who is actually behind this game; William looks like hired help. It could be that it was one of the men at the table — O'Malley knows Sarah too well to consider her — or someone else altogether. Michael, perhaps? More likely Jack or Alfred. He makes a mental note to ask Steve when he gets the chance. He is curious.

As it nears midnight, they take a break. Jack wanders off downstairs to smoke. O'Malley stretches his legs, and chats to Sarah about her recent travels, while they fix themselves drinks at the bar. Bobby Q and Alfred get on their phones, checking whatever there is to check. Danny and James the dealer both choose to flirt with the anonymous server, who wears a look of polite disinterest in whatever they are saying. Sarah wanders back to the table — all business, and keen to get the game restarted. Danny has given up on the help, and scurries over to the bar, grabbing O'Malley's arm.

'Hey, O'Malley, you'll never guess what I saw when I went for a smoke.' He's about to elaborate when Jack returns to the room, and William addresses the group.

'Shall we get back to the cards, ladies and gentlemen?' He ushers the players back to the table, keen to keep the commission coming from the game.

'Tell me later,' O'Malley says to Danny, and retakes his seat. It's getting late, and he has age on his side. He's hoping the older players will flag as the night wears on, and their concentrations slip. Instead, he promptly loses five grand to Sarah. So much for staying out of her way. Maybe staring at a computer screen for most of the day is taking its toll.

A couple more rounds and he figures it is time to call it quits. He's up nine thousand dollars, which isn't bad for a few hours' work. He could leave now, and still catch Claire awake, or grind it out until the early hours. He chooses the first option. He's done enough to get another invitation, and he knows when fatigue is blunting his judgement. He throws a black chip James's way, to thank him for dealing, and William cashes O'Malley out, swapping his chips for notes.

O'Malley needn't have hurried home.

As he makes his way back to the side street where he left his car, he calls Claire. She's beat and tells him that booty calls are off the table. He tries a bit of O'Malley charm, but she holds firm. He knows when he's beaten and gives up, heading straight home instead.

He puts his money somewhere safe and lies down on the couch. Dead to the world.

He wakes with a thump. He's on the floor, alongside the couch, sweat covering his body and soaking through his shirt, and for the moments that it takes to realise he is awake he is terrified. He was dreaming of silent attacks, Bobby Q transformed from poker player to assassin, come to slit his throat. He sits up, aware that his heartbeat is in danger of waking the neighbours, and focuses on his breathing, trying to calm himself down and stop fear and anxiety turning to panic. He stays where he is for two or three minutes, letting himself fully wake up, distancing himself from the threats that he invented in his dreams.

It's a shitty way to wake up, but as he sits in his kitchen, drinking the first coffee of the day, O'Malley figures there's an upside. It is six-thirty, and his day is beginning, not ending. That alone is a novelty. He thinks he may as well embrace it. He packs a bag to get him through the stakeout ahead: plenty of water, some protein bars, and a couple of apples. An empty bottle if he needs it. Thinking way ahead.

He takes the stairs down to the basement, to his truck. He grabs a few lengths of timber from the small lock-up that sits against the wall alongside his vehicle. He throws them in the flatbed of the truck, securing a couple so they stick out of the rear of the ute.

Now, if he's spotted near the Browning property, he's just another builder. He grabs a few tools for good measure and chucks them in with the wood. He's ready to roll.

O'Malley's client is pretty demanding for a man who's asked a favour. There's an early text waiting for O'Malley when he checks his phone before he sets off: Loto, asking for a progress report. O'Malley can't blame him. Every day that passes without news will be an anxious wait for the worried father. But he's not getting ahead of himself, and he might be about to embark on a wild-goose chase, so O'Malley texts back letting Loto know he's made some progress but hasn't yet found Sefina. Loto's response is less grateful than O'Malley was expecting.

*Find her.*

That's the plan.

# CHAPTER SIX

The traffic works in his favour. He's heading north, away from the city centre, and the cars flow freely, a stark contrast to the jams that stifle progress in the opposite direction. He is usually asleep at this hour, and he marvels at the patience of the drivers coming into the city, persuading themselves that this is a reasonable exchange for the lifestyle they have wherever they live — and presumably only see in the dark. Not my problem, he thinks, smug in his well-stocked cabin; forty-two minutes to his destination according to the map on his phone.

He crosses the harbour bridge that connects the city centre to the northern suburbs and beyond, rising up over the still waters beneath, the low morning sun reflecting sharply off the boats that sit enticingly on the surface. O'Malley wouldn't know one end of a boat from the other, but on mornings like this he sees the appeal. Auckland is a proud ocean-going city, with more boats per capita than anywhere else in the world, but it's not a world O'Malley is familiar with, and he wonders how many of the boats he sees are used more than once or twice a year. It's a sign of the wealth gap that New Zealand suffers just like every other country in the world. For every family enjoying weekends on the water, there's a family like the Tupuolas, struggling to make ends meet. Reuniting this one family is O'Malley's way of making a difference. If he can.

It doesn't take long to reach the outer limits of the city's urbanisation, vast green hills replacing villas and concrete and glass. He stops briefly at a gas station, filling the truck and grabbing a coffee to go, and an energy drink as back-up. Stalking people is unhealthy work.

Whitehills Road is a long stretch of track that passes through what was once prime dairy country, but has more recently succumbed to the inevitable spread of urbanites with romantic dreams of living on the farm. Planning zones have not yet caught up, leaving the land relatively untouched, rolling fields maintaining the privacy of distance between neighbours. It is going to be difficult to go unnoticed for too long, sparsely populated as the area is. As the dot on his map starts to get closer he lowers his speed, scoping out the surroundings, wondering where he might be least conspicuous. He approaches the driveway that presumably leads to the Browning home, and notes a rest area on the roadside, a white van parked up with a couple of maintenance workers setting up ladders around a power pole at one end of the gravel parking area. He drives on, intending to do a recce of the property, in search of other entries. The next available right turn is nearly 2 kilometres down the road, and it takes ten minutes to loop back around to the rest area where he started. O'Malley thinks he's covered no more than eight properties in this time, and there are no obvious in-roads at the rear of the Brownings' property. It's time for some proper legwork.

He parks up in the rest area, putting as much distance as possible between his truck and the power workers. He doesn't need to make any new friends this morning, nor does he entirely have faith in their ability to do their work without dropping something from the top of the ladder. He likes his truck and wants to keep it out of harm's way.

O'Malley hops out of the truck and stretches — just a builder limbering up before a job. He's wearing tan worker's boots, an old pair of jeans, and a plain black t-shirt, over which he's opted for a lightweight jacket. It will soon get too warm for the jacket, but he needs the pockets it provides, in which he's loaded up a couple of protein bars and a small pair of Bushnell binoculars. He grabs a water bottle and strolls across the road towards the Browning property. He's hoping the maintenance guys pay him no attention, but if they do, he looks very much the tradesman going for a morning walk, maybe looking for somewhere discreet to water the plants.

A couple of hundred metres down the road he finds a gate that leads to farmland. Ignoring the sign discouraging walkers, he hops the gate and makes his way through the field ahead, sticking closely to the tree-line that will hopefully keep him hidden from sight. The field rolls uphill towards a large farmhouse a few hundred metres from where he stands. He won't be able to identify Sefina from this distance, and he certainly won't have the opportunity for a fireside chat. He isn't sure what his plan is, but it will have to involve more than a walk in a field.

He can't see any signs of activity at the house itself, but there's a cluster of buildings about a hundred metres to the right. A barn, a shed and what looks like a small cottage — the sort of thing you'd build for guests or ageing parents to live in. He catches a glimpse of someone entering the barn, and figures he'll get closer to check it out. Following the trees, he is able to work his way along the field and up into a copse that sits on the hillside behind the outbuildings. He puts his weight on his right knee, holding an elbow steady as he uses the Bushnells to get a closer look.

The back door to the cottage opens out onto a small courtyard where a small table and chairs show signs of recent activity: a coffee cup sits on the table alongside a neatly folded newspaper, a vaping device alongside it. He's still trying to focus the binoculars when he catches a glimpse of someone entering the cottage through the back door. Someone female, dark-haired, and very much like the girl he's looking for. O'Malley tries to see through the doorway and windows, but the sunlight is against him. He'll come back to the cottage, but first he has a look across the rest of the property.

Scanning across to the barn that sits 50 metres from the cottage, he sees three vehicles lined up with their rears facing the open barn doors. An old Toyota truck, covered in mud and dirt, alongside a pristine black Range Rover that looks like it would squeal with distaste if it went through a puddle. The third vehicle is a beaten-up old red Toyota Camry — the sort you give your kid as a first car. It will get you from A to B, but at speeds that would struggle to kill you in the event of a crash. Baby Bear's car.

Three men emerge from the barn, and as he focuses on them through the binoculars he feels a knot in his stomach. Two of the men are big units: gym muscles bulging beneath their jackets, which are black leather, motorcycle-club standard-issue, and the patches on their breasts suggest O'Malley's case just got a whole deal more delicate. No one said anything about gangs. But here are two proud patched members in conversation with a third, older man, who holds himself with authority despite the threatening physical presence of the men on either side of him. O'Malley is quickly trying to join these new dots together, and what bearing they might have on Sefina's disappearance, when he senses movement behind him.

O'Malley lowers the binoculars and begins to turn around, but his movement is interrupted by a tree that seems to come to life and hit him squarely across the shoulder blades. He falls onto his face and turns to see that the tree is just a thick branch, being held at arm's length by a kid who looks just like Jesse Browning. O'Malley doesn't like the odds of lying down for a fight, so he ignores the pain that is building in his back and works his way onto his hands and knees. Jesse has obviously read the same training manuals and doesn't want his opponent back on his feet. He swings the branch towards O'Malley's face, and, before it makes contact, O'Malley has time to congratulate himself for being on the right track.

He isn't out for long. Long enough, though, for Jesse to have called for help, and O'Malley is vaguely aware of being dragged down through the trees towards the barn, a leather jacket on either side of him providing both support and restraint. Escape seems out of reach for now, so he focuses on walking and remembering what day it is. Jesse walks quickly alongside the man on O'Malley's left, calling ahead to the older guy who's stayed put in the barn.

'I found him up in the trees, spying on you. He had binoculars and was watching you, so I took him down.' It's an accurate recap. A little needy in tone, but maybe he won't get praise without seeking it. Damn snowflake.

'Well, let's find out what he wants,' says the older man; Jesse's father, if looks are anything to go by. O'Malley's guards place him in a chair within the barn, away from any other prying eyes that might be hiding in the trees. Browning Senior addresses him calmly, his low voice carrying more by way of threat than any outburst could do. Jesse is obviously no stranger to the technique, and he unconsciously backs away a half-step, keeping himself out of harm's way.

'You've got a minute to tell me who you are, what you're doing on my property, and why you're spying on us. At this stage, it's not looking good for you, boy.' Boy? O'Malley has never responded well to that appellation. But given the context, he's going to let it pass for now.

'My name's O'Malley. I'm helping out a friend who's lost his daughter. I think Jesse there knows her, and I came to see if she happened to be hanging out here. Her name's Sefina.'

The look that passes between father and son is sufficient to confirm it's been good detective work so far. It also tells O'Malley that Jesse will be held to account for drawing attention to the farm.

'You didn't think to use the front door?'

There's nothing to say to that.

'O'Malley. What are you, some sort of private detective?'

'Sort of like that' is O'Malley's answer.

'Check his pockets,' Browning says, nodding to the makeshift guards — Shrek One and Shrek Two. They come up trumps: a protein bar for each of them, and a wallet to share between them. Shrek Two has a quick look in the wallet then tosses it over to Browning, who takes a look, pulling the driver's licence out to confirm that his guest has been telling the truth so far. It also gives him O'Malley's address, which he'll worry about later.

'You here on your own?' Browning asks. It's one of those trick questions. Answer yes and become swiftly disposable. Answer no, and maybe the big guns come out. O'Malley opts for the truth.

'Yes. Just a man looking for a girl,' trying to soften the mood. The reference is lost on his audience.

'Well, that makes things simpler, I guess.' O'Malley doesn't like where that leads. No one else seems in a rush to contribute to the conversation, which tells him the pecking order among his new friends. What Browning decides will be final, so O'Malley thinks he'd better keep the conversation going.

'I'm sorry if I ignored the sign on the gate — it's easily missed. I'll give it a bit of a clean on my way out, if you want. But since we're all here, can I ask if Sefina is around? I've got a message from her father.'

Browning raises an eyebrow, half-surprised, half-impressed with the balls on this guy. Shrek One develops some unwelcome initiative and gives O'Malley a good backhander, which opens up a small cut above his left eye and leaves an annoying ringing sound in his ears. Another time, another place, he'd put him straight about the line of command, but now just doesn't seem the time.

'*If* Jesse had a friend over, then I am sure she'd be well looked after, and I'm sure she'd have her reasons for wanting a bit of peace and quiet. But I don't think we've got any guests at the moment, do we, Jesse?' Jesse shakes his head. He's lost his voice.

'I'm wondering if you're going to cause me an issue down the line, O'Malley. As a businessman, I'm always keen to solve problems early before they have a chance to develop.' That doesn't sound promising. As Browning weighs up O'Malley's prospects, there's a welcome interruption to the silence: Shrek Two's phone ringing insistently. Perhaps he'll be saved by the bell.

Shrek Two holds his phone up towards Browning, as if to

explain the source of the noise.

'It's the boss, boss,' he explains. 'I'd better take it.'

'*Your* boss,' Browning corrects, with irritation, but he nods and tilts his head towards the barn doors, suggesting the call be taken outside. Leaving it a little more spacious inside: just the four of them now. O'Malley's having naughty thoughts. He's really only got to make it through two of them before Phone Shrek makes it back, because he figures Jesse-without-a-stick will run for help as soon as he sees trouble. Despite losing to Jesse-with-a-stick, O'Malley's pretty handy with his fists, though he prefers to avoid confrontation wherever possible. A hangover from his past. But needs must.

He focuses on his plan of attack. He is starting from a sitting position, which isn't ideal. But it puts him level with Shrek One's lower half, which is where his weakness lies. A strong palm well placed through his kneecap will bring him down quickly, allowing O'Malley to follow up with a strike to his head. Then he'll need to close the distance to Browning Senior and put him down. That will have to be improvised. And it will only work if junior does a runner, doesn't try to repeat his heroics on the hill. Still, it's the only plan he's got. He counts down from three.

O'Malley gets as far as one when Shrek Two comes back. He's missed his chance.

Rather than return to stand over O'Malley, Shrek Two approaches Browning, and whispers something. They whisper some more, glancing in O'Malley's direction a couple of times. Something is up. Browning speaks over Shrek's shoulder, addressing O'Malley.

'Do you know Jimmy Tua?'

He does. From long ago. 'Yeah, I know Jimmy.' Wonders where this is going.

'He says you're a stand-up guy. Keep out of other people's business. I don't know why, but he says this might be best put down to a misunderstanding.'

'He's a smart man,' O'Malley speculates. Jimmy Tua *is* smart, but he is also a brutal man, capable of extreme violence when it suits him. O'Malley crossed paths with him when they were both victims of the justice system, and O'Malley did him a solid favour. Jimmy Tua is a gangster, but he's got a code that he lives by. Seems it's playing out now.

'And you're a lucky one, it seems. I guess we don't need to take this any further. No harm, no foul.' Browning is a businessman, and he'll take a testimonial, if it comes from someone with Tua's stature. Besides, O'Malley guesses that Tua's goons have instructions to leave him alone, which leaves Browning with little room to move. Still, he's owning the decision, saving face.

'It's a one-time deal, O'Malley. Get off my property, and don't come back. You need to forget about us and stay out of our business. Agreed?'

'Agreed,' O'Malley replies. There's enough wriggle room in that contract to let him honour it.

'And forget about the girl: I'm sure she's fine and well looked after — wherever she is.'

'Uh-huh,' mumbles O'Malley, confirming that he's heard him, but not necessarily agreeing.

'Go on, get the fuck out. G, make sure he finds his way out.' Shrek One has a name, it turns out, or a letter at least. He hauls O'Malley to his feet, and nudges him gently towards the courtyard, the violence of earlier forgotten. O'Malley walks slowly out of the barn, giving Jesse a final once-over. The young man is staring at the floor, wondering where this leaves him. His earlier heroics have already turned to blame, and now that O'Malley's off the hook, he is wondering what that means for him.

O'Malley's thinking hard, too. He's found Sefina, sort of, but he hasn't determined if she's there voluntarily or if she is in danger. He ponders this as he goes on a romantic stroll across the fields with G. G says nothing, and O'Malley isn't looking for further conversation. As they near the gate, G pauses, and watches

O'Malley climb over it and then turn to give the no-trespassing sign a little rub with the sleeve of his jacket. O'Malley's way of getting the final word in.

He crosses the road to the parking bay and his truck. The white van is still in place, and a ladder leans against the power pole, suggesting work in progress, but the men he saw earlier are nowhere in sight. Smoko, he thinks. Or maybe they were inspired by O'Malley's earlier adventures and went for a nice country walk.

He hopes theirs is less eventful.

# CHAPTER SEVEN

O'Malley checks the time as he pulls out to begin the journey home. It is close to midday; he's achieved a lot for a man who doesn't usually rise until late morning. He's found Jesse Browning, stumbled upon some sort of criminal enterprise, been beaten unconscious, unsuccessfully negotiated his release, taken another blow to the head, confirmed Sefina's whereabouts, planned an escape, and gained a last-minute reprieve from an old acquaintance.

His captors, meanwhile, have unwittingly avoided the beating of their lives. Possibly. He feels victorious for a moment, and then looks at himself in the rear-view mirror. The bruise is already beginning to show on his face, and dried blood covers the left side of his face, which hurts when he touches it, and his back is complaining. He hasn't actually confirmed that it was Sefina he caught a glimpse of. Some might call it a draw.

The drive home is uneventful, and before entering his apartment he takes a minute to replace the tools and wood he'd pulled out of storage. He strips as he walks towards the bathroom, and he's a bit ginger as he bends down to unlace and remove his boots. He takes a long shower, letting the water and steam relieve him of the scars of battle.

O'Malley reflects on the question Claire put to him: what now? Does he tell Mr Tupuola that his daughter is safe, holed up on a farm with a man in league with a motorcycle gang, and let him decide what to do with the information? Or does he look for another way to cross paths with Sefina, and see if he can make her see sense and go home? Loto is a big man, but he doesn't strike

O'Malley as a fighter. Sending him to the Brownings' is likely to cause him more pain and put more distance between the man and his daughter. O'Malley needs help.

As he dries himself, he texts his confidante.

*Hey babe. You free this afternoon? xx.*

No assumptions that she'll drop everything when he clicks his fingers.

*I am. Where are you? Thought you were on a stakeout?*

No text-speak, no emojis. Standards, even on text.

*Been, done, made some progress. At home now. Might have run into a little trouble …*

He doesn't want to worry her, but she'll see his face soon enough.

*Shit. What trouble? I can be there in an hour or so. Want food?*

It hasn't occurred to him, but O'Malley is starving.

*Yes, but plenty here. I'll do something for both of us. See you soon xx.*

He goes to the bedroom and pulls out a fresh pair of jeans and a shirt.

Looking at himself in the mirror, he decides he doesn't look too bad. More like a boxer the morning after a big fight, less like a guy taken by surprise by a big stick. He returns to the kitchen to prepare a late lunch. He tears off a large chunk of sourdough from the loaf on the counter, keeping his hunger at manageable levels until Claire arrives. Then he pulls together a simple meal, his version of a Greek entrée — tomatoes, halloumi, roasted red peppers, marinated chillis, and puts some pitta breads to one side, for the grill. He puts some olive oil and balsamic alongside, ready to dress the salad. He might not be able to sleep in the company of others, but he is broadly domesticated.

Another text from Claire.

*How did you get on last night?*

It seems like a lot has happened since he left the poker game, and he's put it out of his mind — always easier to do after a win. But Claire keeps him honest, making sure he doesn't forget the losses either. But it was a decent night, so he reports back to that effect, no details. She never asks for specifics, so he doesn't know if Claire is aware what sort of money is involved in his day/night job. It might be pennies, for all Claire knows or cares. But she asks, because that's what couples do.

*Good job, O'Malley. See you in 5.*

He is looking forward to it.

'OK, let's start with the obvious. You look like you got hit by a bus. Does it hurt?'

'It was more like a log, and only when you touch it. Like … there. Yep, that hurts.'

'Well, what happened? You obviously found *something*,' Claire says, gently stroking O'Malley's face as she speaks.

He gives her the long version, emphasising how much trouble his captors were in before his escape got derailed. She nods along, not wanting to hurt his feelings. But gets to the point anyway.

'So what did you walk in on? What's this guy Browning got going on that involves a gang, and how does Sefina fit into it all?'

'I don't know. Drugs, most likely. Stolen property, maybe. Whatever it is, I want to keep far away from it. But that doesn't help me with Sefina. Jesse doesn't strike me as a criminal mastermind. I think he's along for the ride with his father. Sefina's dumb luck that she's shacked up with the wrong son.'

'So how will you get to Sefina without crossing Browning's path?'

*How* will you get to Sefina? Not, *will* you keep at it? Claire has decided he is in this for the long haul. He doesn't contradict her.

'I don't know yet. I'm just getting used to my new face,' he says, with a smile.

'Yeah, me too. I may need to shop around if it doesn't get back to normal.'

Claire leans in and kisses him, tentatively at first, until she establishes there is nothing wrong with his mouth. Then a little harder. O'Malley's enjoying the role of wounded soldier. But Claire's bedside manner could do with a little work. She pulls back, pats him on the side of the face, causing him to wince, and walks across to the kitchen.

'Toughen up, O'Malley. You promised me lunch, remember?'

He gets to it. Drizzles some oil and balsamic over the salad like a pro, while the bread warms up under the grill. He has to slap a tattooed arm away a couple of times as Claire tries to pick at the salad before it is served. A few minutes with Claire, and O'Malley forgets whatever problems are waiting for him. If they lived together, it would be called domestic bliss. More so when she returns to the kitchen wearing one of his old shirts, which barely covers the naked body underneath. O'Malley guesses they are having a siesta after lunch. It will be medicinal.

'Best get it while we can,' Claire suggests, 'in case your back gets worse overnight.' He'll push through the pain, but agrees it is prudent to pre-empt his declining physical health.

They eat quickly, throw the plates in the sink, and make their way to the bedroom. The blackout blinds are already lowered to three-quarters, letting in enough light for them to appreciate each other, but preventing any passing cruise ships from enjoying a free show. He removes the clothes that he has only recently put on, but from there Claire takes over. She insists he take it easy and let her do the work. He mostly complies, reflecting that she remains perfect from any angle, and this is a just reward for his morning heroics.

While Claire sleeps lightly, her head on O'Malley's chest, he reads.

He's always been a reader. As a child, a book was a treasure, an escape, and he would take any opportunity to immerse himself in a good story, quickly exhausting the limited selection his school possessed. When he discovered the local library, he learned of worlds that were far removed from his reality, though he often found it hard to relate to the characters he read about, whose lives seemed so comfortable and delightful.

Prison compounded his love of fiction, enabling him to pass the time imagining himself on the other side of the concrete walls that surrounded him. It was here, ironically, that he discovered the world of crime fiction, and the heroes who navigated the mean streets of Los Angeles, the bayous of the American South, and the wastelands that sat between those two vastly different worlds. He followed Cole and Pike, Bosch, Robicheaux, Easy Rawlins, and Leonid McGill as they pursued the truth, stood up for those without a voice, and wrestled with their own inner demons. It was good to know that he had company, though he knew he wasn't in their league.

He isn't quite asleep, but he's definitely losing focus on Easy's latest mission when his phone buzzes from the pocket of his jeans, which lie on the floor alongside the bed. The interruption is unwelcome, but it might be a lead in *his* case. Maybe Sefina has tracked him down and wants to meet. Or it's the library calling for their books back. Either way, he can't let the call pass, so he extricates himself from the warmth of Claire's body and grabs his jeans, heading into the lounge as he takes the phone out of the pocket and answers it.

'O'Malley,' he announces, not looking at the caller ID.

'Buxton.'

One word, and O'Malley is transported back to a time when he was a scared little boy. *Sergeant* Buxton and O'Malley go back some. He was the man who saw that O'Malley went to jail, although it brought him no satisfaction. O'Malley had only recently turned eighteen when they first met, and those early encounters were unpleasant for both of them. Buxton's commitment to the law gave him no leeway in the young O'Malley's fate, but he was decent despite his role in that loss of freedom.

When O'Malley came out, Buxton showed up again, keen to ensure that the young man didn't become a repeat visitor. He'd vouched for O'Malley back when Grant was considering giving him a break, and they've crossed paths now and then since that time. He doesn't particularly like O'Malley's hobby, correctly predicting that it will lead to situations that are a lot harder to explain away for a man with a record. But he sees something in O'Malley that makes him worth taking a risk on. Despite years of dealing with people's worst sides, Sergeant Buxton still likes to see the best in people and do what he can to help those who need someone like him looking out for them. But he doesn't give people many chances, either. And it sounds like O'Malley is about to discover what happens if Buxton finds his faith misplaced.

'Sergeant Buxton. This is a surprise. What's happening?' O'Malley asks, because he genuinely doesn't know.

'O'Malley.'

There's a pause that makes him flinch. Something is up.

'Can you explain to me why I've had enquiries about you from a surveillance team? Specifically, why you and your vehicle were seen — and photographed — at a location of current interest? And don't tell me you stopped for a piss, because from the sounds of it you must have tripped very heavily over your own dick to get the injuries you came back with.'

The white van. So there's nothing wrong with the power in the area. O'Malley's case just keeps on giving. His mind turns. If the police are interested in Browning and act anytime soon, Browning will connect it to O'Malley's uninvited visit, and Jimmy Tua will do the same. International travel is suddenly on O'Malley's mind.

He chooses his words very carefully. He needs Buxton to know that he's still one of the good guys, but he doesn't want to over-share. The police have a tendency to look at the world in a more binary way than O'Malley does, and it will be easy to lose control of the situation once someone like Buxton gets involved. But he hasn't heard Buxton this angry before, so he needs to think fast.

Instead, what he says is: 'Whoa, whoa — hold on with whatever you're thinking.' God knows what he'd have said if he *hadn't* thought carefully about it.

'Don't piss me about, O'Malley. I shouldn't even be talking to you — you're now a person of interest in a live investigation. If you are involved in something, you better tell me now. And don't even think of sharing what I'm telling you. Again: what are you mixed up in?'

'OK, OK, look, I promise you I'm not doing anything that would get on your radar, unless going for a walk on someone else's land is now a serious crime. I'm looking for someone, is all, and I had reason to think they might be up in that neck of the woods. I was wrong. So I won't be going back.'

'And the bloody face? How does that fit?'

'I'm a city boy, as you know. I'm not used to country walks. I slipped on a hillside and landed face-first on a tree stump. No big deal.'

'That all sounds like first-class bullshit, O'Malley. Even if some of it is true, you're in something you shouldn't be anywhere near. I don't buy coincidence, so you're mixed up with people you need to stay well away from. And if you're actually involved in a crime, I'll take it very personally. I'll make it my mission to put you away for the maximum this time. Don't make me regret giving you the benefit of the doubt.'

He's not talking about O'Malley's current predicament. He gave O'Malley the benefit of the doubt thirteen years ago, and that help resulted in a slightly lower sentence, even if it didn't keep O'Malley free. There is a debt there, and he knows O'Malley takes that seriously, which is the only reason he is willing to give any leeway right now.

'Whatever your involvement, it stops now. If you're in deeper than you're saying, then come to me and I'll try to figure how to get you out of it. But this is what happens when you go around pretending to be a detective, O'Malley. Why do you have to keep putting your fingers near the fire?'

'I'm just helping an old man out, Buxton. You should understand that.' He doesn't need to know who, and he doesn't need to know how, but O'Malley owes him a *bit* of context.

'It's Senior Sergeant Buxton to you, and don't compare us today, O'Malley. I help people because it's my job and I've got the law on my side. You, on the other hand, are a soft touch with a record. You turn up in all the wrong places, and this time you're like a deer in headlights: you're on record in the vicinity, you lit up the database, and I'm the poor schmuck who gets dragged into it because you're connected to me. You're now of interest to people I have no sway with, and my guess is that if they draw a blank on their current approach, they'll be back to breathe down your neck soon enough. I were you? I'd take that way-too-good-for-you girlfriend of yours and go on a trip.'

Anger aside, there it is. Buxton is looking out for O'Malley once again. He's got friends he doesn't think he deserves. O'Malley wants to give Buxton some further reassurance that he is still worthy of his trust, but the policeman hangs up, leaving O'Malley feeling bad for letting him down. But he didn't set out that morning with ill intent, and he still can't point to anything that is actually his fault, except for ignoring a stop sign fixed to a country gate. And who hasn't done that?

# CHAPTER EIGHT

'What now, baby?'

The way-too-good-for-him girlfriend is awake.

She's picked up the gist of the conversation with Buxton, but she lets O'Malley tell it.

'Turns out I wasn't the only one snooping around the farm this morning. The Brownings are under surveillance. Which means I'm now on the cops' radar, too.'

'Shit,' says Claire, which is as good a summary as any.

'On a couple of fronts. Whatever Browning is up to, it's bigger than we thought, and I stumbled into it like an idiot. So if the cops make a move on him, he'll blame me. And now the cops have got me down as part of whatever it is that Browning is doing.'

'Shit,' Claire says again. For emphasis.

'In my favour: I've got nothing to do with any of it. I'd have to be very unlucky to get wrapped up in it, wouldn't I?' This is half-statement, half-question. He isn't sure he believes it himself.

'True. But you have a past, O'Malley. Once a criminal, always a criminal is how I hear most cops talk. It's easier to do the job that way. Look at it from their side for a moment. You emerge from the bushes looking like a cage-fighter who's just done five rounds. If pushed, you say self-defence. They say, how many times are you going to use that line?'

She's right. He's a perfect match for a suspect. *What did he look like? He was big, you know, like over six feet. Wide, too. Thick neck. Threatening. He looked like a fighter — like his nose had taken a break or two, you know? Black or white? Kind of in between, olive-skinned. Could be a bit of either. Not* bad-*looking, though, if he wasn't covered in blood.* OK, maybe not that last bit.

He looks the part, is the point, and when he walked into a crime scene while the cops stood watching, he guesses he can't blame them for jumping to conclusions. Claire is also right that using the same excuse several times is going to wear thin. Dogs might eat homework, but rarely more than once. Maybe if he doesn't go looking for trouble, he'll have more success staying out of it.

'I've got truth on my side, is all I'm saying. It might not be a golden ticket, but it's a start. Besides, I'm not intending to go back. So I'm good with the cops. I'd prefer to be off their radar completely, but if I do no wrong, they'll leave me alone. It's Browning and the gangs that I need to worry about. I might have spooked them a bit this morning, but that could go either way. If they accelerate whatever it is they're doing, and they're being watched, it could go bad. But they might just as easily lay off for a while or change their plans.'

'That's a lot of ifs,' Claire says. 'Maybe it's time you changed *your* plans for a bit?'

Maybe. But O'Malley prefers to see what's coming his way. If he lies low, he won't be any wiser when he comes back up for air. Sometimes you've got to walk into the storm.

'I don't think so. For now, it's business as usual. I'll find another way to track Sefina down that doesn't involve the police or Browning. She won't stay holed up forever.'

'Really, O'Malley? Why don't you just let that one go? Tell the father where she is and be done with it.'

'I can't do that. I'd be sending him into the lion's den.'

'Then tell him you've come up empty.'

'I can't do that either. That would be lying, and what did we say about telling lies?'

'Oh, shut up. This is different. You play poker for a living — if I call it a bluff does that make it more acceptable? This is serious, O'Malley.'

'I just can't. I said I'd find her and try to get her home. Now I know where she is, it's even more reason to get her back to her father. She's caught up in this even more than I am. So I'll do what I need to do. But I promise I won't go back to the farm. I promise I'll keep my nose clean with the cops, and I'll try to find a way to stop anything splashing back on me.'

Claire closes her eyes and exhales through her nose. O'Malley thinks he hears her count to three. He can be infuriating at times, admittedly. But all the reasons that are making her mad are also the reasons she gives for being with him. So, you know, swings and roundabouts.

'Oh, and I might need to borrow your car tomorrow.'

'My car? Why— Oh, because they'll be looking for yours. But you said you weren't going near them.'

'I'm not. But I'll need to be in the vicinity. So I'll need another vehicle.'

Claire lies back on the bed and pulls the sheet over her head. Conversation over.

O'Malley gives it five minutes before venturing back into bed with Claire. They get over their differences, but quickly because she has work soon. O'Malley checks his phone for messages while Claire showers. Nothing of note: a couple of messages asking if he'll be going to the poker room that night, a few news alerts, a video of Trump saying something dumb again. He returns to the texts. One from Sunny, telling him he missed a good game last night, suggesting tonight will be similar. The other is from Big Tone, wondering if they can get a decent-size game going tonight. O'Malley doesn't have anything else in his diary, and it will pass the time while Claire works.

*Sure, I'll be there around 8.*

This he sends to both Sunny and Tone.

He hears the water stop in the bathroom and gets out of bed to join Claire in the bathroom. Nothing kinky. He takes over in the shower, and watches Claire dry off and fix herself up for the night ahead. There isn't much involved: she kept her hair dry in the shower, so all it needs is a brush, and she is minimalist when it comes to make-up. She rubs in some moisturiser, which O'Malley enjoys watching, and wanders out to retrieve her clothes from the bedroom. He ponders if it is too late for her to call in sick, make a night of it in front of the TV, or just go back to bed, but she is already on the move.

'Hurry up, O'Malley, or I'm leaving without you.' She knows him better than he knows himself. He's only just decided to go and play cards, but she is way ahead of him. What else would he be doing to keep himself busy?

'Two minutes, babe. I'm making myself beautiful.'

'You'll need a few more days for that. Settle for some deodorant and get a move on. This little package needs delivering to its place of work.' She motions with her hands to accentuate the curves of the package in question. O'Malley's throat makes a noise that could have been a cheetah looking at a gazelle. He's closer to caveman than he likes to think.

'Coming.'

'Good. Now some rules. You're on a tight leash until I've decided otherwise. Drop me off at work, and be back at one-thirty to pick me up, OK?'

'Yes, boss. Understood, boss.' He likes the structure Claire provides. Often wonders how different his life might be if he'd had the same discipline as a child. He might be working in a bank, wearing a suit, sleeping without monsters. In other words, bored. But there's nothing boring about Claire. She has a strict reward system in place when he follows the rules, to make sure he associates good behaviour with treats. Like with dogs. And now they are going for a walk. He thinks about that for a minute.

Nowhere juggles hope and despair quite like a casino. O'Malley walks through the main entrance, passing security, then skirting around some promo girls trying to look happy as they stand in their underwear handing out wristbands for whatever prize-draw is on offer. He passes the bar that overlooks the main gaming floor, and passes the slots zombies. O'Malley figures everybody has a right to get through life however they choose, free of judgement. But slot machines test his libertarian instincts. He hates them. Hates how they turn people into drones, parts them from their hard-earned money in exchange for a flash of lights and a shot of endorphins. The game is rigged, obviously, but knowing that doesn't stop people playing. Because there's always hope before the despair. O'Malley finds himself speed-walking through to the poker room to escape their misery.

The card room is in full swing. Several cash games are fully seated, and there's a regular tournament game in its early stage, taking up half a dozen tables. There's a list showing the names of those interested in a bigger game — with five-ten blinds — and O'Malley will be seventh on the list. It will be enough to get the game started, so he registers at the podium and trades down some of his chips into smaller denominations. There are plenty of people to say hello to, players and dealers alike. It's one big dysfunctional family. Both Sunny and Big Tone are already there, passing the time in a smaller game while they wait for the decent game to get off the ground. Tone folds his hand and stands up from his table, coming over to catch up with O'Malley.

They take seats at an empty table and shoot the breeze.

'What happened to your face?'

O'Malley's forgotten he looks different. Says the first thing that comes into his head.

'Oh, nothing. Sparring got out of hand this morning. How's your night?'

'Slow, but you're here now, and Shaun's on his way, and I think Sarah might be coming, too. Should be a decent game. Sunny's already down some, and getting dark, so that should be entertaining.'

O'Malley's known Tone for years. They met in the casino back when O'Malley was just getting into the game, and Tone's been a constant in the card room ever since. He's well liked because he'll play big, but never deviates in temperament — he is level-tempered and magnanimous no matter if he's winning or losing. It's a rare and engaging personality in a world where the mercurial and volatile dominate. He's successful in the world of commercial property development, but dialled down his interests when the economy was against him, so he's been more or less a fixture in the poker room since the bankers took the economy for a nosedive back in 2007. O'Malley missed those early years of post-apocalyptic gloom, preoccupied, as he was, with prison life. But he met Tone a few years later, and they enjoy each other's company at the table.

'I haven't seen you around so much, recently. Have you been having a break?' O'Malley asks, wondering if Tone's falling out of love with the game, as happens from time to time.

'I'm spending more time on work again, now that demand has picked up. But I've hardly been hiding — I saw you the other night but you left early, and I was in last night. What about you? Where were you last night?'

'Oh, I had things to do,' O'Malley says, leaving it cryptic. Staying discreet. It wasn't his game to talk about.

'Really? I thought you were going to that game that Steve had an in with?'

Tricky. O'Malley didn't like outright lies, but this might just be a bluff from Tony.

'Nope. Gave it a miss. Had to be up early for training,' O'Malley says, doubling down on his own bluff and pointing to his injured face, maintaining the story.

'That's probably for the best. I was going to warn you to give it a wide berth. I'm not sure it's on the level.' Well, if it was a fixed game, it seemed to be fixed in O'Malley's favour, but he can't argue that point now.

'Good to know for next time.'

'Yeah. Just something I heard somewhere. Steer clear, I reckon.'

'Will do. So let's get this game going, because I'm on a curfew — I can't stay all night.'

So they stand up and wander over to the podium from where the managers marshal the games. O'Malley and Big Tone give them a subtle hurry-up to find a dealer and open the new table. Then they've got to cajole the other players to leave their current seats and join the bigger game. It takes the best part of half an hour to get it underway. O'Malley orders a coffee to pass the time while they wait, and turns his thoughts to Sefina and the world she's found herself in. He feels a responsibility towards her, despite the fact he still hasn't met the girl. A plan is forming, but he will need to do a bit more homework online when he gets back home. And he'll definitely need another car.

But his thoughts are interrupted, because the poker room is suddenly alive with activity, and O'Malley's problems are just getting started.

# CHAPTER NINE

It takes a lot to bring a poker game to a halt. Global terrorist attacks. Hurricanes. Floods. Still the game continues. If they were playing on the *Titanic*, you can probably find eight men at the bottom of the ocean, still waiting for the next card to be dealt.

But now, something major is going down, because slowly but surely each table is coming to an abrupt halt.

It starts on Table Two when Gerald, a lovely old guy whose trousers are cut too short, like he's had a growth spurt since he left the house, stands up abruptly and shouts, 'Oh, my God!' His table soon gets the news, and it gets passed on from there. Dealers stop what they are doing, players dart across the room to share the news with those not yet informed, and even the tournament clock gets paused, as people take in the news.

Danny Cain is dead.

One of us, is what people are thinking. A member of this strange, dysfunctional, socially challenged group is dead. It's there in black and white — colour, actually — on the *Herald*'s website.

*City murder: Local businessman killed.*

A body has been found on the outskirts of the business district, rolled into a scrub of parkland connecting the commercial properties of downtown to the university campus that straddles the central city. He's been beaten to death, and the cops are calling it a robbery gone wrong. They're appealing for witnesses.

The news has rocked the poker room. Not the death, so much. This is a group that runs the odds. Probably more accurately than the actuaries. The demographics and lifestyles of most of the players suggests a high morbidity rate. So a death among them is not a surprise. But a murder is long odds. This is New Zealand, not America. Murder is something that happens to other people, not someone you know. And most nights, Danny is someone everyone knows, someone who should be sitting here among them now, throwing chips in the pot and abusing the dealer.

The news reaches O'Malley.

His mouth goes dry: he was with Danny last night. Probably only a couple of hours before he died. O'Malley gets a strange feeling of guilt, like he was involved somehow. He's lied about his whereabouts already tonight, and that somehow makes him feel complicit. He looks around the table in case people are looking at him, like they know he was with Danny. But they're all dealing with the news themselves, in their own way.

'Fuck me,' Sunny says, on behalf of the table. 'Fuck. I only saw him a couple of nights ago.' Sunny looks genuinely shocked, and he's talking too much because he probably doesn't know how to cry.

'He looked so healthy.' That raises a few eyebrows.

'The fuck?' says Shaun, laconically. 'He was murdered, Sunny.'

'Yeah, yeah, but you know what I mean. Didn't look like he'd be dead in a couple of days, is all.'

'That's generally how murder works, mate.' Shaun again. You can't accuse him of sentimentality.

'Anyone see him last night?' Tone asks. Heads shake all round. O'Malley's, too. He isn't yet sure what is going on, and he needs to think before he speaks.

'He wasn't here last night,' Sunny offers. 'I got a text from him saying he wasn't going to make it in.'

'Where was he going, then?' Tone asks.

'He didn't say.'

'Huh,' Tone says. Is he looking at O'Malley when he says it? Does he think O'Malley has had something to do with it?

When O'Malley looks back up, Tone has his focus elsewhere, and he shakes off the paranoia.

The sombre chit-chat continues, but the game gets back up, too. No one says it, but they all know that if Danny were here and one of them were in his place, he would have already asked the dealer to get on with it.

It doesn't mean they don't care, but frankly it just feels awkward to be sitting around the table and not doing anything. And it isn't like the murder happened *in* the poker room. That would be a serious interruption.

O'Malley continues to play, but he is distracted. He *did* see Danny in the hours before he died. He could help the police with their enquiries. And he *did* see something that might mean his death wasn't random. But he's hesitating.

His recent chat with Buxton notwithstanding, O'Malley doesn't make a habit of talking to the police. He'd had four long years to adopt that principle. And he's already crossed paths with the cops once today. Twice would start a trend. But he's got other considerations, too.

He is making enemies at a great pace, and he doesn't need any more. Bringing heat down on the private game and those who attended it would make him deeply unpopular.

At worst, Danny's death is actually related to the game, and O'Malley would be poking a stick into a nest of rattlesnakes. It's a tough spot. He decides to keep his cards close to his chest and see how things unfold over the next day or so.

His phone rings then, which is a welcome distraction. O'Malley steps away from the table to an empty space out of earshot. It is Sarah.

'Have you heard?' O'Malley asks.

'Yeah, five minutes ago. Nobody gets killed for a fucking slow roll, right?' It has been on O'Malley's mind, too.

'That's what I was thinking. You know, maybe, if we were on a riverboat a couple of centuries ago, and it was heat of the moment, then sure. But after the fact? No way. Besides, it wasn't even that bad, right? Bobby's hot-headed, but he was a businessman in China, not a gangster. And does he look like someone who could beat someone to death?' O'Malley flinches a little at his own question, wondering how *he* looks to other people. Another reason not to volunteer himself to a policeman looking for a suspect.

'I don't know, O'Malley. I'm a poker player, this is out of my field of expertise.'

But not mine, O'Malley thinks. Maybe why Sarah is calling him. Because he's the sort of person who might know what's happened to Danny or knows how to find out.

'He was found about half a mile from where we played,' he tells her. 'So it sounds like he got jumped on his way home. Were you there when he left?' Maybe something else happened after O'Malley took an early bath.

'We all left about the same time. The game wound down around four.'

'Was he up?'

'Some. If he did get mugged, whoever did it would have got a nice surprise. Not many people wandering around with that much cash in their pockets.'

There's a pause then, both of them working out what comes next. Sarah breaks the silence.

'You know, I'm not sure I want to get pulled into this. It won't take the police too long to figure out where Danny was before it happened. Right now, I'm not involved, and I'd prefer to keep it that way. There's a game I've been invited to in London. I was going to go anyway, but I'm definitely going now. I'll be off the grid for a while.'

Nice for some. Getting on a plane is getting more appealing by the second.

'Fair enough. I'll let you know if there's any progress.'

'Thanks. What about you? I were you, I'd put some distance between you and that game. I know what you're like — don't go sniffing around. Let the cops handle it.'

She's got O'Malley's number. He is getting curious, and that usually leads him places he shouldn't go. But she's now the second person to warn him away from that game this evening. Too many coincidences are piling up.

'Noted. Good luck in London.'

'Ha-ha. I'll need it.' She will. O'Malley knows where she is headed: the game was getting some attention online. The tournament buy-in would stretch to a house in most cities in the world. Even so, it seems like the best choice at this moment. Get out of town, let things settle down. Unfortunately, away from the table, O'Malley's not so good at making the smart play.

He hangs up and returns to his seat.

He adds the mystery of Danny's death to his growing list of problems.

Sefina, Browning, Jimmy Tua, Buxton … and now Danny.

O'Malley's got nothing to do with any of them, and yet he's involved with them all. Whether he likes it or not.

He drifts back into the card game, but his heart isn't really in it.

Conversation has turned to gallows humour. It was never going to take long. So now the usual table chat, the sledging and sniping, has death as its theme.

'That's bullshit,' Shaun complains, after Sunny has taken down a hand with an oversized bet. 'You had nothing. You robbed me.' A beat, then: 'Where were *you* in the early hours this morning?'

A collective *whoa*.

Shaun looks up, raises his eyebrows, asks: 'Too soon?'

'It's hard to rob a man who gives his money away, Shaun,' Sunny replies. He could stop there, but doesn't. 'And if I was going to beat you to death I'd do it right here, in front of your friends. Besides, I'd need to take a ticket and get in line.'

'Definitely too soon. Tone it down, fellas.' The dealer gets involved. They have to listen to a lot of bullshit to earn their wage.

'Sorry,' Sunny says to the dealer. Then back to Shaun: 'See, even Frankie thinks you're a dick.'

'He was talking to you, Sunny. He'll probably be asking for a cab home tonight in case you're following him down the street.'

On it goes. The Germans have a name for it. *Witzelsucht.* Literally, a joking addiction, an inability to read the room. These guys have it in spades. Like small children who don't know when to stop, it often ends in tears; either someone is politely asked to leave the room for the night, or on rare occasions there's a physical confrontation that ends with a trespass notice. But tonight, it's just a way to process the news. Guys like Sunny and Shaun haven't caught up with the idea that talking about your feelings helps, so they're trying to laugh it off instead.

O'Malley's deep in thought, and he doesn't see the conversation turning his way. So Sunny catches him off-guard when he turns to O'Malley and makes a half-arsed attempt at another joke.

'Hey, O'Malley, I'm sorry. I hope *you* didn't take offence. You know, talking about beating Shaun to … You know. I wasn't thinking.'

The table goes quiet.

A few players are holding their breath, because Sunny's definitely gone too far this time.

Because what Sunny knows, what half the table knows, is that O'Malley has killed a man. And he beat that man to death.

# CHAPTER TEN

O'Malley was born Roy Christopher O'Malley.

His father was an Irishman who left his homeland as soon as he could, finding himself criss-crossing the islands of the South Pacific doing whatever work he needed to do to pay for the next ticket onwards.

Those who knew him said he had a certain roguish charm, and his mouth got him out of as much trouble as it led him into. That same charm worked on women, too. O'Malley's mother fell victim, and to make matters worse, fell pregnant, too.

O'Malley Senior made all the right noises about taking responsibility, and that lasted a couple of years. Just long enough to uproot his new bride from her birthplace and leave her stranded far from home with a young boy to raise. Mr O'Malley would reappear from time to time until he returned to Ireland permanently, seeming to have exhausted his aspirations as a rolling stone.

O'Malley's mother did her best with what little she had.

What she lacked in material possessions she made up for in femininity.

She was a knockout in her early twenties — a real Polynesian beauty. The sort of natural appeal that made Bligh's men abandon ship. There were plenty of men lining up to replace O'Malley's peripatetic father, but it was the mother they were interested in. The child was a mild irritant to the various men who passed through their household.

O'Malley's mother wasn't promiscuous. The poor judgement in men that led her to O'Malley Senior was no aberration. Mean and unreliable. She could pick them.

When one moved on, survival instinct led to another being admitted.

O'Malley's first memories were not bad ones. He remembers a certain stability with a man named Joseph, who, when O'Malley was four or five, he probably took as Dad. He's got vague recollections of the sort of family outings that others take for granted — playgrounds and swings, digging sand on the beach, that sort of thing. His mother told him once that he was a happy child at that time, and he's seen photographs that suggest the same.

But even then the need for income meant that both Joseph and O'Malley's mother were barely home, working multiple jobs to keep their heads above water. O'Malley learned to be alone at an age when he should have been learning to socialise with others, and those times were difficult for Joseph and Tehei, too. On his sixth birthday, O'Malley found his mother crying in bed, the empty space beside her the cause of her tears. It was the beginning of the rot. Joseph was the only man Tehei truly loved. When he left, he took a bit of her with him.

Other men followed, but none stuck around for long. O'Malley made the best of it.

He was an average student, though he liked to read. Kept himself to himself. Him and his books. As he got older, and bigger, there was plenty of trouble to get into. O'Malley, though, steered clear. With little guidance at home, he took his moral compass from the heroes in his books, and learned early that there was no shame in walking away when trouble found him. But he also learned how to take care of himself when backing down wasn't an option. He found a boxing gym that would let him train if he turned up regularly and didn't mind doing a bit of cleaning up. He got handy in the ring.

Rodney showed up when O'Malley was fifteen.

He had a sour face, and no obvious sense of humour. O'Malley was pretty surly himself — but he was a teenager, so he had an excuse.

Mum's beauty was fading, eroded by hard work and disappointment.

Even so, her bet on Rodney seemed to be a sign of defeat.

O'Malley was still punching the clock at school, but he'd taken a job at McDonald's to pull his weight in the household.

Rodney didn't appear to have the same sense of duty. He drank, mostly in bars where he could watch the sports that he bet on. He'd turn up for dinner, making it clear that the lounge was his territory, and O'Malley should make himself scarce.

The abuse was slow to show itself. O'Malley wasn't there to see the slow, insidious ways in which Rodney began to control his mother. He pounced on her fragility, confirming her belief that no one else would have her. His need for dominance was intense, and he'd apply shame and guilt liberally alongside fear and intimidation. But it was subtle, and there would always be a way to frame his behaviour that put the responsibility back on O'Malley's mother.

O'Malley saw the effects, but not the cause. His mother became timid, jumpy and subservient. Later, O'Malley wished he'd done more to help her back then. But he was a kid, and he assumed this was how life worked, and all too often in his neighbourhood that was true.

As he got older, he noticed Rodney's drinking accelerate. Rodney had control of Tehei's wages by then, so he had more money to throw at his hobbies. He would lose more on the horses: a sport that he appeared to know very little about, but which he continued to put faith in.

He'd drink more and get a little looser with his hands. Maybe he decided his words weren't getting through. So, a slap here, and a shove there, and O'Malley started to notice the odd bruise that his mother would try to hide or explain away. Nor was O'Malley immune. When he wanted the remote control, Rodney simply kicked O'Malley out of his chair, and took his place as if he'd been there all along.

O'Malley retreated that first time. Shocked.

But he was becoming an adult in size, and a bigger than average one at that. He also possessed the defiance that comes during those teenage years, and the next time Rodney struck him, O'Malley stood his ground. Rodney cuffed him across the cheek, for whatever, and no doubt expected the boy to scuttle off to his room or cower. O'Malley did neither. He stood tall and owned his space. They stood staring eye-to-eye, and, like most bullies, Rodney was the first to cede his ground. He muttered something unintelligible and left the house, returning later having found an outlet for his anger elsewhere.

O'Malley pleaded with his mother to leave him. She defended him instead. Took the fall, blaming herself for his anger, and explaining that he would get better. He'd promised as much. But a damaged man doesn't heal unaided. His violence came back slowly but surely, as the realities of his lowly place in the world set in once again. O'Malley was a few days past his eighteenth birthday when both men left that house for good.

It was a gloomy Thursday.

Payday for Rodney, who'd found someone who would pay him to labour on building sites.

Payday for Rodney, which meant everyone needed to look out.

He'd cash his cheque after work, and head to whichever bar was desperate enough to allow him in. There were fewer as the years went on. Rodney was drinking with some other guys after work and took affront when one of the younger guys made fun of him. Rodney had no mechanism for dealing with those with sharper wits than he possessed. His inability to fight back with humour left him humiliated. So he used his fists.

He threw a punch, but when his opponent brushed it off and stood up to him, Rodney's humiliation intensified. He threw his beer to the floor and walked out of the bar, intent on finding someone to punish for his own failings. O'Malley's mother was there to oblige.

O'Malley had finished his shift flipping burgers.

He could hear the music before he got to the front door. Rodney had a habit of turning the radio up LOUD when he was giving a lesson. Macy Gray was singing about addictive love. One of the many songs that O'Malley learned to associate with anything but love.

The kitchen was small, and the floor was covered in a combination of cooked mince and broken ceramics, the meat and sauce tracing arcs on the cupboards and walls.

Dinner had been served and rejected with emphasis, and the cook was now curled on the floor, backed up against the still-hot oven door, a gash above her eye bleeding freely. Rodney stood over her and struck her twice more before he realised he had an audience.

In his hand he held a rolling pin, covered in a mixture of pastry and blood.

He turned to O'Malley and snarled. He'd grown wary of the boy of late, the boy's size and growing strength serving as a warning that he was no longer to be ignored.

O'Malley expected him to back off, walking away to leave his mess behind him. But Rodney's blood was up.

'Get the fuck out of here,' he spat in O'Malley's direction. It took him a beat to realise O'Malley hadn't gone anywhere. 'Get out! This has nothing to do with you.'

O'Malley begged to differ.

'Get away from her now, Rodney.' O'Malley rarely used the man's name. It didn't seem necessary. But it had the desired effect. Even O'Malley was looking down on him now. It was a trigger.

Rodney moved swiftly towards O'Malley and struck the boy's forearm with the weapon in his hand. O'Malley didn't feel a thing. He felt calm. He let Rodney strike him twice more, this time around the head. He was focused on getting hold of Rodney's shirt. Twisting his body around, O'Malley was able to manhandle Rodney away from his mother, and through to the small lounge.

He heard his mother from the kitchen.

'Please, Roy — walk away.' He never worked out if this was said for his benefit or Rodney's.

Rodney had more strength than O'Malley credited him with.

He dropped the rolling pin, which he realised didn't have the heft to do much damage, and grabbed O'Malley's shoulders. He swung him around sharply, the two of them in a brief violent waltz in the front room. Momentum took over, and O'Malley let go, feeling himself propelled backwards, crashing into a free-standing shelving unit that had somehow survived Rodney's previous outbursts. It survived no more, falling apart with O'Malley's weight and velocity, but not before its wooden shelves hit him hard in the back, knocking the wind out of him and connecting with his spine sharply, like rabbit punches to the vertebrae. Rodney was enjoying himself. Maybe he was surprised by how it felt to fight something that put up resistance.

O'Malley's calm deserted him. As Rodney lunged towards him they looked into each other's eyes, and they both realised that there was no walking away from this encounter. It had been brewing slowly for too long. It would only end with one of them incapacitated. If it's me, O'Malley thought, then one day he's going to kill us both. Me and my mother. It was incentive enough.

Rodney hit O'Malley twice as he pulled himself up from what remained of the shelves. O'Malley wasn't feeling the impact, adrenalin doing its thing, but his strength was fading.

He needed to slow the other man down.

He punched Rodney square in the balls, because Queensbury Rules were long gone. It didn't slow Rodney down. His adrenalin was working overtime, too. Or it was the booze.

O'Malley followed up with his head, launching himself towards the older man, aiming the top of his crown at Rodney's chin. It connected, and Rodney's head snapped back, absorbing the blow in his jaw and neck. It rocked him. O'Malley watched him stagger back on his heels. Willed him to give it up.

He didn't.

Any chance of this remaining a clean fight disappeared when Rodney reached for the poker that leaned against the small fireplace that kept the house warm in winter. It was iron, and short enough to be swung with force in the enclosed space in which they fought. Unlike the rolling pin, a well-aimed blow from the fire iron would break O'Malley's bones. If Rodney chose to use it a different way, O'Malley would find himself skewered.

The odds had changed.

Rodney swung, and the metal rod hit O'Malley on the shoulder, which slowed it down, but not enough to stop it bouncing upwards and across his ear onto his head.

O'Malley felt the contact in all three places, and he saw a pink mist in his peripheral vision, as the iron opened up the flesh on his ear. He needed to close the distance between them. O'Malley rushed forward. There was nothing elegant about it. He waited until Rodney pulled back for another blow with the fire iron. Then he pushed forward with everything he had.

Rodney fell, momentum carrying him backwards and his calves hitting the low coffee table that sat behind him. He landed on his back, the poker thrown from his hand as it hit the TV. O'Malley landed on top of him and was first to adjust to their new position.

O'Malley threw two punches at Rodney's head. And then he threw some more.

# CHAPTER ELEVEN

Ten more, according to the coroner's estimate.

O'Malley was aware only that he needed to stop Rodney.

He didn't remember making a conscious decision to stop. His arms simply got tired. He was sitting back against a wall, exhausted, when the police arrived in response to a call from neighbours. The lounge was unrecognisable. So was O'Malley. His ear was still bleeding enthusiastically, along with a variety of cuts on his face and body. His eyelids were already swelling up.

O'Malley's mother, curiously, had begun to make a cup of tea.

She'd gone off-planet for a while.

O'Malley looked across at Rodney, and saw his chest rise, so he was still breathing. For now.

The police realised pretty early on that no one was talking.

Rodney couldn't, Mother wouldn't, and O'Malley didn't know what to say.

They settled for letting the medics take over. They cleaned Rodney's face up as best they could, and put an oxygen mask on him, carefully transferring him to a stretcher and out to a waiting ambulance. They checked O'Malley out where he sat, and once they had ascertained he could stand, they walked him out to a second vehicle, to take him to hospital.

O'Malley guessed they did the same with his mother, unless she'd spirited herself away in body as well as mind.

The next twenty-four hours were a blur.

O'Malley spent a few hours in the hospital, tended to by a series of kind, professional staff who kept their boredom behind masks, as they patched up another DV statistic. They weren't party to the facts, so O'Malley could have been perpetrator or victim, but they fixed him without judgment. Photographs were taken, stitches sewn, and bandages applied.

Rodney faded fast. He died in hospital, twenty-three hours after his first post-work drink.

O'Malley met Sergeant Buxton in the hospital. He'd come to take a statement before Rodney took a turn for the worst. Buxton didn't get much out of O'Malley. It hurt to talk, for one thing. But O'Malley also assumed at this point that he was the victim. Rodney had been the aggressor, so he figured whatever he said might be used against Rodney. You don't snitch where O'Malley grew up, so he kept tight-lipped, despite the pain that came with using any muscles around his face.

Buxton was unimpressed but unsurprised.

'Have you asked my mother?' O'Malley asked, with discomfort. To his ears it sounded more like *voo asped my other*. Buxton was bilingual, though, so he got the drift.

'Yes, we have. She isn't saying much. She wondered what she should make for dinner.'

That sounded about right. She could teach an ostrich a thing or two.

'Huh.' O'Malley chuckled at the absurdity of it all.

The next conversation with Buxton was under caution, in an interview room that had seen better days. The table between them was immoveable, bolted to the floor, and bore the scratches and affirmations of those who'd been there before.

A duty solicitor sat beside O'Malley, his dirty fingernails and worn suit doing little to instil confidence. He had an unfortunate coffee stain that straddled the buttons of a once-white shirt, and looked every bit the disillusioned lawyer whose role in life had been reduced to keeping his clients silent. Guilt was assumed, but self-incrimination could be avoided.

Buxton, by contrast, wore none of the signs of the jaded cynicism you might expect from someone who saw what life was really like among those who began the race far behind the starting line. He still believed in the benefit of the doubt, getting to the truth, and giving people enough rope to hang themselves.

'Why don't you tell us what happened in your own words, Roy?'

O'Malley thought on this for a while. He now knew that Rodney was dead, and that he was responsible.

But he also couldn't see how he would have done things any differently. On balance, the worst thing he could do now was try to lie. If he was going to be punished, he should let his judges have the full story. His mother was currently safe from physical harm, and he took solace from that fact. So he told his story as he remembered it to Buxton and the tape recorder, the duty solicitor there to bear witness.

Buxton made few interruptions. O'Malley's co-operation must have been refreshing. Buxton let him tell it as best he could, and only joined in when he was running out of steam.

'So let's focus on something for a moment. You've both fallen to the ground. You're on top of Mr Young?'

'Yes.'

'And you've overpowered him at this stage?' The solicitor started to fidget.

'I wouldn't say that, no. He wasn't done.'

' "He wasn't done?" What do you mean by that?'

'I mean he still had fight in him. He wasn't giving up.'

'OK. And you hit him how many times?'

'I don't know. I don't remember.'

'A couple? Five times? Can you make a guess?'

Fidgety man wasn't letting that go. He whispered in O'Malley's ear. Buxton changed tack.

'All right, would you say you were in control at this point? Did you stop when you saw that he didn't "still have fight in him"?'

They were getting to the nub of it.

'It happened quickly. I don't remember exactly.'

'Well, I guess the autopsy might tell us more.' A fact that sounded like a threat. 'OK, let's talk a bit about the past,' Buxton said, maybe giving O'Malley time to regroup a little bit.

'OK,' he said, unsure.

'Has this happened before? Mr Young beating you?' O'Malley looked to the lawyer for guidance. He shrugged, but it could have been his boredom peeking through.

'Beating me? Maybe a couple of times.'

'And what happened on those occasions?' O'Malley thought about his answer. He kept it honest.

'First time I walked away. Second time I didn't. So he did.'

'OK. So you stood up to him, and he backed down, right? So he was scared of you?'

'No, I don't think so. He just liked easy targets better.'

'Easy targets like your mother?' The conversation was going too smoothly. O'Malley got the sense he was being guided down a dark alley, and he'd find some of Buxton's mates at the end of the street, a streetlight busted out for cover.

'Yes, like my mother. He's been beating her for years. When I got there yesterday, he was beating her again.'

'But what was different this time? Didn't you try to stop him the other times? You didn't ask for help?'

O'Malley felt the shame creep through him, a physical sensation that made him check his bladder. He didn't give any response.

'You've got to help me understand why this was different, Roy.'

'*He* was different. He wasn't usually stupid enough to hurt her in front of me. Why fight two people when you can hurt one without a fight?'

'OK?' Buxton coaxed for more.

'But this time he just didn't care. He started on her and then he came for me. I never saw him that bad.'

'Maybe,' Buxton considered the answer. 'But maybe *you* were different this time. Maybe you'd had enough, and when you found Mr Young once again hurting your mother, you decided to put an end to it, once and for all.'

'Is there a question in there?' Mr Fidget had found his voice.

'Yes, OK, here's the question. Did you, in fact, decide that enough was enough? Did you decide that Mr Young had hurt your mother enough, and you would do something to stop him, once and for all? Did you want to kill Mr Young?' He had to ask.

'No, I did not. I didn't. He attacked my mother, and then he attacked me, and I just needed to stop him. I fought back when I was attacked.'

'Thank you. OK, we'll stop it there for now.' Buxton seemed satisfied. O'Malley wasn't sure if that was good for him or not. He turned to his solicitor for a sign, but Mr Fidget was now Mr Still. Some help he was.

The police didn't have much choice. A man had died, and at O'Malley's hand. A charge was inevitable. O'Malley had their sympathies, but if he was to be exonerated it would be by judge or jury, not the cops.

O'Malley didn't blame them: a man was dead; he was the cause.

His mother remained an unhelpfully silent witness.

Buxton, for what it's worth, treated O'Malley with kindness throughout. His gut told him O'Malley was a good person in a bad situation, but his guideline book told him to charge the young man with manslaughter.

He said as much once the tape was off and he'd finished formally charging O'Malley.

*Rodney Young was a shitbag* were his exact words. *Find a good lawyer and you might get a sympathetic jury*.

O'Malley discovered much later that Buxton himself had made sure that a decent lawyer found the case. But a jury trial is always a coin-flip.

There wasn't much interest in O'Malley's fate. In fact, the only person who sat in the gallery each day was Buxton, who had to be there as the officer in charge of the case. The wheels of justice moved slowly, too. O'Malley spent five months on remand, waiting to be heard. Bail had been set, but he had no one to pay it, and nowhere to go if he got it. He wasn't allowed to go back home, as he would be living with a key witness. They'd conspire and get their stories rehearsed.

If only they knew his mother.

She didn't reveal much of herself in the trial, either. Her memory didn't improve in the months between the incident and O'Malley's day in court. Her answer to most questions was *I don't remember*. She was testing the judge's patience, as both prosecutor and defence tried in vain to elicit a more detailed response from her.

O'Malley didn't really recognise her. Her capacity for reason had deserted her the moment the men in her life had come to blows, and she no longer knew where her loyalties lay. It should have been obvious, of course, to be on her son's side, and all she had to do was tell the truth about what had happened that day and the years of abuse that had preceded it. But her trauma was deep, and she now mourned her abuser. His control of her reached from beyond the grave, and she stayed firmly on the fence, unable to recall much of anything.

O'Malley followed his instructions to the letter, and recounted events as he had now been coached to do. It was the stark brutality of the medical reports that did for him.

The jury needed to believe that he did only enough to ensure his own safety, but the clinical reporting and photographic evidence that accompanied it were intimidating to twelve people whose lives sheltered them from what real violence looked like. People over-estimate how they themselves would respond in circumstances that are hypothetical. No one on that jury looked like they brought experience to the table.

In any event, the jury took their time deliberating. O'Malley's lawyer said this would be a good thing. They might be looking for ways out on his behalf.

In the end, they didn't. When they finally returned a verdict, it was guilty. Only those twelve know if it was a close call. It might have been a slam dunk, or maybe they just didn't want to take any chances, releasing a monster.

O'Malley was sent away for sentencing at a later date. Nothing about the justice system suggested urgency. It was as if they wanted to tease it out.

Buxton waited it out, too, and returned to see it conclude on O'Malley's day of sentencing. O'Malley had ended a man's life and was given four years to reflect on that fact.

# CHAPTER TWELVE

Sunny doesn't regret much that comes out of his mouth, but he's backtracking furiously now. O'Malley's one of the good guys, and Sunny thinks he should have got a medal not a prison sentence. But it's too late now, and he's hoping O'Malley will forgive him. He's embarrassed O'Malley and shared his business with people who don't need to know what happened all those years ago. But O'Malley chooses to take it in his stride and defuses the situation.

'No offence taken, Sunny. I reckon Shaun would take you, anyway.'

The tension passes, and one of the other players takes O'Malley's lead, suggesting odds for Sunny and Shaun in a variety of combat situations. Sunny only comes out favourite in sumo.

Inside, O'Malley is rattled. Danny is dead and Sunny has reminded everyone that O'Malley has form. Give it a couple of days and the entire poker room will be looking at him with suspicion.

He decides he better find out what did happen to Danny, before he becomes prime suspect.

O'Malley plays long enough to put distance between Sunny's comment and his departure. He wins two big pots against Sunny, too. It is the least he can do.

O'Malley says his goodbyes, cashes out, and heads for the exit. On his way out, Sunny calls out after him.

'Hey, O'Malley, what happened to your face, anyway?'

O'Malley definitely needs to find Danny's attacker.

He checks the *Herald* for any updates on Danny's story. There's nothing new. He'll have to find out more on his own. He heads over to The Brandling, hyper-aware of his surroundings, on high alert for unknown assailants or open manholes he could fall into.

The biggest threat he encounters is a group of young women intent on painting the town red. The detective in O'Malley tells him that the girl at the centre of the group, carrying a large inflatable cock, is soon to be married. He feels vulnerable approaching the group: he is on his own, and in the semi-darkness of the city at night might be considered tall, dark and OK-looking. He feels like a sardine who's been separated from the shoal; eight hungry predators approaching from all sides. One of the alphas in the gaggle makes him an offer on behalf of the group, which he politely declines, holding his arms in the air and shaking his head as he makes a sideways dash through their midst.

Their giggles fade as O'Malley regains his composure and carries on unscathed. The ladies have already forgotten him, turning their attentions to an unfortunate parking attendant who soon finds himself mildly assaulted and the unwilling centrepiece to some rapidly arranged group photos. Men in uniform, eh?

'You look tired, baby,' Claire says, as he approaches her at the bar. She is sitting customer-side, sipping a gin and tonic through a metal straw.

'I am,' he replies. 'I could do with a lie-down.'

'We can do that,' she laughs. 'Do you want a drink first?'

'I'll have a rum with a squeeze of lime if you're buying.'

Claire gets down from her bar stool and works her way around to the business side, pulling a stout, dark green bottle from the shelf.

'A new one for you to try today, sir. Diplomatico, from deepest, darkest Venezuela.'

It is very good. O'Malley nods and makes a humming sound to register his approval.

'You're very welcome. How was poker? You look like you spent a grand and won a dollar.'

'It's a long story, and I don't think you're going to like it. Let's save it for later. But yeah, I won.'

'Very cryptic, O'Malley. I could just shake it out of you now, you know?'

'I think you might need to get in line, honey. It'll keep.'

'All right, don't go all gloomy on me. Let me take your mind off it.'

Claire is now back on O'Malley's side of the bar, and she presses her lips on his, pushing her chest against him. He is restored. She pulls back from him and pushes her hair over her shoulder, turning her head to the few remaining customers nursing last orders.

'Now, Mr Detective, tell me what you see.'

He likes this game. Claire will test his powers of perception, before pulling the rug out from under him with her deeper powers of deduction. He pretends he's Holmes, but in her shadow he is always Dr Watson.

'OK, the two suits over there have been celebrating. They're in real estate, or commercial property, something like that. They've closed a deal and they're the bee's knees, and they'll be looking for a strip club to finish the night in style.' He looks for confirmation from Claire, but all he gets is Mona Lisa. He plods on.

'The couple on the left have had an argument, but they're in make-up mode now. He keeps looking at the pack of smokes on the table. He's desperate for a cigarette, but he doesn't want to leave the table and lose the positive momentum they've achieved. The three guys playing pool don't have much of a story. They're just out shooting the breeze; and they haven't been drinking long, so probably all work late hours, maybe a restaurant. The guy in the blue shirt keeps looking over. He's got the hots for you, but he's a decent guy and his ego hasn't taken too big a dent with my arrival. He can still appreciate your beauty. Oh, and Clint has a date lined up. He's smiling, which is a giveaway.'

Clint works the bar alongside Claire, and they live vicariously through his tales of woe on the singles scene. O'Malley figures this guess is a dead cert.

'Four out of ten, O'Malley,' Claire says with a smug grin. Cute, but smug.

'Tell me, oh oracle.'

'OK. The suits won't be going to a strip club. They got married today — civil union — and that's what they've been celebrating. Wrong, too, on profession. One's a TV reporter, the other's advertising, something like that.'

'Hmmm. Well, I'd have got there, you know, if I'd been serving them drinks all night.'

They get competitive over the smallest of things.

'Right. Of course you would. The couple? No argument, and it's not his cigarettes he's looking at. He's watching his phone, wondering when his wife is going to call him to find out where he is. His wedding ring is in his pocket, but the band on his finger is still there if you want to look for it. The girl knows, but doesn't know, if you get what I mean. She's trying to get him home with her, and he's making excuses.'

O'Malley's zero for two.

'So, no points there. You're only part right with the guys at the pool table. They've *all* got the hots for me, dummy. Dom's just a bit more protective than the other two. He's checking you've got good intentions.'

Dom?

'My intentions are pure. Tell Dom he can stand down.' Aiming for cool, but coming off as a touch jealous.

'You're so dumb. Anyway, you're right about Clint. He hit it off with a group of girls out on a hen party earlier on. He got a phone number.'

O'Malley says nothing to that. But he reckons he's done alright on the test.

'Well, I got most right,' he says, hoping his maths won't be scrutinised.

'No, you most certainly did not. But I won't hold it against you. You're still alright, O'Malley. Let's get out of here, leave Clint to clean up before he realises the phone number he's got isn't real.'

Later, O'Malley tells Claire about developments as they sit in his apartment.

It's not well received.

'Seriously? You need to go and see Buxton and tell him everything. If you know something that could help find who attacked Danny, then you should tell the cops.'

'Yeah, I could do that,' he agrees. It is what O'Malley believes is known in business circles as a Japanese yes. Yes, I understand you. Not: yes, I agree and will do what you suggest.

'But?'

'But I think it's too early to play that card. I'll have to tell him more about Browning, too, and that could bring more problems. And I don't even know what the Danny situation is yet. They might already have someone in lock-up for all I know. I'd be making a bunch of enemies that I don't need right now if I brought the game to the cops and it had nothing to do with Danny's death.'

'You've got twisted logic sometimes, O'Malley. It's going to get you hurt, or in jail. Let me spell it out for you. Someone you spent several hours with last night was found dead two or three hours later. He'd been beaten up. You have a police record that matches the crime. The dots join themselves. Staying silent just does it in big, thick marker pen.'

He thinks better of telling her she looks beautiful when she is angry, the way her nostrils flare and the colour rises in her cheeks.

'I get that. The fact remains I've done absolutely nothing wrong. Putting myself forward at this point will just send them down the wrong path and puts me in their crosshairs. A couple of days won't make much difference — and I can bring Buxton in when I've got something concrete for him to work on.'

He raises his eyebrows towards Claire, asking her to see it his way.

'Seriously, babe, what makes you think you'll get to the truth faster than the police? There's only one of you, and you can't exactly force people to tell you anything.'

He probably could, actually, but he doesn't argue the point.

'Two days, Claire. If I haven't got anywhere in two days, I'll have a word with Buxton,' he says, drawing short of a promise. He's learned not to under-deliver.

'And what if you cause more problems in the next two days?'

'Then we'll know I'm making progress,' he says.

Claire stays at O'Malley's: Claire in the bedroom, O'Malley on the couch. She's past trying to persuade him to share the bed, and tonight maybe he'd have found himself on the couch anyway: he pushed his luck a little too far, and he'll be tiptoeing his way back onto her good side for a while yet.

As it is, he wakes up unnaturally early, his phone buzzing urgently a little after eight in the morning. Too many rude awakenings and he'll have jet-lag.

He answers the phone without looking.

'O'Malley speaking.'

'Mr O'Malley. It's Loto. Loto Tupuola. I wondered how you were getting on?'

# CHAPTER THIRTEEN

*Sefina.* She'd fallen down O'Malley's priority list when Danny turned up dead.

'Some progress, Loto. But not enough to share with you yet. I believe that she is safe, though, which should give you some comfort.'

Safe, as in not shackled to a lunatic's basement wall.

'She is not safe until she is home, O'Malley.' He feels rebuke in the words. Loto won't be any happier if he knows O'Malley has been close to Sefina but hasn't found the time to chat.

'Well, I'm on the case, Loto,' he says, but wonders why he is doing *all* the work. 'Have you heard anything? Anything that might help me?'

'I have not. I have spoken with all her friends' parents, and they assure me no one has heard anything from Sefina. It has been two days since we first spoke. I don't mean to sound ungrateful, but what have you been doing?'

Ungrateful? Why would he sound ungrateful?

'Let me worry about what I'm doing, Mr Tupuola, and assume I'll be in touch when I've got some news.'

He hangs up. He needs coffee. O'Malley feels a little bad speaking to Loto so tersely. If he was being paid he'd call it bad customer service. But he isn't being paid and his face hurts — actually, his whole body hurts. If he makes it to the end of the week without further injury or jail time he'd call it a result. So he forgives himself the lack of early-morning manners and makes his way to the kitchen.

He has slept well, so the only tidying required from his night on the couch is the blanket that needs folding. It can wait. He makes his coffee, taking care to tamp the grounds firmly, letting the machine warm up before pouring just the right amount to ensure the flavour and strength meet his standards. Like everyone else in Auckland, he's turned into a coffee snob. Claire's happy with granules, so it's all the more galling when she floats past him, taking the coffee from his hands as she does so.

'Thanks' is all he is getting for now.

He needs another sentence or two to gauge her mood and his wellbeing.

She stands in the middle of the kitchen, cradling the coffee mug with both hands, studying O'Malley as she takes a drink. He studies her right back. She's wearing a simple black thong, which makes her legs go on forever, and a pink cropped shirt that reveals her tight stomach muscles. The gap between the shirt and her skin looks like a wonderful place to warm his hands, but O'Malley resists. He isn't yet sure if it is safe. Claire's hair is tousled from sleep, and it falls around the mug as she raises it to her lips. Claire can sense where O'Malley's mind is.

'Go and get dressed before you embarrass yourself. Then let's make a plan.'

That's good. Plans are good. He goes through to the walk-in wardrobe that connects the bathroom and his bedroom and takes about thirty seconds to choose what to wear and get dressed. It would have been quicker, but he dithers between maroon and black for the t-shirt that will match his jeans. He opts for maroon, which matches his sanguine mood.

He chooses boots over trainers, in case someone accidentally drops something heavy on his foot. If it comes to it, he'll run equally well whatever he wears, but a broken toe might slow him down. He comes back out to find Claire fully dressed, and back where he left her in the kitchen.

'You took your time, princess,' she says playfully.

'Got to look good for you, baby.'

'Well, let's keep you that way. What's your big strategy, O'Malley?'

'Find Sefina, talk to her, reunite her with her father, stay out of Browning's way, and confirm if Danny's death had anything to do with the game the other night,' he replies, making himself a coffee to replace the one he lost.

'That sounds like a list of objectives, hon, not a strategy. How are you going to achieve those objectives?'

Claire would make a very good business coach.

Well, she'd be good at whatever she put her mind to, but for now she is determined to keep O'Malley honest. And alive.

He tells her what he has in mind.

She makes some tweaks to his plan, and insists on regular check-ins, which he accepts reluctantly. He's still got pride.

It's hard to be a hero and gain Claire's admiration and approval if she does all the thinking. Besides, his first day as hired muscle got him a smack in the face from a beanpole. He isn't sure his brawn is something he can rely on.

But every relationship is built on compromise.

He'll let Claire think she is in charge, for an easy life.

She throws her keys his way.

'Walk me home and be sure to bring my car back in one piece.'

O'Malley grins and nods all at once.

'Oh, and O'Malley?'

He looks up at her enquiringly.

'I'm tracking your phone, so don't go thinking you can change the plan once I'm out of range.'

O'Malley's in charge alright.

His plan is loose.

He's got two lines of enquiry to follow, and one of them has to be in person.

He figures Sefina isn't being held against her will. His guess is she was shacked up with Jesse Browning against Browning Senior's better judgement. This was fine until O'Malley turned up, drawing attention to whatever business is going on around love's young dream.

The arrangement will be getting a little uncomfortable on the farm, and the teenagers will be itching to get out from under the disapproving glare of Mr Browning.

Sefina might already be realising that the grass is really just the same shade of green whichever side of the fence you're on. They won't stay cooped up for ever. O'Malley's just got to be there when they come up for air. He could wait at the end of their driveway and follow them from there. But he'll run into more snap-happy power-company employees with powers of detainment. That's a bad idea.

So he will need to take a gamble on where they might be heading if they emerge from the driveway.

He figures there's not much to interest a couple of teenagers if they take a right — it's just more farmland and rural views, and they have plenty of that where they are.

They will take a left and work their way over to one of the more populated areas towards the coast. With no better plan in mind, O'Malley sets himself up on Pine Valley Road, and adjusts his rear-view mirror, hoping that his instincts are right and at some point a battered old Toyota Camry will come into view.

It is boring work, but he has come prepared. He's swapped yesterday's protein bars for potato crisps, water for Red Bull, and is saving an apple and a bag of nuts in case things get desperate. When he's tired and stressed, diet is the first thing to suffer. He'll work it all off in the gym sometime. For now, he is focused on how he'll get out of Claire's VW Golf if he gains too much weight.

Traffic is light out this way, so he doesn't need to remain constantly vigilant. For all he knows, Romeo and Juliet will wait a few more days before they get stir-crazy. He'll just have to wait, too. He's got plenty to keep himself occupied.

He needs to find out more about the private casino he'd been at before Danny's untimely end. He'll pull some threads and see where they lead. Starting with Chinese Steve, who brought him into the game in the first place. O'Malley calls him hands-free, so he can keep eating crisps.

Steve takes his time answering.

'Hey, O'Malley. It's early, man, what's up?'

'Never mind the time, what do you mean, what's up? Don't you read the news?'

'Yeah, sure, but different newspapers to you, I'm guessing. Why? What's happened?' He sounds genuinely clueless, so O'Malley fills him in. He stays quiet a while. O'Malley keeps his eyes on the road behind him, multi-tasking.

'Nah, man, that's not Bobby's style. He blows up hot — you know that — but he's not a violent man.'

'Well, he had a pretty good temper on him on Friday.' What O'Malley saw looked like a tendency to violence.

'Yeah, but he's all mouth. Look, if he did have anything to do with it, he'll have already disappeared. Let me find him and check it out. But honestly, I don't see it, O'Malley.'

'It's too much of a coincidence to be random, Steve. That game has something to do with it, even if it's not Bobby Q. Whose game is it, really?'

'I don't know. I know William, and he invited me, said to bring another player. But he's just hired help. For a set-up like that, you need juice. That's not William.'

O'Malley considers this. Everything Steve says is true, but could also be deflection.

'So it would need to be someone well connected in the community, with cash, and the right phone numbers to call if there was any trouble?' he asks. It was a predominantly Chinese game, and that's the community he is pointing to.

'Yes, I think so.'

'So someone like you?'

'Hey, fuck off, man. How long have you known me? If it was my game I'd have told you that from the start. I don't know who's behind it, OK? And anyway, why does it matter so much who's running the game?'

'Because if Bobby Q didn't kill Danny because he got slow-rolled, there's something else going on that I'm not seeing. I want to know what that is.'

'And what are you going to do if you find something, O'Malley? If you're right, then you're walking into trouble. Why would you want to do that?' O'Malley isn't about to share his reasons. And not with Steve, who is still on the list of suspects until O'Malley can look him in the eye and rule him out.

'Danny wasn't the best guy on Earth, but he got killed and I figure someone should find out why.'

'Always the saviour, O'Malley. I think you like getting into shit.' Maybe. Or maybe shit finds him. Chicken and egg.

'I don't. But it feels like now I'm in it, I better keep moving forward or I'll drown in it.' It isn't a pretty image. 'How do I find William?'

'Fuck's sake, O'Malley. If this is what you say it is, you're going to drag me into it with you.'

'Not if you're telling me the truth; I'll keep you well out of it. But I need to have a conversation with William, so where will I find him?'

Steve's sigh fills the car, in surround-sound.

'He's just a kid, hangs out with all the other kids. Comes to my bars pretty regular, likes the VIP service — you know, bottle of vodka for the table, showing off to the girls. I don't want you turning up and causing trouble, O'Malley. No offence, but you stand out a bit next to my customers.'

'I said I'd keep you out of it and I will. I know you'll tell your door staff to turn me away anyway. But it's Sunday night tonight, where will he be?'

Another long sigh.

'Probably bar-hopping. But he might end up at the Shanghai Club on Pitt Street around midnight. Fuck, man. I do not need to be involved in this, O'Malley.'

O'Malley figures he'll probably hear that a lot before this is over.

'If you're not, you won't be. And call me when you find Bobby Q,' O'Malley replies before hanging up.

He calls Claire and gives her a brief update. She is in the middle of a tutorial, so O'Malley's able to keep it brief and one-way. He's sure she'll call back to object to his night-time plans before the day is out. But he's got time to work on a rationale.

There's no sign of Sefina and Jesse, so all he can do is sit back and wait.

He puts the radio on, changing stations until he finds some decent music to keep him awake. He stumbles on an old Aretha track, and when inexcusably that's replaced with something from the eighties he switches to a Motown playlist from his phone. He's an old soul at heart.

He gets bored playing with the air conditioning, switching seat positions, opening and closing the window. He finds a near-empty Pringles can in his backpack. One of the small packs that contains about twenty crisps when it's full. He eats the remaining contents, just to empty the pack. Then he tears the foil from the top of the pack, and places it on the middle of the back seat. He then resumes his position in the driver's seat, and plays basketball, throwing nuts over his shoulder towards the Pringles can. It takes a while to get his aim in — and he remembers a little too late that it isn't his car, and he's been instructed to look after it. He'll have to stop and vacuum the car before he returns it.

He is getting pretty good at peanut basketball. He's worked out how to compensate for the lack of uniformity in the nut's shape, and he's hitting about seventy per cent. He is ready for challengers.

He considers giving Claire another update to let her know his time isn't being wasted when he sees a tatty red car approaching in the distance. It's the closest match he's seen by a long way, and he gets that sensation in his stomach that you get when you think of someone and next minute they're calling you up out of the blue. Serendipity or coincidence? He'll take either. He grabs a baseball cap from the passenger seat and puts it on, low over his eyes. He slumps down in the seat, the way he's seen people do in the movies.

He's parked as close as he can to the intersection, so cars would naturally begin to slow as they pass him, buying him a fraction more time to look at the occupants.

It's a red Camry, and the glimpse he gets of the girl in the passenger seat reminds him of the partial profile he found on Instagram only a couple of days earlier. 'Follow that car,' he instructs himself, waiting until he sees it turn left at the intersection before starting up the engine and heading in the same direction. He spills more peanuts on the passenger seat in his haste.

# CHAPTER FOURTEEN

O'Malley follows the Toyota to the state highway, allowing a silver Prius to slip between his VW and the Camry ahead. It gives him cover and a little more time to react to Jesse's route.

He expects Jesse to cross the highway and carry on to the cluster of retail outlets on the other side, but, instead of going straight on, Jesse indicates a right turn, which will take them onto the highway and back to the city. Maybe Sefina is going home all on her own? O'Malley will be able to tail them to her front door and put his arm around her as she steps back into her father's embrace. Job done. But they're not going back to the city. Instead, they take a slip road that peels off the main road. O'Malley lets the Prius carry on, and then follows the Camry.

The slip road leads to a dead end: a car park that sits at the bottom of a hill, on which a large indoor artificial ski slope has been built. It's incongruous, and would be even on a winter's day, and O'Malley's not dressed for skiing.

Serves him right for stalking a couple of teenagers.

Outside it's bikini weather, and Jesse and Sefina are going skiing. Maybe they've got dreams of running off to the Alps and starting a new life.

O'Malley parks a safe distance from where the Toyota has pulled up, and when he's sure they are here for the snow he gets out of the VW to stretch. He's a tight fit in Claire's car, and sitting stationary for the morning has done nothing for his already aching body. He tries to touch his toes a couple of times. Fails. Then follows Sefina and Jesse inside.

The kids are at the counter paying for entry, so O'Malley loiters around in the shop that charges a premium to those who've driven all the way here and forgotten something. He looks for a pair of gloves that might fit, thinking ahead in case he finds himself on the slopes. He finds a pair big enough, but the price makes him remember why he's never taken up winter sports. He puts the gloves back and watches the kids disappear through turnstiles and into a fitting room where they'll pick up their hire gear before hitting the snow.

O'Malley goes into the café that sits alongside the slope of artificial snow that everyone is here to enjoy. Thick glass acts as a divider between the relative warmth of the café and the wintry conditions that people have paid good money to endure on the other side. He orders a coffee and buys a newspaper, taking a seat close to the glass, appearing, he hopes, like every other anxious parent watching over their child as they play in the snow.

His coffee arrives, delivered with world-class indifference by a surly boy not much older than Sefina. The server puts the cup down in front of O'Malley, making sure to spill some of its contents onto the saucer that comes with it, before removing the number that O'Malley has placed on the table to identify his order. All without wasting any words on his customer. He has found his vocation.

O'Malley reads the paper, keeping one eye on his target.

Sefina is no skier.

It looks to be her first time on the snow, and she alternates between standing still and moving at speed on her bottom. She is loving every moment of it. Jesse, to his credit, is laughing with her, and helping her up whenever she falls. It's a good choice of date, and O'Malley wonders whether Jesse might have some redeeming qualities after all. Sefina certainly looks happy, and if that is Jesse's doing, then O'Malley can't blame her for building her dreams on the wrong boy. Maybe if they can stay away from their fathers, there is hope for them.

But O'Malley's not here as a relationship coach. He needs to get five minutes with Sefina and encourage her to reconnect with her broken-hearted father.

He doesn't find anything of interest in the newspaper. The report on Danny's death is word-for-word identical to the online version he's already read. The story is tucked below the fold on page four, already drifting from the headlines. O'Malley has a valiant attempt at the cryptic crossword — Claire has been teaching him the rules — but it's one thing to watch someone explain how they got the answer, and another to get there yourself. He stops trying.

He returns his attentions to the ski slope, enjoying the slightly hypnotic repetition of the skiers getting pulled up to the top of the hill, and zig-zagging their way back down. Sefina is improving, getting better at controlling her speed, her skis pointing inwards and following her instructions. As she gains in confidence she lets herself go a bit, picking up speed and letting out a scream of delight as she does so.

Her progress is short-lived.

An experienced skier has been making swift work of the slope but finds himself with nowhere to go, caught between a small, accomplished child and Sefina's unpredictable progress.

He puts the brakes on, avoids the child, but clips Sefina as he does so. Not enough to knock her down, but enough to interrupt the delicate calculations she is making to stay on her feet.

She falls once again, and again she takes it with good grace.

Jesse, less so.

He doesn't stop to help her, but instead chases after the other skier, meeting him at the bottom of the slope and getting as close as his awkward footwear allows. O'Malley can't hear what is being said through the glass, but Jesse's body language makes it clear he is unimpressed. Chivalry and testosterone make for a heady cocktail in young men, and it looks like the situation might boil over, which O'Malley is quite looking forward to. It's not every day you get to see a ski fight. With all the equipment they are wearing, it will be like two team mascots rolling around on the sidelines. Entertaining, with little chance of injury to either party.

O'Malley's hopes are dashed when Jesse's opponent is joined by a friend. Two against one is enough of a suppressant for Jesse's anger, and he backs off, still giving plenty of verbals, as he shuffles sideways back up the slope, back to Sefina, who has been watching it all as she sits on the snow.

The date loses steam after that. Sefina shakes her head in frustration, and encourages Jesse back to the ski-lift, trying to help him to get his head back in the game, but on their next descent Jesse is still distracted. He's been denied the opportunity to defend a lady's honour, and he's out of sorts. They give it a couple more runs and then call it quits. They head back to the changing rooms to return their equipment. O'Malley will get his chance to speak to Sefina when they emerge, but now he'll have to contend with Jesse's latent anger, too. O'Malley's in no mood to indulge him.

O'Malley rolls his newspaper up and leaves the café, thanking the surly boy for his coffee on the way out. The server looks confused, unsure why O'Malley would be thanking him. It's a small victory.

O'Malley taps out a beat on his open palm with the newspaper, walking across the car park until he reaches Jesse's car. He makes himself comfortable on the car bonnet, resting one foot on the bumper.

He waits. Begins to think there might be a back exit from the snow dome, and he's been stood up, but after about ten minutes Sefina and Jesse emerge through the main entrance, arm-in-arm, Sefina carrying a bottle of juice in her spare hand.

Jesse and Sefina make their way across the tarmac, but before they begin threading their way through the cars something catches Jesse's attention, and he stops in his tracks.

He turns towards an SUV parked in the first line of cars, and O'Malley looks across to see what he is looking at. The guys who made Jesse back down on the slopes are now putting their gear in the back of their vehicle.

O'Malley sees where this is heading but lets it play out.

The two guys see Jesse looking over and share a private joke.

Jesse isn't going to be denied again. He breaks away from Sefina and heads their way. The skiers are both bigger than Jesse, but they don't look like brawlers. O'Malley still doesn't rate Jesse's chances. Sefina stands her ground, calling after Jesse to leave it, but his blood is up.

'Hey, fuckhead. You owe my girlfriend an apology.' O'Malley wonders how Jesse has survived this long.

'Look, man, it was an accident. Let it go, OK?' No apology, but no attempt to escalate either.

'You like pushing girls over? Is that your thing?'

This boy has definitely got some unresolved anger issues.

'Now you're just being a dick. We don't want any trouble, so just back off, OK?'

The guy is warming to the idea of a confrontation, but still trying to talk Jesse down.

He's wearing a long-sleeved red t-shirt, and he rolls the sleeves up now, showing Jesse he's ready if it comes to it.

Jesse launches his hands into Red's chest, pushing him back with both arms. 'You like pushing girls?'

Red is prepared for the shove, and holds his balance, but not his temper.

'For fuck's sake,' he says, and responds to the push with a shove of his own.

That is all it needs to kick off.

Jesse responds by throwing a punch, but it lands innocuously on Red's shoulder.

In return, Jesse receives a punch in the face. Sefina lets out a little cry, and O'Malley decides it might be time to intervene. But he doesn't rush. A tired and defeated Jesse will pose less of an issue when it is time for O'Malley to talk with Sefina. He'll let Red soften him up a little bit before he gets involved.

O'Malley slowly stands up and off the car he has been sitting on and walks across to the mess that Jesse has created. Jesse is losing valiantly. Red's got him pinned beneath him now, and is trying to tire Jesse out, but Jesse keeps struggling, showing no signs of giving up.

When O'Malley reaches them, Red's companion takes a step towards him in defence of his friend, but he backs off when O'Malley threatens him with the newspaper in his hand. When he sees O'Malley up close he realises he's out of his depth and steps back.

O'Malley puts an arm around Red's neck and pulls him off Jesse. Red resists and turns to face O'Malley, ready for more. His dander is up. But he, too, backs off when he takes a look at the man in front of him.

'I think that's enough, don't you, guys?' O'Malley waits for a response.

Nobody seems in a hurry for more, and O'Malley takes that as agreement, pointing his head towards their car, suggesting they get on their way.

Red doesn't need any further prompting, and silently gets into his car.

O'Malley turns to Jesse. Sefina is kneeling by his side. If he is expecting sympathy he's in for further disappointment. Sefina is busy telling him he's a fucking idiot.

O'Malley sees that Jesse is lying in the path of Red's SUV. Red probably won't mind if Jesse stays where he is, but O'Malley thinks he better help Jesse avoid further punishment. He reaches under Jesse's arms and drags him backwards out of harm's way. Sefina follows.

There's a grass verge to the left of the car park. O'Malley dumps Jesse down and lets him catch his breath. Jesse looks up at O'Malley and realises who has come to his rescue. How bad could his day get?

'You! Shit. Come on, Sef, we need to get out of here.' He's not so brave without a lump of wood in his hand.

O'Malley is getting a little tired of young Jesse. He pushes him backwards gently with his foot, and holds it in place on his chest, pinning him down.

'Not yet. You've had enough for one day, so why don't you just stay where you are for a few minutes? I haven't come to hurt you, but I could change my mind very quickly if you don't calm down.'

Jesse is aggressive but not entirely stupid. He keeps quiet and stays where he is.

O'Malley turns to Sefina, who's getting more confused by the second.

'What's going on? Who are you?'

Jesse obviously hasn't mentioned yesterday's heroics. O'Malley feels Jesse struggle under his foot. A bit more pressure and he settles down.

'Hello, Sefina. My name is O'Malley. I hoped you would give me five minutes of your time.'

He wants her to see he is a reasonable man.

'Do I have a choice?' She looks at the big foot resting on her boyfriend's chest. Now she realises that O'Malley's here for her, not Jesse, and her defences are up. She has that staunch look that teenagers do so well. She crosses her arms to confirm she's unhappy.

'Your father came to me because he's very worried about you. He doesn't know where you are and is scared for you. He asked me to find you and talk to you. So can we talk?'

Sefina's arms get tighter and she leans back from O'Malley.

'Your father is very concerned. He said to tell you he wants you to come home and he will try to do a better job of listening to you. Can you do that?'

'No,' Sefina responds. What was O'Malley expecting?

'No? That's it? Look, I know dads can sometimes be a pain, but parenting is difficult — I'm sure you can work it out.' He's making it up as he goes along. What does he know about fathers and parenting?

'I'm not going back, so you're wasting your time. Please let us go now,' she says, glancing again at the foot that is preventing her beau from getting up.

O'Malley doesn't know what more he can do, but he figures he better give it one last push. He looks down at Jesse but speaks to Sefina.

'Well, there's a problem with that, Sefina. I'm not sure you're in a safe place right now. I can't drag you home, but I can tell your father where you are — and I'm not sure that would work out so well.'

'Go ahead and tell him. I don't care. What's he going to do? I'm perfectly safe with Jesse, and Mr Browning wouldn't let my dad on the property. Would he?' She is asking Jesse for confirmation.

'No, he wouldn't,' he replies to her. Then to O'Malley: 'And you've been warned already. I wouldn't mess with my dad.' Playground talk.

'You're right. I wouldn't advise Mr Tupuola to come and visit. But you're still a minor, Sefina, and your father has every right to be worried about you. He might ask the police to come and check in on you, maybe bring you home.'

That gets Jesse's attention.

'Look, O'Malley,' he interrupts. At least he remembers his name. 'Sefina's better off with me. Can't you leave it alone?'

Now he is trying to be reasonable. He doesn't want Daddy to get upset. O'Malley takes his foot off Jesse's chest, letting him sit up a bit and get comfortable.

'Look, kid,' O'Malley says, patience running out, 'I've been asked to help out a man who's missing his daughter. I've had a glimpse of where she is living, and it doesn't seem to me to be a safe environment. I don't know what you're into, and I don't care. But I promised I'd do what I can to make sure Sefina is safe, and you're not giving me any confidence. You can't even leave the house without getting into a fight. So, what am I meant to do?'

The testosterone and adrenalin have run low in Jesse's system and he looks his age, and out of his depth.

'It's not permanent, OK? We want to be together, and I'm working on a plan to get us our own place away from everyone. Away from both our fathers.'

'And how's that plan going?' O'Malley doubts Jesse's ability to plan a trip to McDonald's.

'I'm getting there. You don't need to be a dick about it.'

O'Malley's pretty sure he's not being a dick, trying to reason with a kid who only yesterday hit him with a log.

'I'm not. I'm trying to look out for her,' O'Malley says, pointing to Sefina. 'I'm trying to stop an old man who's already suffered a lot from experiencing any more pain.'

'Hmph.' Sefina contributes a dismissive grunt to the conversation. 'What has Dad told you?'

'He told me about your sister and your mother, and I know your brother isn't around to help out,' O'Malley replies.

'Yeah, poor Dad. Life's really thrown him some curveballs.' Heavy on sarcasm, light on empathy. 'I don't think you know him at all.'

'Why don't you tell me, then?'

'You don't have to tell him anything, Sef,' Jesse pitches in. 'Take my word for it, O'Malley, we may be kids, but we know what we're doing. We just want to be left alone.'

'You and every other teenager I've ever met,' O'Malley replies, and then appeals to Sefina's sense of reason. 'You can't go running off every time your dad says something you don't like.'

'Man, who made you the law? Haven't you got anything better to do?' Jesse pitches in.

'Plenty. But a promise is a promise.'

Sefina has heard enough.

'Leave us alone. We're leaving now. If you're concerned about my welfare, please don't tell my dad where we are. If you want to find out what sort of man you're trying to help, speak to Scott Cranshaw.'

'Who the hell is Scott Cranshaw?' O'Malley asks.

'He was driving the car when my sister died.'

'What's that got to do with this?'

'Plenty.'

'That's it? That's all you're giving me? Where would I find him?'

'You found me, didn't you? I'm sure you'll work it out.'

Sefina's had enough, and pulls Jesse to his feet, not giving O'Malley anything more. He settles for a compromise.

'OK, I'll speak to Scott. Listen, I'll do you a deal. I won't say anything to your father. Yet. But in exchange, Jesse, you've got to get off the farm.' He's thinking of the gang members, and the police surveillance out front.

'We're fine there, for now.'

'No. You're not,' O'Malley says firmly, hoping it might get through his thick skull. 'Find somewhere else to go. Or call me, and I'll find somewhere for you.'

O'Malley hands Sefina a card with his phone number on it. Hoping she'll hold onto it.

They walk away, leaving O'Malley with a clear sense that he's been wasting his breath.

# CHAPTER FIFTEEN

O'Malley gets back in Claire's car, deflated. He's trying to close leads down, and all he seems to be doing is gathering new ones.

The sensible thing to do would be to walk away from the domestic squabbles he's wandered into. But he wasn't bluffing when he told Jesse they were in danger. Whatever his father is up to is drawing heat from the police, and his business partners aren't known for putting their hands up and going quietly. If Jesse and Sefina get caught in the middle, they'll have way more to deal with than unwanted parental interference.

O'Malley's sense of responsibility has shifted from Loto to Sefina. He's determined to help *someone*. But now he's unsure who actually deserves it.

He writes Scott Cranshaw's name down in his detective notepad and gets to work clearing peanuts from the passenger seat. At least he can measure progress with that task.

His phone buzzes.

He's got three missed calls. One from Chinese Steve, two from Claire. Steve will be brief, and O'Malley's curious about what he might have discovered. He calls him first.

'Steve, it's O'Malley.'

'Hey, bro. I found Bobby Q.'

'And?'

'And he says he didn't do it.'

'Oh, OK then. Mystery solved.'

O'Malley is running low on patience.

'I laid it out for him, and he went pale, man. Even said it looks bad for him. He wants to meet you.' Fuck *that*.

'Where? Down a dark alley? At the docks? In his basement?'

O'Malley isn't *that* stupid.

'Not like that. You choose, he said. He's scared, O'Malley. He doesn't need any more issues with the authorities. He knows how this looks. It helps him if he can help you.'

'You're not playing me, are you, Steve?'

'Come on, O'Malley. You asked me to find Bobby, I found him. I took you to the game, so I owe you that. I'm not involved in this, I've told you that. After this call, I'm out of it. Nothing to do with me. I've got businesses to run. I still think you're digging into things you're better leaving alone.'

O'Malley is losing friends as well as making enemies.

'OK, Steve. I trust you.'

Which he thinks he does.

'Tell Bobby to meet me at the bar in Huami. Nine pm?'

'OK, bro. Don't bother letting me know how it goes. I don't want to know.' He hangs up. Either he's a great actor or O'Malley's pissed him off. So be it.

O'Malley calls Claire as he drives back to the city. Tells her what progress he's made.

'So you found Sefina but didn't persuade her to go home, and you've set up a meeting with a man you think might have had something to do with Danny's murder?'

*Put like that …*

'I know, I know, so much progress in such a short time,' O'Malley responds, refusing to let his positive mood evaporate.

'Always the optimist, O'Malley,' Claire says, then a pause. Her tone changes.

'I like having you around, O'Malley. That's all.'

'I know you're worried, Claire. I'm being careful. But if I don't find out what's going on, I'm worried that I'll end up in the frame. Soon as I've got something, I'm done, alright?'

'No, but yes.' And then another pause. 'I'm not working tonight. Can we do something?'

O'Malley draws a deep breath. He's not going to win any popularity contests anytime soon. He hasn't told Claire when he is meeting Bobby, and he's forgotten to mention that he's planning on tracking William down after midnight.

He tells her and prepares himself for her response.

'OK, O'Malley. This is what is going to happen. You're going to pick me up at seven-thirty. We're going to go to Masu for cocktails, and then you're going to book a table for nine-thirty at Huami. I'll make myself scarce while you speak to Bobby Q, then we're going to have a long Chinese dinner, involving dumplings, Peking duck, and whatever else I fancy. You're paying. Then, when we're done, we'll roll our fat bodies to the car and go looking for the mysterious William. Together.'

Some men don't like being told what to do by a woman. O'Malley finds it irresistible.

But his Neanderthal brain still has something to say.

'I don't think it's such a good idea you coming with me to find William. I can't ask him what I need to know if I'm worried about you at the same time.'

'How do I cope when you're not around to protect me? Idiot. You're not going to *ask* him anything. If we find him, we're just going to see where he goes. Hopefully we'll find out where he lives. Then you can keep tabs on him tomorrow.'

'How does that move things forward?'

'Well, you *could* rough him up tonight. That way, if he's involved, you'll signal to the world that you're on to them, and still not know who you're actually dealing with. If you follow him, though, he might lead you to the people you're really after.'

'There might be some logic to that,' O'Malley concedes.

'Very gracious. Also, the idea of you skulking around the city at midnight on your own depresses me. You'll scare the pigeons. Whereas with me on your arm, we'll just look like a couple out on a stroll.' She isn't going to lose this debate.

'With you on my arm, I will be invisible,' O'Malley concedes.

'Well, yes, but I didn't like to say so.'

He can hear a smile return to her voice, which makes it a good time to wrap it up.

'OK, gorgeous, your plan wins. I'll see you at seven-thirty.'

'Good. Try to stay out of trouble until then. Bye, hon.'

Even O'Malley can manage that.

It's not all work, this detective lark.

O'Malley's got a few hours to kill before he meets Claire, so when he gets home he opens up the doors that lead to his balcony, makes a cup of tea and watches the world go by. It's another sunny day, the clouds mere wisps with little breeze to move them along. The restaurants below are doing great business, hosting lots of important meetings that require chilled wine and oysters.

His apartment is positioned on the second floor, allowing some privacy from the throngs below, but enabling O'Malley to observe the al fresco diners without resorting to binoculars. People-watching is addictive. It was here that Claire and O'Malley developed their deduction game, inventing narratives to explain the sometimes-incongruous mix of people who inhabit the tables below. Sometimes they see people they know and take a wicked pleasure from observing them without their knowledge.

The apartment is a privilege. It is also a curse.

Prime real estate, and beyond the reach of a man of O'Malley's means.

It was a final gift from O'Malley Senior, from beyond the grave.

The only gift O'Malley ever remembers. And one that comes with baggage.

An unexpected visitor delivered the news of the old man's death, an unfamiliar lawyer sitting across from O'Malley in the sterile surroundings of the prison visiting room. Turns out, O'Malley's father had lived a very full life once he was free of the shackles of the Southern Hemisphere. He died a wealthy man, leaving behind many assets and three families. O'Malley never pursued those other descendants, figuring they wouldn't have much interest in an ex-con; one abandoned to make room for them.

The lawyer was also there to tell O'Malley that he was a beneficiary in the will. As his mother struggled to make ends meet and keep her child fed and clothed, his father had been busy accumulating wealth and investing in property where he saw opportunity. As Auckland emerged from its shell and began to expand, he smelled opportunity, and purchased an apartment that was built in the late nineties to capitalise on the impending yacht race that would bring well-heeled visitors from around the world and provide a fillip to landlords who saw the chance to hike prices and get rich quick. Right up O'Malley Senior's street.

Maybe he invested here because he dreamed of one day returning to New Zealand and reuniting with his first family. If that was the case, he never mentioned it. Instead, he owned property and received rent just 10 kilometres from where his first-born struggled.

*What a man.*

So, then he died. It felt spiteful, leaving the apartment to O'Malley. He could have helped them, all those years, and maybe O'Malley's mother would have met a better class of loser, and maybe he wouldn't be in a cell.

But now, from beyond the grave, the wandering Irishman was letting his son know that he'd done OK. In case he was worrying.

Saying sorry, perhaps, from beyond the grave. Because he didn't have the balls to do it when he was alive.

O'Malley wanted to shoot the messenger. Tell him to shove his apartment up his arse.

But sense prevailed.

He had few prospects to look forward to, and now he was a landlord with rental income accumulating that he could not spend. It was something.

O'Malley spent a good deal of his remaining time inside

evaluating this gift from the devil. He still had hopes he might reconcile with his mother, who remained estranged from the son who reminded her of her own miserable life. He hoped this might wane, and then he would happily see her take residence in the apartment — though she need not know its origins. She might finally get some relief. But she did not mellow and rejected any attempts to rebuild their relationship.

So fuck it. Pragmatism won out. A few months after his release, when he was still living with a houseful of internet misfits, his tenants moved out, and O'Malley moved in.

He's had enough of people-watching and self-reflection. He's got about an hour to fill before he needs to get ready for his hot date. He follows the breadcrumb that Sefina dropped for him. It's probably a wild goose chase, but he doesn't have any better ideas, and he really wants to close the book on the Tupuola saga.

He's got a new name to chase, and it takes all of five minutes to track down Scott Cranshaw. Actually, O'Malley finds two, but as one of them is a forty-six-year-old marine biologist, he focuses on the other. Scott is now twenty, and a student at the university. O'Malley doesn't need any Venn diagrams to locate him, either. He finds an email address and a mobile phone number easily enough. He also finds a couple of news reports about the accident that killed Sefina's sister Talia.

It's unlikely that Scott will meet willingly to discuss events he's spent years trying to forget. So, O'Malley resorts to another small bluff. He sends him a text.

*Hey, Scott – you don't know me but I think I found a folder of yours in the Science Fac. Don't understand what's in it (!) but it's got your name on some of the papers. Can I find you somewhere tomorrow to return them??*

See if that gets a bite. Now he's had enough of the Tupuolas for one day. He takes a long shower to forget about them and thinks about what he's going to eat for dinner. How much duck is too much?

# CHAPTER SIXTEEN

O'Malley is waiting for Bobby Q.

Claire stays put across the road where he left her, chatting to the bar staff as she sips sake.

From where she sits, she's got a view of O'Malley as he stands at the bar on the other side of the street. He's refrained from anything alcoholic so far, but his nerves are getting the better of him, and he needs a steady hand for the conversation ahead.

Bobby Q is an unknown quantity. O'Malley knows *of* him, and now he's played cards with him, but he doesn't really *know* the man. He has a reputation, has even had several column inches devoted to his exploits, but much of it is sensationalist, betraying the xenophobia that's never too far away from the surface when local reporters write about Asian immigrants. He had fallen out with the authorities in his homeland. But either by negotiation or leverage, he'd been allowed to return to New Zealand, chastened but not imprisoned. Whether he is the fraudster and thief he's been painted as, or he's simply fallen out of favour with the Party, O'Malley doesn't know. But if he *is* a criminal, he is not small-fry. Settling a slight with violence is more than plausible. And so O'Malley's nervous.

He orders a gin and tonic — which comes with a flowery narrative to justify the price — and waits for Bobby to arrive.

Bobby keeps O'Malley waiting.

When he arrives, he is accompanied by two younger ladies, who he waves away into a corner of the bar out of earshot. He joins O'Malley at the bar, and orders a Scotch, simply by pointing to the bottle on the shelf behind the barman. He's short on niceties.

'We meet again, Mr O'Malley.' So he's got a sense of humour. Playing up to his villainous reputation.

'Bobby,' O'Malley manages, offering his hand. Hoping that the size and strength of it will level the playing field.

'I am sorry about your friend. I hear you suspect me? It was not me.' His English is better than he revealed the last time they met, but it's still patchy, and he speaks slowly, thinking about each word. 'But maybe it looks bad for me, yes?'

'Yes,' O'Malley confirms. He's opting for strong and silent, letting Bobby do the talking.

'But why would I kill a man? For winning a poker hand? No. That does not make sense. It is … illogical.'

'And yet. Danny was killed a few hours after upsetting you.'

'No, no, no. I do not accept this. These are two events. Not connected. I get excited at the card table. I admit. But I do not hurt people. How would I hurt someone?'

He points to his own physique with indignation.

He's got a point — he doesn't look in great shape for murder. He's slim and looks like a man who's sat behind a desk for much of his life.

O'Malley has already looked for signs of damage to Bobby's hands, but they are soft and well-manicured, and his knuckles are smooth. All that indicates is that he hasn't done any dirty work. Maybe he lets others do his dirty work. The women in the corner might be Bobby's Amazonian guard.

'So, you get someone else to hurt Danny. Maybe they went too far?'

'Why would I?' Bobby's pitch is getting higher, the more he protests. 'I do not even know this man. He showed his hand too slow. So what? I am angry that I did not win. I am not angry so much with the player. If I kill the dealer, maybe?'

That sense of humour again. Sunny and Shaun would love this guy.

'This is very bad for me, Mr O'Malley. I have my own … problems. You find who did this. I will appreciate it.'

O'Malley considers Bobby Q as he sips his gin. He's not warning O'Malley off. Quite the opposite. If he is responsible for Danny's death, he isn't scared of what O'Malley will uncover. But he's a poker player, too. He might just be playing a very strong hand. But O'Malley's not reading him that way.

'Tell me about the game, Bobby. How did you find out about it?'

'I do not have trouble finding the games, O'Malley. They come to me. People like to play with me — I think you know why.'

Because he's a whale: games are built around players like Bobby Q. He's got money, and he's a reckless gambler. He feeds the poker economy.

'Who came to you about this game?'

'I have been playing at that place for many weeks. Alfred, Jack, me — we all are regulars. You are the … newbie?' Pleased he's got the right word.

'So, who's in charge? Alfred? Jack?' O'Malley thinks about who else was present that night.

'No, no, they are just players like me. I think William is in charge, yes?'

Maybe.

'So, it was William who came to you and invited you?'

'Oh, no. Not William. Tony recommended me. Tony Jones.'

Big Tone. He warned O'Malley off the game, but apparently he encouraged Bobby. That makes no sense. Which makes it interesting. Might actually be the first real clue O'Malley's uncovered.

'Big Tone? Are you sure?'

'Yes, Big Tony. I was in the casino. He asked me if I was looking for a good game. Then William contacted me and gave me the address.'

Tone knows more about the game than he's let on to O'Malley. But then O'Malley told Tone he didn't play in the game. All these bluffs, O'Malley's thinking, make it hard to think straight.

'Anything else you can tell me about the game, Bobby?'

'The game, no. But the house — there is more than poker there, I think.'

O'Malley remembers the Sic Bo room that William showed him, and the pretty girl in the towel, running across the hallway.

Bobby's comment triggers something in O'Malley's brain, and he remembers Danny's whispered comment.

*You'll never guess what I saw when I went for a smoke.*

Danny didn't die because of a slow roll. He died because he saw something he shouldn't have.

O'Malley pushes Bobby for more. 'Such as?'

'I am not sure. More gambling, certainly. Maybe other things,' he says enigmatically.

That's all O'Malley's getting. Bobby Q drains his glass.

'I am not the man you are looking for. Please call me if I can help you with this.'

Bobby gives O'Malley his number and shakes his hand.

Another casual gesture and his female companions are on their feet and by his side. They're gone before O'Malley realises the drinks are on him. Bobby has expensive tastes.

O'Malley turns to look across the road and give Claire a wave to let her know the coast is clear. He needn't have bothered. She's already alongside him. His own Amazonian guard.

'Well?'

'Not him. I think.'

'Well, let's eat. You can tell me more when we've ordered. I'm starving.'

They take their seats and study their menus in silence. Claire's thinking about the food. O'Malley's thinking about the house in Parnell, and what secrets it holds.

They over-order. They've got bang-bang chicken, assorted dim sum, and a whole duck with pancakes.

O'Malley talks while Claire constructs a pancake, heavy on duck, light on onion, plenty of plum sauce. She's listening, but the food keeps her mouth occupied. O'Malley talks until he runs out of steam.

He's pretty sure that Bobby Q is not guilty. When it comes to Danny, at least. But Big Tone's got him confused. O'Malley knows him well, better than anyone who he's met through cards, but then it never pays to fully trust a poker player. He just can't figure out how Tone would be involved. Claire finishes another mouthful and joins the conversation.

'So, Tone could have been happy to send Bobby to the game, but keen to keep you out of it? Maybe he was protecting you because he knows there's other shit happening over there? He could have been looking out for you.'

'Could be. But he didn't give me the impression he really knew much about the game — just rumours he'd heard. Yet he got Bobby into it weeks ago.'

'What did you say he does for a living?'

'Construction. Commercial stuff. Property. All above-board.'

O'Malley puts his chopsticks down as it hits him.

'God, I'm stupid.'

'What?'

'I've been focused on the game. But if there's more going on in that house, and Danny saw something that led to his death, it's not the players I need to focus on. It's the house. I need to know who owns the house.'

'And how do we do that?'

'With six bucks. You can get a title search online. It'll take about five minutes.'

'Well, what are you waiting for? Find the name, get dessert, we can be home and watching a movie by midnight.'

O'Malley gets to it. Gets his phone and credit card out and orders a title search. He's interrupted midway by a text. Scott Cranshaw responding. That can wait. O'Malley's on a mission.

'Got it. OK, let's have a look. Title, blah, type, blah, date issued, register type, current owners: *Morbius Holdings Trust Limited.* Damn. That's annoying. No name.'

'Can't you find out who owns the company? Follow the money, as they say?'

'I can. But not on my phone. I need to do a few searches — better done at home.'

'It's a start. Horrible name, by the way. Morbius.'

'A vampire. Someone's got a dark sense of humour. Or an honest one. The house always wins, bleeding its customers dry.'

'Well, what do you want to do? Go home and keep chasing this, or stick to Plan A and try to find William?'

'William. He's involved. He's still in this, somehow.' O'Malley recalls the scar on William's face, thinks now that it was probably earned the hard way.

'Let's do it. Thank you for dinner, by the way, it was amazing.'

To demonstrate, Claire leans back in her chair and attempts to push her stomach out, blowing air into her cheeks for good measure. Still beautiful, still funny. Still the boss.

'Pay the bill, O'Malley. I hope I was expensive.' O'Malley looks at the bill and confirms she is.

'I'll need to have another win soon, or it'll be beans on toast next time.'

'Beans on toast, on the sofa, with a movie? Perfect. That would beat this every time,' she says, not ungratefully. 'Can we pop upstairs before we go looking for William? Can we go into the poker room just to watch for a few minutes? Would that look weird? I'd like to see where you spend all your time — and put some faces to names, you can point them out to me.'

'We could do that. What are you thinking?'

'I'm thinking there's only one of you, and your list of people to follow is getting very long. You need to share the load. I can't follow people if I don't know what they look like. I know what Bobby looks like now, but I don't know any of the others. They might be upstairs.'

'I don't really want you to get involved, Claire. We're talking about murder here.'

'And that's man's business, right? Get over yourself, O'Malley. We're not chasing a serial killer. I can look after myself,' she says, pulling a can of pepper spray from her bag to demonstrate. 'You, on the other hand, can't go for a country drive without getting beaten up. I'm helping. End. Of. Story.'

He's got nothing to say to that.

# CHAPTER SEVENTEEN

O'Malley is hesitant as they walk into the poker room.

A lot of these guys don't get out much. A woman who looks like Claire is going to be a novelty, and some of the players will find it hard to internalise their appreciation. O'Malley hopes his presence will keep their adolescence at bay.

As they approach the podium, he senses heads turning at the tables that surround it. Claire feels it, too, but she is used to the attention and can tell the difference between men who pose a threat and those who just need a few social skills. She leans into O'Malley and whispers in his ear.

'Wow, O'Malley. If these are your usual friends, you're really punching above your weight, aren't you?'

'I've never said otherwise, baby.'

Frankie is behind the podium, directing traffic to the tables.

'Looking for a seat, O'Malley? Two seats?' Gentleman Frank.

'Not tonight, Frankie. We're on a hot date, and Claire just wanted to see what was so special about the place I spend so much time in.'

'He thinks it's a hot date,' Claire interjects. 'I'd say lukewarm, going on warm.'

'Well, it's not going to get any warmer in here,' Frank responds with a laugh. 'Welcome to the home of average service and questionable hygiene.' That makes her laugh.

'Makes you question your choice in men, doesn't it?' Claire responds.

'No comment,' Frank chuckles. 'I'm just here to deal the cards.'

'Thanks for the support, Frank. Hey, any of the big games going tonight?' O'Malley asks, moving the chat away from his life choices.

'Yep, over on Table Eleven,' he says, pointing to the far corner of the room. 'The usual suspects.'

'Thanks, Frankie. I'll see you tomorrow, no doubt.'

'Unless I win the lottery.'

'Good luck with that.'

They drift away from the podium. O'Malley wants Claire to get a good view of the room without going too close to Table Eleven. They stand in between the two tables at the front of the room, O'Malley with his back to the corner he wants her to focus on. He makes like he's explaining the game to Claire, pointing to Table One as he does so. Claire is quick on the uptake and deciphers his code.

'So, Seat One is the one to the left of the dealer, round to Seat Nine on the dealer's right. The button tells you where the next hand will be dealt from. So, you see how the button is on Seat Five? So, Seat Six is the small blind. The *big* one's in Seat Seven.'

Claire is looking over at Table Eleven, counting in her head around to Seat Seven where Big Tone is sitting.

'OK, I get the big blind: that's what everyone needs to match to stay in, right? What's the other one, again?'

Translation: Where's Steve sitting?

'We'll get to that. Let's just watch this hand play out.'

The actual hand, the one on Table One, is turning into a big pot. Some of the guys at the table are aware that Claire is watching. They can't help themselves; the audience is making them bet big. They want to impress her. Jessica, one of the two female players at the table, looks over to O'Malley and rolls her eyes. She'll eat the men for breakfast while Claire has them distracted. They watch it play out, until the small blind has moved where O'Malley needs it to be.

'So, the small blind is in Seat Three.' Where Chinese Steve is sitting over on Table Eleven. 'He's got less to put in to match the big blind, but he'll be first to act after the flop, so it's still a big decision to stay in the game.'

'Got it. I could get the hang of this.'

A couple of the men look up from their cards then, hoping she'll get the hang of it right now and join them at the table.

'But another time. I've seen enough for one night.'

She's seen Tone and Chinese Steve, and that's what she came for. She pulls on O'Malley's arm and steers him away from the action. At least for now.

They take the lifts down to the car park where O'Malley's left his truck. Claire's been here a few times before, but she's always amazed that people ever find their cars again. The car park is confusing, with entrances at either end, and floor numbers that never seem to match the ramps that descend from street level to the lower bowels of the parking station. Navigation has never been her thing, so she leaves it up to O'Malley to get them back to where they started.

They enter the lift and discover they've got it to themselves.

'I felt a bit overdressed in there, O'Malley. Don't they have a dress code in casinos anymore? If you'd warned me, I'd have worn shorts and a t-shirt.'

'I guess they don't want anyone wasting money on clothes that could be better spent on the machines. Besides, if you'd worn shorts someone might have had a heart attack. Wouldn't have been very practical, either, for where we're going next.'

She lets the compliment pass but appreciates it anyway. O'Malley makes her feel good. Every girl should have an O'Malley in their life. She knows she's got plenty of flaws and spends too much of her time dwelling on them, but when she stops to see how O'Malley looks at her she feels ten feet tall. Except she's always been self-conscious about her height, so maybe that's not quite the phrase she's looking for. Whatever. She's not nearly the catch O'Malley seems to think she is — not as clever, pretty or funny as he makes out — but there's no telling him that. Professionally, she would say he has an over-idealised view of her, which is hard to live up to, but she can't help loving how it makes her feel. But he doesn't need to know quite how much. It might cause him to dial it down.

'True. I do look good in shorts. Let's focus on finding the car and get moving.'

'You know, if we go up instead of down, these lifts go to the hotel. We could always call it quits and pretend we're Mr and Mrs Jones.'

'Wow. Five minutes in the poker room, and you're as bad as the rest of them. Focus on the job, O'Malley. We've got a killer to catch.' She lets him kiss her anyway. She'd much rather be spending the night in a room upstairs, and she tells him as much with the kiss, but she also knows that he's on a mission to find out what happened to Danny, and she hopes that if she's with him he won't get himself into trouble.

They get in the truck without too much of a plan. It's only a five-minute drive to Pitt Street, and all they've got to go on is Steve's vague suggestion that William might visit his club on Sunday nights. Not much to go on. But better than nothing.

Pitt Street is one of those empty parts of town that acts more as a connector to places you'd rather be. The edgy nightlife of Karangahape Road to the south, and the arterial roads that lead out of the city to the north. It's home to the central-city fire station and an ambulance hub, and a scattering of reasonably priced commercial office spaces, with easy access to the central city. It's the sort of road that appeals to entrepreneurs like Steve, who knows he can attract a niche crowd to the fringe of town, and benefit from cheaper rents and looser licensing restrictions.

It's 11 pm when they arrive and find a parking spot across the road from the Shanghai Club. They might have hours to fill, just the two of them in the warm cab of O'Malley's Ford. Claire's happy with that and not looking for too much excitement in this pursuit of the truth.

Half an hour of chit-chat passes by. Claire confirms she clocked both Big Tone and Chinese Steve in the poker room. O'Malley suggests they might get another chance to see Steve before the night is through. He doubts Steve leaves his club completely unsupervised on weekend nights.

There are a trickle of young, well-dressed Asians coming through to the club. And an equal number of males of all ages working their way up to the strip clubs and massage rooms that sit on the junction of Pitt and K Road. Claire doesn't judge. If the women and girls who these men come to see are working voluntarily, and the conditions are safe, then it's not for her to question the life choices of others. But perhaps she judges the men, just a little bit. Actually, she judges them a lot. It's a conversation for her to have with O'Malley another time. But right now, Claire decides she's had enough of sitting around.

'Right, we can sit here till dawn and find out the guy's nowhere near here, or we can find out we're at least on the right track. Wait here.'

'Where are you going?' O'Malley's got that look on his face that suggests he's coming over all protective.

'I'm going to see what all the fuss is about at the Shanghai Club.'

'Hold on. If you're going in, I'm coming with you.'

'I've got this. Big scar, paint in his hair. Probably in the VIP area. I'm going into a club that's got loads of people inside, enjoying themselves. I'll blend in better than you, and William doesn't know who I am. It's safe.'

She's right, but O'Malley's face says he's not convinced. Claire realises she needs to give him a little bit more reassurance. And she could do with a little herself, because the prospect of a manhunt is giving her a few butterflies, despite the front she's presenting to O'Malley.

'Have you got a better plan? No, didn't think so. Sit tight. Pretend it was your idea if it makes you feel better. And don't go speaking to any single women walking past. I don't want you arrested for kerb-crawling.' Not much by way of reassurance there, but she hopes the last bit will distract O'Malley long enough to let her get on with things.

Claire makes her way over to the club, giving the bouncer a winning smile, and slipping in, down the stairs, to the venue below. It's all pretty straightforward décor: lots of bling, mock-velvet booths surrounding the main dance floor. There's a raised section towards the back of the club, and she can see waitresses in short, gold dresses fawning over those who've chosen to pay the premium for a VIP experience.

She takes her time, getting a glass of water from the bar, sipping it through a straw to suggest she's got something stronger. It's not her type of club, but she's a big people-watcher, and enjoying this glimpse into a subculture that's clearly vibrant in the city that she thinks of as home, but perhaps doesn't know quite as well as she thought. As she makes her way towards the VIP area, she wonders how O'Malley is coping, sitting outside worrying about her safety. It makes her smile.

Not too well, is how O'Malley's coping. He's feeling bad for dragging Claire into his world. He knows she's right and there's no reason to think she's in any danger, but he worries anyway. His fear of situations being out of his control is rearing up. He's starting to fiddle with the controls inside the car — the air conditioning, the radio, anything to keep himself occupied. But he doesn't have to wait long.

In far less time than it felt to O'Malley, Claire's there again, smiling at the guy on the door as she walks slowly and coolly back across the road to the truck. To O'Malley, it's all in slow motion. He half expects her to toss a cigarette over her shoulder and blow the building up in her wake. It's a soundtrack moment. Then she's back in the car, slapping his knee.

'Hey, lover boy. Been worrying about me?'

'Nah. I lost track of time. Have you been gone long?'

'Whatever,' she laughs.

'Well?'

'Oh, yeah, he's in there. He really needs to do something

about the hair. He's living it up like a lord. VIP booth, chicks, bottle of Grey Goose, the whole cliché. Couple of guys with him, making sure no one spills their drink on his suit. He's king of the hill in there.'

'Good work. Our plan worked out. Now I guess we wait.'

'Sure thing, boss. Good plan, by the way.' She doesn't let him get away with too much.

It's a long wait.

Longer, because Claire insists they listen to talk radio. She says it's a good test of your own sanity. If you start agreeing with the people who call in after midnight, you're nuts. O'Malley doesn't know why listening is required to confirm this. But he listens anyway, and learns that Trump's got some good ideas, that Asians are responsible for New Zealand's housing crisis, and women shouldn't seek public office until they've had their children. O'Malley's getting wound up, which is amusing Claire. He's distracted, too, so he's looking in the wrong direction when William comes out of the club. But Claire's there to save the day.

'Here he comes. Now remember, keep a safe distance. We just want to see where he lives.'

She takes a photo of William with her phone.

'I know the drill, Claire.' They really need to have a chat about who is in charge here. 'Let's just wait to see if he's walking or has a car.'

They watch William light a cigarette and cross the road, diagonally, towards the YMCA and around the corner onto Vincent Street. They both open their doors and decide to follow on foot. O'Malley wears a baseball cap because he forgot his fake moustache.

They keep their distance, Claire looping her arm round his, just a couple going home after a night out in town. They leave plenty of distance, thankful there are a few other people out on the streets making their own way home.

William makes his way down Vincent Street, past a series of

soulless apartment buildings, until he reaches the junction where Vincent merges onto Mayoral Drive. More people on the street down here, closer to the city's heart. They close the gap, in case they lose the potential killer in their sights.

Maybe it's the reality of tailing William in the flesh, but O'Malley's increasingly sure that William's was the last face Danny saw before he died. William walks with a confidence that only comes when you are the threat, not the potential victim. He's got swagger, and the subservience that he demonstrated when O'Malley first met him doesn't marry with the way he holds himself unobserved. O'Malley is speeding up now, but Claire places a hand on his arm and pulls him back.

'Wait. We're getting too close.'

'I think he did it, Claire. I want to talk to him.'

'If you catch up to him in this mood, there won't be any talking. You've got nothing on him right now. And you'll learn nothing by confronting him. Don't you want to know why Danny died? Don't you want to know who's calling the shots?'

She's right, again. O'Malley still needs to work on his impulse control.

They fall back. They follow William along Mayoral Drive as he hangs a left onto Wellesley. The crowds are thicker now, well-oiled from a night out, looking for more action. William takes a right onto Federal Street, where Claire and O'Malley started their evening. If they'd known, they could have just waited it out, picking up William as he passed the restaurant where they were eating.

William crosses the main concourse of the casino, under the shadow of the tower that is now an integral feature of the city. By day, people pay good money to throw themselves from the top of the tower to the street below with only a zipline to protect them, but now, in the early hours, it's just a waiting point for taxis and the homeless. William walks on, crossing Hobson Street, and heading in the direction of the waterfront. O'Malley is beginning to regret doing this on foot, but before he says anything, William stops.

Of all the places to go, William's chosen Denny's.

The diner is not a venue that O'Malley can imagine William frequenting.

'Maybe he's just stopped off for a pee?' Claire suggests.

'Why Denny's? He could have popped into the casino, or the hotel, or any of the bars. I doubt he'd even know where the bathrooms are in Denny's.' It's a good point.

'Well, let's see what he's doing, then.'

O'Malley begins walking the exterior of the diner, trying to get sight of William through the glass windows that face the street.

'He's over there, in the far corner,' Claire says. 'He's with someone, but I can't see them properly.'

O'Malley thinks about their options. He wants to get ahead of Claire at least once in the evening.

'Did William see you in the club?'

'No, I made sure of it.'

'How's your bladder? Need a pee?'

She's on board. 'Yes, I think I do. Wait here.'

She leaves him standing in the road and goes into Denny's. Home of the twenty-four-hour toilet.

She is stopped at the front of the restaurant by a helpful server, and O'Malley sees them exchange words, Claire jumping up and down on the spot and pulling faces, as she charms her way into the room. The server is no match for a pretty damsel in distress, and he points her towards the bathrooms. She gives him a quick hug, which will see him through the nightshift.

She takes her time in the bathroom, and then returns to join O'Malley on the street. He looks at her expectantly, wondering why she's taken so long.

'What? I actually needed to pee.'

'Who is it, Claire? Who's with William?'

'He's with Big Tone, O'Malley. I think we're getting somewhere.'

# CHAPTER EIGHTEEN

Standing outside Denny's in the middle of the night, O'Malley feels sweat roll down his back; part humidity, part fear. He's in over his head, the only person he is sure he can trust standing alongside him.

He's known Tony for many years, one of the few people he's met through poker who he's spent time with outside of the game. Tony had patiently walked around the golf course as O'Malley tried to pick up the game. They'd talked about the pitfalls of the construction business, talked about Tony's wife and child, talked about the Sunshine Coast and the easy living that was to be had over there.

Despite his size, Big Tone struck O'Malley as a gentle soul. But here he is, mixed up with William, who O'Malley is now convinced is a gangster. Why?

*You'll never guess what I saw when I went for a smoke.*

That's the problem. O'Malley can't guess. Danny was wise enough to turn a blind eye. He learned to ask no questions and treat other people's business as their own. It goes with the territory when you're playing with people with suspect bankrolls. Don't ask, don't tell. That way, you don't need to question the money that ends up in your pocket. Whatever Danny saw was sufficient to require his permanent silence.

Now Tony's in this. No way it's a coincidence. O'Malley's thinking about the last few days and wondering if Tony's got any idea what he's mixed up in.

'What now?' Claire asks.

'I don't know, babe. I really don't. But we can't stand here all night. Let's go home.'

'And follow the money?'

'I guess so.'

'And then what?'

'Fuck knows. Maybe it's time I hand it over to the professionals.'

'Buxton?'

'For starters, yes. But I need more than we've got at the moment. Let's go home and do some digging.'

So, they retrace their steps back to the truck on Pitt Street. It would be quicker to just walk home, but then O'Malley would only have to walk back tomorrow to collect the truck.

It gives him time to think. Right now, all they've got on Tony is circumstantial. Why shouldn't he know William, have a coffee buddy with a shared passion for late-night diners? It would explain why he knows about the game, suggested it to Bobby Q. He could have had O'Malley's best interests at heart when he warned him away from the game, knowing that he needs no further brushes with the law.

If O'Malley involves the police at this point, the only person who might find themselves compromised is William. If he was directly involved in Danny's death, that would be some comfort. But there's more going on here, and O'Malley wants to know what led to the murder. If Tony is in this, money will be involved, and however smart he is there will be a trail. O'Malley just needs to find it.

When they get back to O'Malley's apartment, he needs another shower. All that walking has made him ripe, and he needs to freshen up. A *hot* shower remains a luxury that reminds him he's a free man, and he doesn't need much of an excuse to wash the grime away. Invigorated, and ready to do some online stalking, he finds Claire in the kitchen, making herself a post-midnight snack.

'Dinner wasn't enough for you?' he asks. She grins.

'The trouble with Chinese food is it fills you up but you're always starving again an hour later,' she explains. 'Besides, you put the idea in my head when you mentioned beans on toast. I was thinking about it all the way home.'

Her brush with danger has done nothing to diminish her appetite, then.

'Will I disturb you if I watch a movie?' she asks.

'Go for it,' O'Malley replies, grabbing his laptop and getting comfortable on the sofa. Claire takes her place next to him, crossing her legs effortlessly to create a makeshift table for her plate of beans. She grabs the remote and begins scrolling through Netflix. O'Malley forces himself to focus on his work, looking for something concrete to connect Tony to the house in Parnell that is at the heart of his concerns.

The first task is to attach a name to the entity that is on the property title. Morbius Holdings Trust Limited is an opaque company, designed to keep distance between whoever owns it and the assets that sit within it. But nothing is truly anonymous.

A quick search with the Companies Office, and he's got an address.

The company is registered with Lomas, Howarth & Partners, with an address on Halsey Street, not ten minutes' walk from where O'Malley is sitting.

There is one director listed: Paul Howarth, with a home address in the old part of Remuera.

O'Malley searches for Lomas, Howarth & Partners. Their website is slick, describing a law firm that specialises in property and immigration issues. It seems an odd combination of services, but makes more sense when O'Malley reads the biographies of the titular partners.

Lomas is, the website boasts, one of the country's pre-eminent commercial property specialists, with an impressive list of qualifications that O'Malley glosses over. Lomas is, the site claims, your first and only stop for all your 'trust and asset protection' issues. The biography page features a gallery of photographs of Lomas that project wealth and power. O'Malley reckons he's the sort to have a photograph in his office showing him alongside a world leader or two.

In the main portrait on the website, Lomas wears a blue pinstripe suit, a red tie and a glint in his eye that suggests he can't believe he's come this far, either.

Howarth, meanwhile, is the man to go to if you are trying to overcome the irritations of international borders. If you are high net worth and want to add a New Zealand passport to your résumé, Howarth is your guy. He's a cheerful-looking man, with a complexion that speaks of good red wine and bonhomie. His cheeks seem to be hiding gobstoppers. He reminds O'Malley of a convivial hamster.

O'Malley guesses it's not unusual for lawyers and accountants to act as passive partners in corporate establishments, providing a convenient address and front for their clients' businesses. There is nothing illegal in that.

Certainly, Lomas, Howarth & Partners look every bit the legitimate and formidable law firm. They are probably responsible for hundreds of legal entities, charging handsomely for their services each time. It's a good way to support a high lifestyle.

O'Malley does another search, this time looking for Lomas as a director.

The list is long.

O'Malley needs a pen and paper. He puts his laptop to one side, getting up to retrieve his notebook from the desk. Claire is now curled up like a cat, her knees pulled in towards her chest and her head resting on a cushion that lies against the arm of the sofa. She is engrossed in her movie, *L.A. Confidential.* It's an O'Malley favourite, and they've watched it together before, but Claire's eyes are glued to the screen, as if experiencing it for the first time. O'Malley's not sure that the violence of Ellroy's LA is the best way to escape their current realities, but it's on the money with its depiction of man's moral flexibility and individual struggle to define what is good. His own struggle to find justice for Danny is taking him to places he should probably avoid, but he's committed to going there, nonetheless.

O'Malley makes a list of all the companies where Lomas is listed as a director. Lomas is a busy man. He looks for any sign of Tony Jones in the details. There's nothing. If he is connected, he's doing his best to remain nameless. If the search of Howarth's directorships is equally productive, O'Malley's got a long night ahead. It is probably a waste of time. Time probably better spent watching Russell Crowe and Guy Pearce going toe-to-toe. But he sticks with it.

Howarth, thankfully, is less productive than Lomas, and his list is shorter, but no more revealing. There's no shortcut to this work; it is the safer side of detective work but comes with much more tedium. O'Malley's eyelids are heavy. At this rate, he'll settle for the blunt approach tomorrow, and shake the truth out of someone.

Most of the companies on the list are simply paper entities; further online searching reveals nothing tangible. As the movie comes to an end, O'Malley's losing the will to live. He'll need an army of forensic accountants to uncover anything interesting. With nothing to find, no websites to trawl through, he moves from search to search pretty swiftly. Claire stirs, emerging from her movie-buff reverie, wondering about his progress. He gives her a one-minute update.

'Well, I'm going to bed. Keep at it, champ. Feel free to join me when you're done.'

She knows he won't, but she always asks.

'OK, baby. I love you.'

'That's inappropriate, O'Malley. We work together now, remember?' She kisses him inappropriately anyway.

'Night, boss.' He's given up pretending he can do this alone. Truth is, they make a pretty good team. Beauty, Brains & Brawn Incorporated. Two-thirds Claire, one-third O'Malley.

He gets back to it. Keeps finding dead-ends. Blank, after blank, after blank. He's pretty much on autopilot. Enter company in search box, skim results, find nothing, repeat. It is thankless work. He can handle boredom, though. Had four years to practise in his youth. Optimism is the key. Either he'll find something, or simply get to the end of the list with nothing. Either way, an end will come.

His patience is rewarded, a little before five in the morning.

He has exhausted Lomas's list, and is on the home straight of Howarth's interests, when he searches a company called Lucky Country Construction.

It has a website, which is progress — most companies on the list seem to live only in the Companies Office.

Lucky Country Construction is a commercial property developer on Auckland's North Shore. It stands out from the other names on Howarth's list purely because it is actually trading in something.

The website features the variety of commercial developments that are in the company's portfolio. But it is short of detail: there's no information about staff or owners, just a standard info@ email address to make further enquiries.

O'Malley's not going to be put off. If the company is legitimate and trading, it will have left a trail somewhere. He finds what he is looking for in the archives of the *North Harbour News*. There has been some opposition to a new development proposed by Lucky Country. Whichever intrepid journalist wrote the article contacted the company for comment. The managing director declined to comment. Tony fucking Jones.

O'Malley's got his link. It is slim, but more than enough to whet his appetite. Tony Jones is connected to the lawyers who are connected to the house in Parnell. Auckland is a small town. But it's not that small. It is too much for coincidence to explain away.

He finishes the list without any further revelations. His gut tells him Tony is lurking behind other companies and trusts, but he's been well insulated by the expertise of Lomas and Howarth.

He returns to their website, staring at their photographs in the hope they'll reveal some hidden clues. He gets nothing. He's reached the point of diminishing returns. He returns the laptop to the desk and gets comfortable on the sofa. He's dog-tired, but his mind won't rest. He turns the television back on and takes his turn rewatching *L.A. Confidential*. He's asleep before Officer White has protected his first broad.

O'Malley wakes to find broken glass where his coffee table should be. He's lying in it, and he's cut himself on the arm fighting whatever foe visited in his sleep. Claire is in the bedroom doorway, looking in on him, and putting shoes on to protect her feet before coming to his aid. She is cautious of him until she sees that he's aware of his surroundings. He can't blame her. He's a liability to them both.

'O'Malley. Are you awake?'

'Yes, I'm awake. You're good. I'm sorry, baby.'

'Don't be sorry. Are you OK? You're bleeding.'

'Yeah, but you should see the other guy,' he says, pointing to what is left of the table.

'Let me look at your arm,' she says, moving towards him.

'Are you a nurse, as well as a doctor?' he asks.

'I'm not a doctor yet, and even when I am I won't be qualified to stop you bleeding. But I'm all you've got, so come on, let me have a look.'

O'Malley raises his arm towards her, thankful he has such an understanding woman in his life. 'I think it's just a couple of scratches, babe, I'm fine.'

'I'll be the judge of that. Now shush, and let me look.' She holds his arm gently and checks for glass. She doesn't find any and helps him up. 'Go and wash that arm, leave this mess to me.' He does as he's told.

He checks himself out in the bathroom. He's got off lightly. The cuts on his arm are shallow, and the bleeding is superficial. He is still shaken. Whatever control he tells himself he has over his life still stops when he sleeps. While other people seek sanctuary in their dreams, he finds dread. He returns to the lounge to find Claire scooping what remains of the tabletop onto newspaper. He gets out the vacuum cleaner to remove the rest of the evidence. She takes it from his hands.

'Coffee, O'Malley. We need coffee.' O'Malley complies.

'Do you remember anything?' she asks, over the din of the vacuum.

'Not really. I was sharing a cell with Big Tone. Then I was wrestling a croc. Not sure after that.'

'You've got to get this sorted. You'll run out of furniture.'

'I know, I know. What I really need to do right now, though, is find out who Tony Jones really is.'

He tells her what he found out before he fell asleep.

'So, take what you've got to Buxton. Let the cops do the rest.'

'It's not enough. I need something more to go on.'

'Like what?'

'I need Tony to come out of his cave. I'm going to rattle their cages and see what happens.'

'And if I tell you not to?'

'Then I'll tell you that I love you, and I respect you, but I'll do it anyway.'

'That's what I thought. Fuck, O'Malley. You just can't help yourself, can you?'

'Danny deserves the truth to be known.'

'Keep telling yourself that. You just can't stand not knowing. Fine. I get it. But if you insist on putting yourself in harm's way, this is how you're going to do it.'

She tells him.

He takes notes.

# CHAPTER NINETEEN

O'Malley enters the offices of Lomas, Howarth & Partners at exactly 11 am.

He's taken the lift to the fourteenth floor to get there, and the reception area gives an impressive view of the harbour and those countless boats people buy but don't know what to do with.

He's greeted by a striking receptionist on the cynical side of thirty. Her face makes it clear there will be no opportunity for the O'Malley charm to work its magic. Her defences are up, but O'Malley's not here to cause her grief. She is just the messenger.

'Can I help you?'

'Yes, I do hope so. I'd like to speak with Mr Lomas or Mr Howarth please.'

'Appointment?' she asks, using her words sparingly, in case she needs them after work.

'No. I was hoping to catch them if they're free. I have some questions about a couple of companies they look after.'

'You need an appointment.' It was going pretty much how O'Malley thought it would go.

'Can you just check if they're free?'

'What makes you think I wouldn't know if they were available?'

'Fair enough. You seem very … organised.' Hoping that doesn't sound sycophantic.

'Neither Mr Lomas nor Mr Howarth are available. I'm sorry, you've wasted your time.'

She doesn't look sorry. He sees the corner of her mouth twitch. She looks positively delighted. The only way to nudge this case along is to walk straight into it.

'Perhaps I can leave my details with you? What I'm looking for?'

'You can. But they are very busy, and Mr Lomas is overseas. I can't tell you when we might get back to you.'

'That's OK. Here's my name and number.' She looks at his note.

'First name, Mr O'Malley?'

'Mr O'Malley is fine, thank you. Here are the companies I'm enquiring about.'

He hands her a piece of paper with three names on it. Morbius, Lucky Country and Smegma Holdings. The last one he'd chosen randomly, but it sounds like a bullshit company and the other two will be enough to get the reaction he's looking for. Big flags waving in the wind.

The staunch receptionist looks briefly at the list, but her face betrays no reaction.

'I'll see that Mr Howarth gets it when he is available.'

'Thank you,' O'Malley replies. He smiles, pausing for a beat. Nothing. She is happy to stare him down, confident he will break before she does. She is right. He turns on his heels and leaves the building.

As his feet hit the pavement, he nods ostentatiously. Claire is out there somewhere, keeping watch. He has delivered the message.

O'Malley returns to his truck, parked expensively in a sixty-minute spot lining the road. All they can do now is wait. It might be a long shot, but in the movies they watch, smart crooks never do important business on the phone. There is always a meeting. He figures that these guys are smart, and probably take their cues from the movies just like everyone else. So he fights the tiredness that consumes him, desperate to be awake if Howarth delivers to their plan. He loses the battle, drifting off. He settles into a dream. His phone rings, jolting him back to the present.

'Look lively, lover boy. He's on the move.'

O'Malley rubs his eyes and finds focus. Howarth has left

the building. He is walking at a brisk pace towards the Viaduct Harbour, where businessmen like him expense their lunches. Claire decided they needed to cover all options. She is on foot, but O'Malley will need to be on wheels, in case Howarth taxis away to his destination.

'I'm on it,' Claire says, enjoying herself by the sounds of it. 'No point driving aimlessly. Stay put. I'll let you know where we end up. You can come over if he settles somewhere.'

O'Malley's getting used to playing second fiddle. He mumbles agreement.

'Oh, and O'Malley? Stay awake this time.' She has the Eye of Providence. Most women do.

He wishes she'd stayed on the phone. He isn't worried about her; he's got over himself in that regard. A running commentary would be nice, though, keeping him feeling involved, playing a part.

He doesn't have to wait long. Claire calls him back five minutes later.

'He's in a restaurant in the Viaduct. He's on his own, but it's a table for four. Out front, so I'm going to take a table at the Italian opposite. I'll have a perfect view. Don't come yet. You might stumble into whoever he's meeting. I'll text when his lunch date arrives.'

Always one step ahead. He can't argue with her logic. He stays where he is. A minute later his phone rings again. He is expecting it to be Claire but doesn't recognise the number.

'Hello. O'Malley speaking.'

'O'Malley, it's Sefina.' There's something tentative in her voice, getting O'Malley's spider-senses going. 'You said to call if I changed my mind?'

'What's going on, Sefina?'

'I'm just … I don't know. There's stuff going on here, Jesse's dad, he's … I'm scared.' The teenage bravado he witnessed when he first met Sefina is stripped away. She sounds every bit her age now. His phone buzzes. It's a text from Claire. Shit.

'Sefina, look, it's a bad time, I'm in the middle of something I can't get out of. I'll help, but can I call you back?' He feels bad as soon as the words are out of his mouth.

'No. Don't call me. Jesse doesn't know I'm calling you. I'll call you back.' She hangs up.

Shit. It will have taken a lot for her to pick up the phone, and he is stretched too thin to help her. It will prey on his mind. But she'll call back, he hopes, and he can't leave Claire to do all the dangerous stuff. He reads her text. *Tony Jones at table with Howarth.* O'Malley guns the engine and heads over.

He enters the Viaduct from the rear, sneaking through a hotel lobby to avoid the walkway directly in front of the restaurant Claire has pointed him to. He joins Claire, keeping his back to Howarth and Big Tone. They know he's onto them, but he doesn't want them to see him right now, and not with Claire.

'What's going on?' He waves away a waiter as he asks Claire for an update.

'Tony arrived and Howarth looks angry. He's pulling lots of faces. Tony is doing a lot of pacifying: you know, calm down, calm down, with his hands. I think we've pissed them off, O'Malley.'

'That was the plan. So now we know: Morbius and Tone are connected. Maybe Smegma, too, if that's actually a company and not a typo.'

'Actually, I looked that one up. Smegma is a thing. The Greeks used it to clean themselves. I think someone got too clever with their naming conventions. Might as well call it Laundromat Inc.'

'Money-laundering makes sense. Lawyers, lots of shell companies, probably an accountant hidden away somewhere, too. Tony has a legitimate business needing big funding. It has to come from somewhere. None of that explains why Danny's dead, though.'

'No, I can't work that one out, either. Still, Howarth is really antsy, and Tony is on the back foot, by the looks of it.'

'So maybe he'll make a mistake,' O'Malley hopes.

'Yeah, that's the bit I'm worried about, O'Malley. If he's as dangerous as we think, won't he come after you? You've put your name in lights.'

'That's sort of my plan. If he's rattled, he'll do something stupid. I just need to be there when he does. Then I've got enough to go to Buxton with, and get out of the way.'

'What if that something stupid is to silence you, like Danny was silenced?'

'Better I know it's coming. I've faced worse.'

The first step to convincing Claire is to convince himself. She puts her hand up to stop him saying more.

'Hold on. There's someone else joining them.' O'Malley sneaks a look. Another suit, distinguished-looking, a man in his fifties, who doesn't shake hands with either man at the table, just sits down.

'Who's that?' he wonders aloud.

'I'm not sure, but he looks familiar, somehow. From his body language, he's not happy with either of them. Even Howarth is backing off.' O'Malley can't take second-hand commentary any longer. He shifts his chair to watch the men directly.

From a distance it is hard to decipher the power dynamic at the table. The mystery man looks like he is used to being the alpha and is chastising Tone and Howarth. But Tone is arguing back. He's gone from pacifying to pointing his finger, and he's regaining control of the conversation. Both Howarth and the new arrival stay silent. Whatever Tony has said is hitting home. The new arrival has heard enough. He looks directly at Tony, gesticulates wildly, then pushes his chair back and leaves.

'You stay here, babe. I'm going to follow the new guy.' O'Malley doesn't wait for a response. The man stops at the entrance to the restaurant, shaking hands with a couple of diners on his way out. He's regained his composure and the statesmanlike demeanour that he possessed before he sat down. He isn't so much shaking hands as pressing flesh. His greetings are brief, as if he recognises those he shakes hands with but can't remember their names. He'll be gone before they realise.

Exiting the restaurant, he takes a left, heading into the hotel lobby that O'Malley arrived through. O'Malley follows, not worrying about keeping his distance. He's got no reason to think the man knows who he is. The man smiles and says hello to people as they pass him, quite the charmer.

As they exit the hotel, he approaches a BMW 7 Series, getting into the back seat and gliding away into traffic, leaving O'Malley no time to take up the chase. The car stirs his memory, though. A driver, still in their parked car, in the lane behind the casino house in Parnell. If it isn't the same car, it is very similar. O'Malley's willing to bet that the mystery man was present when Danny played his ill-fated slow roll.

O'Malley regroups with Claire. Tony is gone, but Howarth remains at the table, drinking rapidly as he tries to recover his appetite. He plays with his phone absently, in the manner of those who dine alone and need to keep themselves occupied.

'Where did he go?' Claire asks.

'Into a car that was waiting for him. I think I've seen the car before. Outside the house in Parnell.'

'Then we're in trouble,' Claire says.

'How so?'

'Because I know who he is. He looked familiar, but I couldn't place him. You know when you see someone out of context, and it takes a while to catch up?'

O'Malley nods, keen for her to get to the point.

'Anyway, I've placed him now. This might be bigger than we thought.'

With that, she passes her phone to O'Malley, and he stares at the photograph on her screen. It is definitely the mystery man. O'Malley reads the article that accompanies the photograph.

Patrick Robertson is a politician. He's more than that. He's a minister, currently in charge of both Workplace Safety and Immigration. It makes sense of the chauffeured BMW. It's a Crown car, used for public engagements. It explains his connection to Howarth, an immigration lawyer. It does nothing to explain why he'd know Big Tone, or why he'd be present at an illegal gambling house. Claire is right; they're in worse trouble than they thought.

'Fuck's sake,' O'Malley says.

'My thoughts exactly,' Claire agrees.

'On the upside, we shook their tree and now we know more,' he says, optimistically.

'Whatever's going on, it hasn't kept him from his lunch,' Claire says, pointing her forehead in the direction of Howarth, who is now occupied with several plates of food.

Comfort eating.

'Do you think I could just go over there and shake the truth from him?' O'Malley asks Claire. It's an option.

'Maybe. Probably not. He's running scared. I think he'd just clam up. Besides, someone looking like you, roughing up someone like him in the middle of the day? There'd be cops on you before you'd said hello.'

O'Malley wonders what she means, someone looking like him. Then he remembers the bruising on his face, the cuts on his arm. No wonder Howarth's receptionist played so hard to get. He isn't at his prettiest, he has to admit. Howarth can wait. O'Malley will push him if he needs to, but left to sweat he'll soften up pretty quick. O'Malley wants to see Tony's next move first.

'So?' Claire asks.

'So, now we split up. I don't think Tone will try anything straight away, but I don't want to take any chances. Go home, catch up on your work. There's someone I need to see.'

'And who's going to watch your back, O'Malley?'

'I'm good. I'll buy a little insurance on the way.'

# CHAPTER TWENTY

He takes his truck home, parking it under the building, and grabs a backpack from the rear seat. It looks like the sort of thing a student would carry their books in, and he wants to blend in. He's heading to the university campus to meet with Scott, to find out what happened the night Sefina's sister died.

Walking across town, he focuses on the more recent death, and tries to piece together the puzzle that surrounds Danny's murder. He saw something worth dying for, and the list of those involved is growing. The names on that list are also now a danger to O'Malley, and, if he isn't careful, to Claire, too. He needs back-up. He's got two options, and neither are good. He'll work out which way to jump after speaking to Scott.

Scott Cranshaw has agreed to meet O'Malley, though he doesn't remember losing any notes. Curiosity got the better of him anyway. He texted O'Malley and told him where to find him, in Building 302, a modern complex on Symonds Street, the heart of the university's sprawling campus.

O'Malley navigates the building's interior unchallenged and pokes his head into the room that Scott's text dictates. It doesn't look much like a science lab, but he's never been in one, so what does he know? There are three tall benches dominating the room, and a mixture of whiteboards and screens lining three walls, the fourth taken up by windows that look out onto the streets below. A young man sits at one end of the middle bench. His checked shirt and glasses are his most distinctive feature. Just another student. Not the joyriding teenage killer O'Malley has pictured. Not at all.

'Scott?'

'Hi, er, yes. Are you Roy?'

'I am,' O'Malley replies, pulling a seat up and placing himself between Scott and the door. He doesn't want to appear threatening to Scott, but he doesn't want him to do a runner either. Scott is amiable enough, if a little nervy. But then O'Malley doesn't look like he belongs here. He looks like a man who's been on a pig hunt, alone. And the pigs won.

'I got your text and was confused. I don't remember losing anything.'

'Well, look, I feel bad about that, Scott. I don't have anything of yours. But I needed to speak to you, and I didn't think you'd meet me voluntarily.'

'Wait. What? What's this about?'

'I'm sorry to do this to you, but I've got a few questions about the accident.'

Scott's face falls. His eyes go to the door, and then to other possible escape routes. He realises there is no easy way out and drops his head. O'Malley knows as well as anyone that past mistakes stick to you, no matter how hard you try to shake them off. He tries to reassure him.

'Scott, what's in the past should stay there, and I'm pleased you've done something with your life to put it behind you, but I need to ask you about what happened. Can we do that, please?'

Gentle.

'What do you want to know?' he asks, addressing the bench in front of him.

'Well, to be honest, I'm not sure. I'm helping Sefina out on something. She's not getting on with her dad. She told me to speak to you.'

Scott sighs long and hard. It might have been a breathing exercise given to him to manage stressful situations. Or he is trying to blow away his guilt. He takes his glasses off, rubs his eyes. O'Malley hopes he'll tell him something that is worth putting him through this.

'Is Sefina OK?'

'She is. For now,' he says, hoping it is still true. He abandoned her when she asked for help.

'Well, her father is an asshole, if that helps.'

'Maybe. How so?'

Scott tells O'Malley what happened on the night of the crash, using words economically, cutting to the chase. Like he's had to replay the scene many times since it happened, and he no longer requires the catharsis of dragging the story out. He wants it over with.

'I met Talia when I was volunteering. I'd help prepare food boxes for families who needed them. Talia was another volunteer. I'm not exactly good with girls, go figure.' He looks at O'Malley as he says this — seeking reassurance that a bit of humour is all right if it's at his own expense. O'Malley nods for him to continue.

'She was nice to me, acknowledged me, and we became friends. Odd friends, really. I'm from a pretty good home: private school, nice holidays — you know, solid middle-class. I started volunteering because it would look good on my résumé. Talia, I could tell she didn't have much of anything, but she still had time to help other people. That struck me as sort of angelic, you know?'

So, Talia was a good girl, big-hearted, and Scott was the boy of privilege doing his bit. OK.

'We'd just talk a lot while we worked. I had a crush on her, if you can't tell. She'd never go for someone like me, though. To be honest, I don't think she was even thinking about boys — she wanted to do well at school, wanted to help whoever she could help, she didn't have time for any fun stuff. But we got on. We didn't mix outside of work; just when we were packing boxes, sorting out food.

'She didn't talk about home much, which I thought was weird. But maybe she was ashamed or something, you know, because she thought I had this perfect life. She'd talk about her little sister, though: Sefina. She was always doing stuff that made Talia laugh — little things, you know? Anyway, we got along. Over time she opened up to me. Her dad was very controlling. Had to know where she was at all times, wouldn't let her do anything on her own. He'd do the same with Talia's mum: she'd have to give him all the money she earned, rely on him for shopping money, that sort of thing. It sounded really bad to me, but Talia said that's just how it was in their house. She accepted it.

'I'd given her my number in case she ever needed anything. You know, wanted my dad to pick her up to get to the warehouse, or whatever. I just hoped she'd call me, really. So, one night the phone goes. It was a landline then, so I remember standing in the hall, trying to answer it quickly because my parents had gone to bed. She was in a state. Her dad was going mental — calling her a slut, getting violent. He was chasing her around the house, getting physical. She said she didn't know who else to call. She was scared. I offered to call the police, but she wouldn't let me. Said he just needed time to calm down — sober up, is what I think she meant.'

'So you went to rescue her? Be a knight in shining armour?'

'She asked me to. Of course it was stupid. But back then I just wanted to help her. I took my dad's car keys and went to her address. The car was an automatic — how hard could it be, right? The biggest issue I had was finding her address. I'd never read a map before, and I had to keep stopping to check where I was going. But I found it. I was scared shitless, to be honest. It looked like a rough street, and I was worried I was going to get jumped. Skinny white kid in a fancy car, I was out of place. I honked the horn to let Talia know I was there. It felt like ages, but then she was running out from behind the house, towards the car.'

'So, tell me about the accident. How did it happen?' O'Malley can't understand how the kid sitting in front of him got it so wrong. He got himself to South Auckland in one piece, but somehow screwed up the return leg.

'Just as Talia was getting in the car, the front door of the house opened. Her dad came steaming out. He was terrifying — to me at least. I took off, as fast as I could. But we got to the end of her road and realised we were being followed. He was chasing us and coming right up to the back of our car, almost touching it. I remember his headlights blinding me in the rear-view mirror. I was panicking, Talia was screaming. She said he'd hurt us both, that he'd already smacked her brother around when he tried to take her side back at the house.

'I tried to lose him. I have never been so scared. I was lost, too, just following Talia's directions. Left here, left again, go straight over. I don't know how we didn't hit anyone else. I guess that was something.'

'But you did hit something.'

'Yeah,' he says, slowing down now, confronting the moment that changed his life. 'I lost control. He was right behind me, up my arse, and those fucking lights, man. I think they blinded me for a second, but frankly I had no control over the car. I was learning to drive during a fucking car chase. I lost it, and I came off the road. We hit a power pole. The airbags exploded, but not quick enough for Talia. She … Well, you know what happened. There was nothing anyone could do.'

'I'm sorry, Scott, I really am.'

It was a sorry tale. It was poor judgement to get involved, but kids do stupid things every day of the week. Scott would be living with this for the rest of his life.

'You know what really sucked, Roy?'

More than Talia dying? Had to be something to top that.

'What?'

'Her dad didn't even stop. We went off the side of the road, and he just kept on driving. When the police went to tell the family what had happened, he pretended he'd been at home all along. Who fucking does that?'

They sit in silence for a minute. They both need the break. Scott is teary-eyed; O'Malley thinks the boy's probably cried himself dry more than enough since that deadly evening. He doesn't need much more from him. He's heard what Sefina needs him to hear. O'Malley's been playing for the wrong team.

'What happened afterwards, Scott?'

'I told the police everything I've told you. Talia's dad denied everything. He made his wife back him up. I don't think they believed him, but they couldn't find any witnesses to say he was there. One of the policemen told me his car was still warm when they got there, but they couldn't do anything. Talia wasn't around to back me up, was she?'

'And what happened to you?'

'Well, I think the police believed me, but I'd still been driving, I had no licence, wasn't in control of the car, and my passenger died. They charged me and I went to court. But I had a good lawyer, a friend of my dad. I got community service and counselling. The court made me apologise to Talia's family. That's probably what still eats away at me. I had to say sorry to her fucking dad. I don't have words for him. Talia's brother contacted me a few months after the accident. He wanted me to know he didn't blame me. That meant a lot. He seemed nice, sorted. But I guess he couldn't stomach his dad either. Last I heard, he was running with one of the gangs. Says a lot, don't you think?'

O'Malley thinks they've got a lot in common, these two boys who had to grow up fast and bear the guilt of another person's death. But Scott got a second chance. O'Malley got hard time. Even so, he thinks Scott probably got the longer sentence. O'Malley leaves Scott to it, wishing him luck in life. He has come this far, which is better than most. O'Malley turns his attentions to Mr Tupuola. His controlling nature resulted in his older daughter's death, illness consuming his wife, his son being pushed into the arms of the gangs and subsequently to jail, and now Sefina is on the run and in harm's way. He chased Talia himself, and now he is using O'Malley to chase Sefina. O'Malley is determined to get her to safety, more now than before. She doesn't deserve to have her life destroyed by her father's skewed view of the world. He is yet another man who doesn't deserve a dog licence, never mind the honour of parenting a child.

# CHAPTER TWENTY-ONE

The university is throbbing with hope.

Students going about their daily routine surround O'Malley as he makes his way through the campus and back home. He's envious of the young people around him, and their opportunity to just *learn*.

O'Malley studied in jail with the permission of a unit manager, reading everything he could, a dictionary by his side to decipher the tough stuff. In his experience, big words were simply a writer's way of hiding their lack of thought.

When they had something decent to say, they tended to cut to the chase.

*I think, therefore I am.*

Nothing wasted there, but those five words gave O'Malley a lot to ponder when he first read them.

He doesn't begrudge these kids their privilege. Some of them will have worked very hard to get here. Many others won't yet know, might never know, how life has been handed to them on a plate. O'Malley roots for the ones who know they are fortunate, because they've seen the alternatives. Scott grew up with privilege, but he knows how swiftly it can all be taken away. He will value every day now, because he's had a brutal moment of enlightenment. In some ways, he is one of the lucky ones.

O'Malley is in a philosophical mood.

He's willingly walked into harm's way. He has no doubt that he will face retaliation. But he's got his opponents rattled, and more likely to make mistakes. He will be there when they do. But a few more eyes can't do any harm.

He makes the call. It is answered before O'Malley hears a ring.

'Twice in a week, O'Malley? I hope you've been following my advice?'

'Scout's honour, Sergeant.'

'Then why the call? I haven't heard from you in months. And even then, you wanted something. So I'm guessing nothing's changed. What can I do for you, sir?' Bit of sarcasm there. Cops don't make a habit of being at the service of those they put away.

'Are you still CIB?'

'Yep. They offered me a stint in the kiddie squad, but I don't have the stomach for it,' he replies.

'Got time for a coffee? An acquaintance of mine was killed last week. There's been no news on an arrest. I'm wondering how you're going?'

'Who was your acquaintance? I mean, I can probably guess, because last week we had three DVs, and they solved themselves. Thankfully, not many unsolveds around here right now. But I've got a fat gambler who looks like he fell down a thousand steps. Am I warm?'

'Danny Cain.'

'Why am I not surprised you knew him. Congratulations, you just made my list of suspects.'

'I take it the list isn't a long one, then?'

'So now I just give you a status report? Want me to check in with you each day? It's an ongoing investigation, O'Malley. I'm not at liberty to say. But you've got my attention.'

It's why he didn't call on Buxton earlier. He has a suspicious mind.

'Ponsonby Road, thirty minutes' time, Sierra Café, on the left coming from my direction,' growls Buxton. 'Unless you'd like to just come straight to the station? I've got a cosy interview room.'

'Sierra is fine.'

'Hmmm. I won't be doing much talking, O'Malley, so I hope you're bringing something to the table. Otherwise, I will just be enjoying the coffee. Your shout, obviously.'

He hangs up. One of the techniques they taught at cop school. Stay in control.

'Danny Cain. Thirty-nine years old. Overweight, unemployed, no priors. Found dead in the bushes at the bottom of Constitution Hill. Twenty metres from a police yard. Ballsy or stupid, depending on how you look at it. Nothing in his pockets, no phone, wallet empty found nearby. No witnesses. Where were you, O'Malley?'

'When?'

'Saturday morning, between four am and five-thirty.'

'I was home. Asleep. No one to corroborate. Probably my phone would back me up, if it came to it.'

'It might come to it. So far, we've got very little, O'Malley. But now I've got a convicted killer asking questions. Occam's law is popular in my line of work, O'Malley. Simplest answer is often the right answer.' *Occam's razor,* O'Malley wants to correct him. Thinks better of it.

'Sometimes. But you know I'm not that stupid. Like the firebugs who come back to watch their own fires burn. I've got better instincts.'

'So why the interest? You know Cain, how? The great fraternal brotherhood of poker?' Buxton doesn't approve of O'Malley's pastime. Says that casinos are just holding rooms for when the jails get full. He'd had higher hopes for O'Malley, once upon a time.

'Something like that. I knew the man, is all. Sounded like a shitty way to go, and he wasn't a bad guy. Needed a woman's touch, for sure. But not *bad*. Call me old-fashioned, but I figure he deserves some justice at the end of the day.'

Buxton can't argue with that. O'Malley's speaking his language. He was the first person to show O'Malley you can still believe in black and white, even if you spend your life in the grey.

'And another mystery for the famous O'Malley to solve. Right?

So, *detective*, what have you found?' Buxton is really getting the hang of sarcasm. O'Malley needs to give him something, but he's not ready to spill his guts. He wants to keep those where they are.

'Not much, but you know, you hear things.'

'You do,' Buxton agrees.

'Danny would play poker 24/7 if he could. He wasn't at the casino the night before you found him. That's unusual. I figured it meant he'd found somewhere else to play.'

'What, he doesn't have a night off? Let his hair down, get laid now and then?'

'You've seen him. Only place he gets laid is at the knocking shop, and he can do that in his dinner break, still be back at the table on time. No, he would complain the casino was shut on Christmas Day. He'd be playing somewhere.'

'Any ideas where?'

'Not exactly. But I asked around. There's a guy in town who they say is the go-to, you want to find a big game.'

'Oh, that's what they say, is it?' Buxton is playing along. He knows O'Malley won't play faster than he wants to. 'This guy got a name?'

'William.'

Buxton nods, wanting more. It's all O'Malley's got.

'William? That's great, O'Malley. I'll be on my way, go speak to William. Fuck's sake. What am I meant to do with that?'

'It's all I've got. But someone pointed him out to me. Would a photograph help?'

'Cute. That's real cute, O'Malley. Yes, a photograph would help. Please may I see it?'

O'Malley opens his phone, shows him what Claire snapped outside the Shanghai Club.

'Great. Do you know how many Chinese call themselves William in this city? More than three, that's for sure. I need that picture. Email it to me?'

Er, no. Too much of a trail. O'Malley shows Buxton how

AirDrop works and sends it to him that way. He's pretty sure Buxton won't remember how he's got it, and it'll be harder to trace back to O'Malley's phone.

'So who is this guy, O'Malley? Why have you put him in the frame?'

'Someone I trust saw him with Danny.'

True.

'In the casino a couple of days before he got killed.'

Bluff.

'Don't suppose you remember who this someone is?'

'Not off hand, no.'

'Right.'

They size each other up then.

Buxton knows O'Malley is putting his neck out.

O'Malley knows that Buxton knows he isn't getting the full story.

He is trying to work out how O'Malley figures in it all.

Doing the right thing is a flimsy excuse for exposing himself in a murder.

They both know that.

'Handy, you having the photograph.' A statement, not a question, so O'Malley keeps his mouth shut.

'Why do I get the feeling you've got me doing your dirty work, O'Malley?'

O'Malley puts his hands up in protest. They both have the same goal. Punishing those who thought Danny was expendable. O'Malley wants William to feel the pressure. With the photograph, the official investigation might get some traction. Maybe there's some CCTV footage somewhere with William making a cameo. Something to warrant picking him up.

And if Big Tone is directly involved, O'Malley wants him to pay, too. But he needs a bit more proof before he can bring that to Buxton. It would overwhelm him. Right now, it just sounds like a conspiracy theory. Occam's razor. Keep it simple, stupid.

Buxton leaves O'Malley to pay for the coffee. O'Malley calls Claire, tells her what is what. He can hear the relief in her voice when he tells her he's met with Buxton.

'So if I, you know, disappear, go to him and tell him everything.' He regrets the words as soon as he speaks them. He was aiming for light-hearted but misses the mark.

'What do you mean, if you disappear? Do you really think they'll try to get to you?'

'Well, I'd say it's fifty-fifty. They might have panicked with Danny, and they can't afford to keep piling bodies up. They might just be closing the hatches on whatever it is we've stumbled on. Or, it's big enough to take the risk and shut me down instead. So, fifty-fifty.'

'So we get out of town for a few days, let the dust settle.' Statement, not question.

'Maybe. But I need to get Sefina somewhere safe, first.'

'You can't help her if you're dead, O'Malley.'

'True, but I'm talking another day is all. Meantime, I need to find out more about our lawyers, and about Tony and Patrick Robertson.'

'How?'

'Well, I could do most of it if I had the time. But it would take me days. Time I called in the experts. It will cost me in favours, but without more evidence we've got nothing.'

'OK. I don't want to know, do I? But listen, come to mine tonight. I'm working, but come afterwards. I want to keep my eyes on you.'

'Done. I'll pick you up from work, around one.'

O'Malley gets going. He's got a lot to do.

If O'Malley's going to find out what is really going on, he needs to go back to his roots — to the guy who taught him how to use the internet properly — using all the doors that it opens.

There is no point trying to set up a meet. The guy's barely

been outside in a decade. And O'Malley doesn't know where he is, anyway. Fucking guy hasn't used his real name as long as O'Malley's known him. Goes by a bunch of names, but O'Malley knows him as Minderbender: a pseudonym he adopted in online poker circles. O'Malley calls him Milo.

Milo is paranoid, which is a hazard of his job, as far as he is concerned.

*When you've seen what I've seen, O'Malley, you wouldn't call it paranoid.*

Milo's got a lot to be paranoid about. He spends his time in places he shouldn't, far beyond the firewalls and encryptions that are meant to keep him out. Mostly, just for kicks. But there's personal gain, too. Milo justifies his occasional transfers of wealth both by being selective with his victims and morally righteous in his choices. Stealing from thieves is a double negative. Which makes a positive. He's like that.

Milo is weird, and he's dangerous. And O'Malley wouldn't call on him unless it was a matter of life or death. But he figures that's where things are at, so he calls as he walks.

O'Malley uses Wickr, an encrypted app on his phone.

It's the minimum level of anonymity Milo will accept, and even then he'll be jumpy.

O'Malley installed the app on Milo's instructions a couple of years ago, and he's never found a reason to use it until now. Milo is the only contact in there. It's answered quickly, like Milo has been waiting all that time for this call.

'Yeah, who's this?'

He knows who it is. Wouldn't answer otherwise. Unlike O'Malley.

'It's O'Malley.'

Milo speaks. A hundred words a minute. He lives on Red Bull and intrigue.

'Hey, O'Malley. How are you? What's going on? You need to watch yourself. This whole trade-war shit? It's just the beginning, man. The US, the Chinese? They're just spoiling for a fight, man. They've both got some really dodgy shit going on in the background — I'm hearing all sorts. The Americans are threatening China with a flu, man. A fucking flu. Got it all locked and loaded, ready to take the Chinks out if they don't play ball.'

See? Paranoid.

'Nobody says "Chinks" anymore, dude.'

'Yeah, whatever. What do you need?'

O'Malley tells him.

Milo sounds bored, like the task is beneath him, but the mention of a government minister perks him up.

'Sweet. I can do that. No problem. When do you need it?'

Yesterday?

'As soon as, it's getting a bit sticky.'

'Well, OK. I guess I can give the security services a break for a little bit.'

Jesus. O'Malley doesn't want to know what Milo's up to.

'Hey, just checking: when you get it to me, it won't be traceable, will it? It might end up in police hands. Don't want to cause you any grief.'

'Ha. You couldn't if you tried. You'll owe me, OK?'

'Yes, I'm good with that.'

'OK, then, O'Malley. I'll let you know when it's done. And seriously, get a fucking flu jab, man.'

Milo hangs up, leaving O'Malley wondering what it looks like inside his mind. But now he's getting somewhere. He's got Buxton on the case, chasing William down, and Milo checking out the legal web that Tony is protecting.

O'Malley's got a spring in his step. He's almost home when his phone rings again. He checks to see who's calling — he's got Milo on his brain — and recognises the number. Sefina is trying to reach him.

# CHAPTER TWENTY-TWO

'O'Malley,' he answers, opening his apartment door at the same time.

'O'Malley, it's Sefina. Can you talk?'

'Yes, of course; I'm sorry about earlier.'

'It doesn't matter. I don't think it's safe here. I need your help.'

'What changed your mind?'

'I went for a walk. When I was coming back I passed the barn near our cottage. Jesse's dad was with some gang members. They said some stuff, scared the shit out of me.'

'What exactly did they say?'

'I don't know what they'd been talking about, but when they saw me one of them pointed to me. Said "throw the girl in and you've got a deal". Then some other stuff I don't want to repeat.'

Nice guys.

'What did Mr Browning say to that?'

'He laughed. Said he'd think about it. Did they want the deal or not?'

'These gangsters. Did you get a good look at them? What were they wearing?'

O'Malley wants confirmation they are Tua's boys. He guesses he's going to need to see him once again.

'Like they all look. Big, scary, leather jackets. Patches.'

'Could you read the patches, Sefina?'

'Yeah. It said Rebels, and had one of those old American flags on — you know, the red flag?'

The Confederate flag. Not Tua's men. Browning is playing with fire: dealing with both sides. O'Malley wonders if they know.

Rebels are an Australian gang, and like the Comancheros and the Bandidos they got a foothold in New Zealand in recent years, when their members were deported from Australia back to a place they'd never called home. With no roots, no connections in this country, they only had each other. So, they just did what they knew: banded together for safety in numbers. Word is that the established local gangs don't like the new competition. Whatever game Browning is playing, it is a dangerous one.

'Where's Jesse in all this, Sefina?'

'Fucking Jesse,' she says. 'I told him what happened. He starts crying like a little bitch. He pretends he's all tough and down with the gangs and shit. But he's a pussy really. He's just trying to impress his dad, but at the same time he's terrified of him. I've tried to tell him his dad doesn't give a shit about him, but he doesn't listen.'

There's an edge to Sefina's voice: she's tough, hardened by the hand she's been dealt. O'Malley hears it and knows he can speak to her on level terms. She's past being spoken to like a child.

'OK, Sefina, this is important. I can get you somewhere safe, but is Jesse with you or not? Does he want out?'

'He's confused. I think if I could get him away from his dad, he'd see sense. Be relieved maybe. But I don't think he's got the balls to run. He's too scared of getting bashed.'

O'Malley gets that. Sefina is a rarity. She's seen the threat at home and got herself out. Most don't. Abusers make sure their victims are emotionally dependent before they go to town on them. It's not weakness that makes people stay. It's fear, love, dependency, belonging. And having nowhere else to turn. O'Malley can fix that last bit, at least.

'OK, Sefina. Where's your nearest McDonald's?'

'Orewa. Fifteen minutes away.'

'You ever go out for a late snack? Is McDonald's a thing for you?'

'Duh. What do you think?'

'Good. Tonight. Say nine-thirty. Tell Jesse you want a

McDonald's. Make a fuss if you have to. Get him to drive you to Orewa. I'll be there. If we can persuade Jesse, great: he comes, too. If he gets shitty, wants to go down the other road with his dad, we're leaving him there. Deal?'

She gives that some thought. Jesse is a pussy and a bitch, but he is all she's got. O'Malley has seen the photos. They've had their good times. Tough call.

'Deal,' she finally says. 'But O'Malley: you're not tricking me, are you? I'm not going back to my dad. I'd rather take my chances here.'

'No, Sefina. You're not going back to him. I'm working for you now, not your father.'

'You spoke to Scott?'

'I did.'

'OK. Wait — tonight? Leave here at nine-thirty or be there at nine-thirty?' She has her head screwed on.

'Either way, Sefina. I'll be there. It might be a one-shot deal, though — I may not be able to help again, so do everything you can to get there.'

'I'll be there. *We* will be there.'

Six pm.

O'Malley needs to find Sefina a safe haven. She/they can't stay with him. Right now, they'd be safer in a lion enclosure. He thinks back to how this all started. Loto came to him on a recommendation. It is time for Grant to make amends. O'Malley calls him at home, one of his stray cats answering and passing the phone to Grant.

'Grant. It's O'Malley.'

'Hey, how are you? Did Loto get in touch?'

'He did. That's why I'm calling. How well do you know him, Grant?'

'Not that well. Just a friend of a friend. Sounded like a man in need.'

'Well, that big heart of yours is going to get you in trouble again. He doesn't deserve your help, or mine.'

'Aw, shit. I'm sorry. But shit, you don't owe him anything. Walk away. I'll check with you next time before I give someone your name. My bad.'

'Too late for that this time, Grant. You got any rooms free at your place?'

'Well, we're pretty full, but I can make it work. What do you need?'

O'Malley tells him what to expect. Either one or two new arrivals.

'Whatever you need, O'Malley. But she's fifteen, you say? And he's eighteen? I know it's a modern world and all, but I can't let them share a room, you know? I'm not blind to what kids get up to, but I still need to go to church on Sunday.'

'Put the boy in the shed outside, as far as I'm concerned. Just keep them safe and keep it quiet. It won't be forever. And you hear anything from Loto, you call me straight away. Don't let him in your house.' He owes it to Grant to let him know what he is dealing with. Gives him the condensed version.

'He comes to my house, he's going to have a man to deal with, not a child. This is on me, O'Malley. I'll deal with it.'

'Good. Thanks. And Grant, don't beat yourself up. If you hadn't sent this my way, Sefina would be on her own out there. You did good, whether you realised it or not.'

'Thanks, bro. I appreciate it. See you when you get here. Don't matter how late.'

Seven pm.

Time to check in with Claire. He makes his way to The Brandling, hoping to catch her before her shift starts.

Too late. The place is jumping.

O'Malley makes his way through the suits and skirts, leans on one end of the bar. He'll make do with broken conversation when Claire can fit him in.

He likes watching her work. She moves effortlessly along the bar, taking the next order while completing the last, keeping everyone happy. She knows who's been waiting, who is muscling in. The latter get no joy from Claire. She'll make them invisible. Focus on the quiet ones who wait with patience. Click your fingers, holler, call her 'babe', you go to the back of the line. She is queen.

'Hey, babe. Still in one piece, then?' she half-shouts as she nears O'Malley's end of the bar.

'So far, so good. Sefina called. She wants out,' he shouts back. Claire is gone again, fixing cocktails for a couple of girls at the other end of the bar. She doesn't take long.

'So, you going to get her? What about the boyfriend?'

'I'm getting Sefina. Maybe Jesse, too. We'll see.'

'OK. Still good to meet me back here?'

'I should be, but if I don't make it, don't worry. I'll come to your place. I'll try to text.' She is on the move and pulls a face. Like she's missed that last bit. He holds up his phone, tries charades. I'll text you. She gets it this time.

'Be safe!' she shouts, above the din.

Seven forty-five pm.

O'Malley is back in his truck. He's got time to kill. It will only take him half an hour, forty minutes max, to get over the bridge at this time of night. He can think of worse places than a McDonald's car park to sit for an hour, but not out of choice.

He wonders about Big Tone. How rattled he is. Or maybe he's just taking it all in his stride. Maybe he's playing cards to unwind from a tough day at the office. O'Malley's got time to check, so he heads over to the casino, finds a park in his usual spot, and gets in the lifts up to Level Two. There's a young couple already in the lift when he joins it. Dressed up, the guy in a shiny black shirt, pants, dress shoes, his girl in a silver dress, on just the right side of too small. They're excited, hitting the casino, ready to make twenty bucks last on roulette, hit the slots afterwards. It's how casinos should be, O'Malley thinks. A harmless distraction, an adventure. Not the inevitable descent into poverty that it is for too many.

Full of happy thoughts tonight.

The poker room is busy, plenty of full tables, a waiting list that extends beyond the capacity of the screen on which it is displayed. All the usual faces, and many unfamiliar ones. Despite the list, there are a few empty tables, the rush catching the casino out so they don't have enough spare dealers to cope with the overflow. It's the least profitable part of the casino, so the first to be neglected when demand is high. Left to their own devices, management would use every square inch of floor space for the slots, but their licence demands that table games are provided. So they dutifully comply, but on nights like this it's easy to see where their priorities lie.

O'Malley nods hello to the staff, says hello to a few of the low-limit players grinding away. He's interested in the bigger game, if it's on. Phil's behind the podium, points to the waiting list, telling O'Malley he's got a long wait ahead. O'Malley swats a hand in the air; he's not here to play. He sees some of the usual suspects sitting at a table near the sports betting lounge. It's warm outside, but everyone is layered up, still complaining that it's cold, the air conditioning so high it's either incompetence or a passive-aggressive move by management to discourage the players from getting too comfortable. O'Malley's money is on incompetence.

Chinese Steve is there, Big Tone, too. So he's not gone to ground. Maybe that's a good sign. The table is full, so there's no pressure for O'Malley to join the game. He stands and watches instead, making easy conversation with the table. Tone's got a big stack of chips in front of him. Winning, relaxed, no sign that O'Malley is a thorn in his side.

'Where have you been, O'Malley? Game's good, you're missing out.' Big Tone, opening the betting.

'Too busy to spend time with you degenerates,' O'Malley replies. Keeping the banter light, avoiding escalation. Tone, who has a lazy left eye, looks alert, pupils maybe a little dilated.

It's a tell, O'Malley thinks, but of what, he doesn't know. Could mean he's got a good hand, or just a reaction to the lighting. But O'Malley's thinking it's because he's enjoying this side game, the elliptical conversation where neither side is saying what they really want to.

'You keep your ear to the ground,' Tony states. 'Any news on Danny?'

There it is, O'Malley thinks. A little push, to see how he reacts. An exploratory bet, to see if he'll push back.

'Nothing' is the reply. Then: 'Cops haven't got anything to go on yet.'

'You been talking to the cops, then?' Tony overplaying his hand, in O'Malley's opinion.

'Just casual, bro, mate of mine in Central.'

'That sucks. Just wrong place, wrong time, I guess.'

O'Malley keeps a straight face, but he's thinking *the gall of this guy*.

'I guess.'

'Well, if you hear anything, let us know, eh? Be good to know there's not a serial killer out there, picking off poker players.'

That gets a nervous laugh or two around the table. Tone's well liked here, his jokes get a response. But it's a joke about Danny, and it's too soon, is what some are thinking. You never know who you're playing against, is what O'Malley thinks.

'Yeah, you'll be the first to know if I find anything,' O'Malley responds. There's nothing ambiguous about that, and it gets an eyebrow raise from Big Tone, but nothing more. The table is oblivious to the high-stakes game that is being played around them. Tone wants the last word.

'It's probably too late, unfortunately. What do they say? First twenty-four hours are critical? But watch your back, anyway, O'Malley. We can't afford to lose any more players.'

Now O'Malley's sure. Big Tone, William, the dodgy lawyers, it's all there; he's just got to figure it out. And stay alive long enough to do so.

# CHAPTER TWENTY-THREE

Eight fifty-five pm.

O'Malley is back in his truck.

He should be worried, but his exchange with Big Tone has left him oddly relaxed. He's looked his opponent in the eyes, and he knows what he's up against. Like lancing a boil, the release outweighs the anticipation. Now if he can put the Sefina saga to bed, literally get her to a safe bed at Grant's, he can make a final push to connect the dots between Tone and Danny.

Give Buxton what he finds, maybe get some sleep.

He heads onto Federal Street, nudging his way through the party crowd spilling onto the road, onto Victoria, connecting to the highway north, to the bridge.

Auckland is a small city, by population, but its boundaries spread far and wide, over some one thousand square kilometres. Bigger than New York. But it's a technicality. The area that would be judged the real 'city' by most observers could fit on a postage stamp. What would be considered a block by a native New Yorker. The rest of Auckland is given over to urban sprawl, a series of satellite suburbs, stretching out to retail and commercial areas that serve a population growing faster than the construction industry can keep up with. It's a low city, its residents long resisting the inevitable requirement to live on top of one another to maximise space. New Zealanders cling onto a dream of owning their own property, sitting on its own land, detached from their neighbours. But this ideal, this idyll, is undone when a third of the country all want to live in the same place. It's stupid, stubborn logic, which leaves seventy per cent of the country uninhabited, and results in the sprawl that O'Malley finds himself driving through to retrieve Sefina.

Once he's over the bridge, O'Malley is in territory that's still unfamiliar, despite the thirty-odd years he's lived in its proximity. As a boy he never made it across the bridge. His world was small, restricted to the confines of his bit of South Auckland, poverty building an artificial boundary to his horizons. Now, as he passes the wealthy northern suburbs, he still feels like he's a visitor, but there's no opportunity for sightseeing at this time of night.

It's not long before the road lighting disappears, full-beam necessary to navigate the stretches of highway that connect the outer suburbs. As he progresses, he passes recent haunts, the artificial snowfield on his right, the last few customers illuminated by spotlights in the car park where Jesse bit off more than he could chew.

He passes Millwater, another suburb that didn't exist ten years ago, pulls off the highway, crossing it once again and heading towards Orewa. It's a coastal town, with a long sandy beach, and calm waters that attract the weekend crowds. The surf club does good food, and acts as the focal point for firework displays that bring people from far and wide. All of which appeals to O'Malley much more than a thirty-minute road trip to McDonald's. But McDonald's it is, and O'Malley has plenty of company.

Even close to closing time, the car park is busy, a mix of teenagers getting out of the house, older guys grabbing dinner after the pub, and late-shift workers too damn tired to worry about nutrition. O'Malley's got a choice. Park out front with a view of the dining area, or down the side, where the drive-thru is doing solid business. He opts for the front, crediting Sefina with the smarts to entice Jesse inside, out of their car. He's got five minutes before she's due, longer if she's playing it casual.

Sefina is nervous. She's done well so far, getting Jesse to agree to McDonald's, especially given the family dinner at eight means cutting it so fine. It was a stressful meal, with Jesse and his dad exchanging stares that spoke of unfinished business, but she guilted Jesse into getting out and going for a drive. Sefina is feeling awkward, she says, like she isn't welcome. Just wants to get out for a bit. Jesse gives in, because he knows she won't stop complaining until he does. It's what girls do, in his limited experience. Sefina plays up the stereotype. They are running late, though, which stresses Sefina out, hoping O'Malley will still be waiting. And there is Jesse to deal with. She isn't sure he'll take kindly to the intervention. But she had been genuinely scared by the way the gangsters looked her up and down, and she is ready to run, with or without Jesse.

It is nine-fifty when they arrive at Macca's. Not a twenty-four-hour one, either, so she hopes they're open. If not, it will be harder still to get Jesse to stop the car, get out for some air. But the lights are on and there are signs of life inside, so she tells herself to chill, act normal. There is no sign of O'Malley. But he's a pro, knows what he's doing, Sefina thinks. Hopes.

They park up, go inside. Wince as they adjust to the bright lights inside, after the dark journey to get there. Jesse is perking up, to give him credit. He's a different character out of his dad's shadow. More like the person Sefina fell for, less like the boy trying to be a man he is at home. Free to be a kid. He orders a soft-serve ice cream, chocolate and strawberry sauce, as if to prove the point. Sefina has hers just with chocolate. Hoping now they can enjoy themselves a bit before O'Malley turns up. Just the two of them, having fun.

O'Malley figures he'll let them chill for a few minutes. They're late, but here. Jesse is going to be a hard sell, but he'll be impossible if he doesn't get to finish his ice cream. O'Malley has a good line of sight on them sitting alongside the window that fronts the restaurant. They look like two kids having fun, getting some free time from their parents. True, on so many levels. But time to crash back to reality. O'Malley prepares himself to ruin the moment. It isn't the place to cause a scene. McDonald's staff would have the cops on speed-dial. Needs to be quick and efficient. Sefina will have to carry the show. O'Malley will be supporting cast. He enters, stage left.

O'Malley moves swiftly, sits down alongside Jesse, blocking an exit.

To Sefina: 'You ready?'

'Ready for what?' Jesse asks. Realising that he is surprised by O'Malley's presence only after he's said it. Adding: 'What the fuck?'

'We've got to get out, Jesse — leave the farm,' Sefina says, putting a hand on Jesse's arm plaintively.

'What? No. Now? No.'

O'Malley wonders what is next in that sequence.

'Yes: now. We've got our chance — now. I'm fucking scared, Jesse. Your dad, his friends ... You.'

'Me? What does that mean? *I* scare you?'

'How you are when you're around your dad. You're either going to get into real trouble, or you and he are going to blow up. Whatever's going on? It's not you, I know it's not.'

O'Malley keeps schtum. She's got this. Jesse looks like he wants to argue, but he can't find the words. Turns his attention to O'Malley instead.

'What? And this guy's going to help us? He wants to take you back to your dad, remember?'

'No. I don't.' O'Malley's voice is firm, but he's not going to elaborate. He hasn't come for a debate. 'I've got somewhere for you to stay. One of you, or both of you. You decide, but do it quick.'

He figures it's safe to leave them to work it out as a couple. Stands, goes outside, takes some air. He keeps one eye on them through the window, because kids, well, they can be dumb sometimes. If he had both eyes on the car park, he might have spotted the Porsche Cayenne sitting idle, two people inside. But he doesn't, and soon enough the conference inside is over, Sefina coming out of the door. Jesse follows, head down, saying nothing.

'OK, you got anything with you before we go? We're taking my car, so last chance to grab anything.'

This hits Jesse hard. Rich kids travel heavy, and he's only prepared for McDonald's. To his credit, he twitches, but nothing more. Sefina has done this before, has a bag stashed in the Toyota; she grabs the keys from Jesse and retrieves it. Jesse twitches again. Probably thinking a heads-up would have been nice. He can make do, O'Malley thinks, probably will get back to pick things up if things go south for his dad, which is likely.

They get in O'Malley's truck, Jesse choosing the back seat, still not ready to embrace his new future. Sefina is up front, making herself at home, changing the radio station, playing with the settings on her seat. Nobody talks for a while. Jesse breaks the silence.

'Where are we going?'

'To stay with a friend. Someone who looks out for kids, keeps them straight.'

'I'm not a kid,' Jesse says, proving that he is.

'Kids, young people like yourselves, it's semantics.'

Jesse stews on that for a while, not sure what it means.

'You can stay there for a while, as long as you follow the rules, show respect, leave trouble outside.'

Silence to that. Sefina is watching Jesse in the mirror that she's pulled down from the sun-visor in front of her. To O'Malley, she looks thoughtful. Wondering what her future looks like, maybe. He's hoping it looks a little brighter away from sinful fathers.

There's not much traffic on the road heading into the city. Most folks are either already in bed, or heading in the other direction, back to their cosy North Shore suburbs. There's nothing cosy about O'Malley's drive, though, because Jesse has recovered his composure and is now arguing loudly with Sefina. They should have stayed where they were, they were safe there, we don't know this guy, and on. Sefina's arguing back, and O'Malley's on the brink of intervening, maybe stopping the car and letting Jesse find his own way in the world. But where they are, the highway is unlit and down to two lanes, all the way through to Albany. It's an accident hotspot, and even Jesse doesn't deserve to take his chances walking home in the dark from here.

But O'Malley's distracted, and he's not alert to what's happening outside of the truck, and he really does need to pay attention, because one moment O'Malley's is the only car on the road, the next, he's blinded by high-beams coming up fast behind him. O'Malley thinks it's an aggressive boy-racer. Another idiot learning to drive on the highway. He'll pull out and pass any second. But he doesn't. The lights fill the inside of the truck's cabin, making Sefina and Jesse turn around to see where the light is coming from.

'What's this idiot doing?' Jesse asks.

'I don't know,' O'Malley says, worry starting to grow. He slows down a bit, let's the guy know he's happy to be overtaken. The car behind just closes in, now about a metre behind. Dangerously close. Then the car whips out beside O'Malley, who tries to get a look at the driver, but sees only dark-tinted windows. The car speeds up, passing O'Malley, then just as recklessly pulls in front of the Ranger, tapping the brakes, forcing O'Malley to push heavily on his own.

'Fuck,' Sefina says, speaking for them all. She's pale, terror on her face. 'Who the fuck are they?'

O'Malley is unsure. Could be Tone sending a message, or Browning chasing an errant child regardless of endangerment, repeating history. He focuses on keeping control, but the car ahead, a new-model Porsche, is swerving to and fro, changing speeds and forcing O'Malley to slow down.

He's got a choice.

Be forced to slow down, and eventually stop, on an unlit, quiet highway, or try to get past the aggressors in front.

Stopping isn't an option.

He's got Sefina and Jesse with him, and he's pretty sure the occupants of the car in front aren't looking for a roadside chat. He's got to get out in front of them and stay on the road long enough to meet other traffic, reduce the risk.

Worst case, he favours his truck to win in a collision with the Porsche. The German cars are built for looks and speed, but the Ranger's built for work.

Sefina is getting louder in her protests. No wonder, given her past. Jesse is beyond words, sitting silently in the back, struck dumb with fear. O'Malley can't worry about them right now; he's got to focus on getting them out of this alive.

He slows down, waits for the Porsche to follow suit, and then tries to pull out, accelerate past the car in front. The sports car is too quick, too responsive, and it blocks the path with ease.

He tries again, this time moving to the right before pulling hard left and going for the undertake. Again, the Porsche moves fast, blocking safe passage.

There's no let-up, and Sefina is shouting at O'Malley to stop, but he knows that's the most dangerous option.

He tries again, is thwarted again.

The highway opens up, a slow lane appearing on the left, widening their options; three lanes to play with. O'Malley sticks to the centre lane, allowing himself two ways through.

There's no way he's going to make it past the Porsche entirely before the faster car closes in. So he's going to have to push his way through, and hope the Ranger is built as tough as they promise.

He moves to the right, waiting for the Porsche to follow suit, closing down the right lane. When it does so, he barrels to the left, aiming for the far-left lane, giving himself as much room to pass as possible. He only needs to get the nose of the Ranger in position to give them a chance.

The driver ahead is good, but he's playing a game of fine margins, and O'Malley makes use of the extra space, nosing the Ranger through. The Porsche has other ideas and swiftly pulls left, but O'Malley's prepared for it and pulls right, pushing the Ranger into the left side of the Cayenne.

The driver isn't prepared for this, and O'Malley senses the

other car losing traction. It pulls out, away from the Ranger, focusing now on keeping control itself rather than controlling the Ranger. It's the gap O'Malley needs, and he puts his foot to the floor to put distance between the two cars.

The advantage is short-lived.

The Porsche settles, then picks up speed, once again drawing alongside the Ranger. O'Malley's change in tactics has changed the game: the Porsche driver thinking *two can play at that game.* O'Malley senses the car alongside moving closer, trying to force O'Malley left, where there's nothing to keep the car from leaving the road; just a grass verge, trees and trouble.

Both cars slow down, neither driver particularly confident of jousting it out at high speed. But the Porsche is intent on driving O'Malley off the road, and it pulls left then out again, encouraging O'Malley to oversteer, off the road and into the beyond.

O'Malley holds his line, ready to push back, which he does the next time the Porsche makes a move towards him. The cars touch, briefly, making a God-awful noise as the Cayenne's wing mirror smashes against the body of the Ranger, a high-pitched noise of scraping matched inside the cab by Sefina's screams.

O'Malley is sweating now, hopped up on adrenalin, too. He wonders how long he can hold the Porsche off, but he glances ahead, and sees light at the end of the tunnel. Several lights. Literal ones as the highway acknowledges approaching suburbia and streetlights begin to guide the way.

There's opportunity, too, because up ahead, in the middle lane, there's a heavy articulated truck moving slowly ahead of the Porsche. O'Malley doesn't wish the truck driver any harm, but a bit of him is hoping the driver of the Porsche doesn't look up and just ploughs into the back of it.

Not quite.

But the Porsche notices the truck late in the piece and has to brake sharply to avoid it. As it does so, it pulls out to the right, thinking it can overtake the truck and resume hostilities where it left off. But O'Malley's lane is branching off — there's an exit road to Oteha Valley, and he takes it without hesitation, the slow-moving truck acting as cover to his right. The Porsche will be past the exit before its driver realises where O'Malley's gone.

He composes himself, turns to his passengers.

'OK, it's over. You both all right?'

Sefina just looks at him. Tears stain her face and drip from her fingers, her cheeks hidden behind her hands, as if they'd offer some protection. O'Malley can't tell if Jesse is in shock or wetting his pants with excitement. But he's aware enough to offer Sefina consolation. He leans forward, puts a hand on her shoulder, whispers something approaching soothing. She shakes him off, turning in her seat.

'What was that, Jesse? Was that your fucking dad? Did he have someone follow us?'

Jesse's face is pure confusion. He hasn't joined the dots like Sefina has, doesn't see the past flashing forward to haunt her.

'Why would he do that? Seriously? How can that have anything to do with my dad?'

'Just like my dad had nothing to do with Talia, you mean?'

Oh. O'Malley sees Jesse finally come up to speed. It is going to be a long night for these two.

O'Malley gets his bearings, works out the fastest way to Grant's that doesn't involve the highway. He takes the Eastern Bays down to Takapuna, rejoins the highway only when he has to; without doing a huge detour back via the upper harbour, there's no other way back across the city to Grant's house. Quickly weighing the odds, he reckons the detour is not worth it. He maintains their path, keeping vigilant, looking for a Porsche Cayenne minus a wing mirror. Doesn't see one.

There's traffic now, and he's finding comfort in it, but he's wondering how long the tail was on him before it made its move. He doesn't think it has anything to do with his passengers. He thinks Big Tone is cleaning house.

# CHAPTER TWENTY-FOUR

Jesse is confused, to say the least.

He's not emotionally equipped to process what's happening to him. He thought if Sefina came to live with him, life would get better. His dad had been different since his mum died. Having a girl around the place would soften his dad up a bit, he hoped, make him feel normal again. Be a normal dad again. But he'd got worse, going through a mid-life crisis that was less new girlfriend, new aftershave, and more new career, new shotgun. He was playing out a macho fantasy, taken straight from *Sons of Anarchy*.

Jesse kind of enjoyed that bit: gangsters visiting the farm, showing Dad respect, making Jesse feel tough by association. But he didn't enjoy what was happening to his father. He had turned cold, treating Jesse like an embarrassment, not smart enough, not tough enough, to be of value. Like he'd decided what he was going to become, and Jesse didn't figure in the plans. Didn't measure up. Jesse had tried hard to impress, but when he inevitably fell short, he found himself fantasising about a physical showdown where Jesse landed a final punch, put his dad in his place. He knew that would never happen, so he just spent most of the time bottling his anger and impotence.

Then they threatened Sefina. He knew he couldn't defend her if it came to anything. So he was happy to run. It would be a second chance. But now he's barely escaped a car crash, forced off the road by some fucking lunatic who Sefina thinks is working for his dad. It's all too much. He wants to curl up and go to sleep, pretend this isn't his life.

He's standing in an unfamiliar kitchen, being introduced to Grant, who has kind eyes, and is asking if he can get Jesse a drink, maybe a sandwich.

'I'm good' is all Jesse can muster.

'Thank you,' Sefina prompts, a little sharply.

'Thank you,' Jesse adds, sheepishly.

Sef's going to be mad with me forever, Jesse's thinking. Maybe sleep will fix that, too.

'You're welcome. O'Malley says you've had a bit of excitement tonight, but you're safe here, and you can stay as long as you need. I'll show you around in a sec, introduce you to everyone. It's quite a full house at the moment. Jesse, you'll have to sleep on the couch tonight, until I shuffle everyone around tomorrow — hope that's all right?'

'Sure.' Then: 'That's great. Anything.' Probably a good thing that he's not sharing with Sef tonight, it'll give him time to work out what to say. She's always so much better with words than he is. Better at most things, if he thinks about it.

'OK, then. O'Malley, I've got it from here. You need anything?'

Fucking O'Malley, Jesse thinks. Everyone loves O'Malley. He sees how Sef looks at him, all my-hero-in-shining-armour. Now Grant's at it, like he owes O'Malley something. But I got the drop on him the other day, is what Jesse is thinking. If only everyone had seen that. But when he thinks about it, Jesse feels bad about that, too. Because O'Malley's actually pretty fucking cool. Handled that car chase like a boss. Jesse's head hurts. It's just all so damn confusing.

O'Malley leaves Sefina and Jesse with Grant. They're in good hands.

Sefina has pulled herself together pretty quickly, he thinks. Jesse, well, another story. O'Malley knows what it is like to be a teenage boy, yearning to be a man. Prison was full of the type. Maybe a bit of time with Grant will get him straight. He hopes so.

O'Malley looks at his truck with dismay. The driver's side is scratched to hell, there's a couple of dents in the doors and a bigger dent on the front right-hand body, where he pushed it into the Porsche. It's a mess. But it's just a car and can be fixed. Harder to fix a couple of dead kids, if it had gone the other way.

O'Malley's feeling lucky to be in one piece, and also wondering who was behind the wheel. His blood is up, and he's hoping he finds out so he can have another round with him. Tomorrow, though. Now O'Malley just wants to get home, get to Claire's, feel the warmth of her.

The drive home is blissfully uneventful; no sign of the Porsche that will probably follow him in his dreams tonight.

O'Malley's thinking about how to take the fight to Big Tone directly. Wonders if Milo has made progress. He'll check when he gets upstairs.

He pulls the truck in, under the apartment building. At least no one will see the damage to it down here, think he's a careless driver.

He's bone-tired, now that the adrenalin has drained. Getting too old for this, he thinks. He parks up, tight against the far wall of the basement that has space for four cars, but tonight holds only one. He grabs his jacket from the back seat and locks the car with his key fob. The lights flash twice in response.

Turning to head to the stairwell that will take him upstairs he hears the scuff of feet on concrete. He looks round and sees the source of the noise. He's not alone.

William stands 3 metres away, and he's brought a friend. O'Malley stands his ground, sizing up the situation.

'You drive well, Mr O'Malley,' William says. Which solves one mystery. 'You know, in my culture, it is rude to ask too many questions.'

Great, O'Malley thinks. Someone else who's watched too many movies. They've already lost the advantage of surprise, and now William's giving a speech.

The stairwell isn't far away, and O'Malley thinks he can make it ahead of them, but both guys are pretty lean, probably fast. It's too close to call, so he stands pat.

He watches their movement, tries to assess the threat.

William and his pal, another Chinese guy who's dressed like William in a suit, but with a dark blue shirt instead of William's white, are standing about 2 metres apart, slowly closing in on O'Malley. They're about two and a half metres away right now.

If they've come with a gun, O'Malley needs to close that distance fast, to give himself a chance of deflecting the weapon. Optimistically, to take it from them.

But when O'Malley looks at his attackers he doesn't see guns but knives. And for a knife fight, distance is good.

But there's two of them, and they're co-ordinating their movements. If they attack at the same time, one of them is going to get through, and O'Malley knows he's finished if that happens. He's had more experience with knives than guns. Back in Pare, a shiv was a very real threat, and he survived two attempts on his life. He intends to make that three.

O'Malley holds his jacket in his left hand, puts a little spin on his wrist to try to twist the jacket together, give it more weight, make it less flighty. It's denim, which is good. He'd prefer leather right now, with its heft and durability, but denim will do. It's tough and will slow a knife down.

He needs to move, take the initiative back, and change his opponents' plans — try to take them one at a time. They're both right-handed, which is a factor. If he can get on the outside of the blue shirt who's standing to his colleague's right, William will need to move further, all the way around, to bring his knife hand into play. A fraction longer before they can double-team him.

Might be enough.

There's about a metre and a half between them now. Much shorter and O'Malley loses options.

He moves fast, forward and right. He swings his jacket down hard, out to the left, where he thinks Blue Shirt's knife will lunge. The jacket connects with his attacker's arm, wraps itself around a bit, causes a nuisance. It gives him enough time to step outside the knife arm and throw a hard right into the guy's face.

O'Malley feels it connect, knows it will do damage, but follows it with another quick hook anyway. The knife hand is free, but William's friend is wondering what hit him, and his brain isn't speaking to his arm right now. O'Malley ducks down, using his size to his advantage, and drives his body as hard as he can into Blue Shirt, using his opponent as a shield that he pushes fast into William, who is moving in with his knife hand pulled back to strike.

O'Malley keeps on pushing, and he's driving both men back, neither of them in control. Drives them into the wall. He hears the connection, William's head bouncing off the wall behind him, sounding like a coconut that's fallen onto a footpath.

Blue Shirt is meat in the sandwich, crunched together between O'Malley's shoulder and William's suddenly unyielding torso. He's still recovering from O'Malley's punches, and now he's feeling the wind knocked out of him, too. He goes down, dropping the knife as he does so. O'Malley pushes himself off the guy, making sure he doesn't go down as well. On the ground, with William above him, he'll be dead meat. He steps back a metre or so.

Blue Shirt is down but not quite out. William is shaking off a headache, and trying to stay on his feet and not get tripped up by his sidekick lying at his feet. He moves to one side, steps forward, and comes for O'Malley, thrusting the knife to dissuade O'Malley from another offensive move.

They move in a circle, William hunched over, his knife hand leading, his other arm held out for balance. O'Malley hunches over, too, trying to reduce his body's surface area, keep his arms protecting his torso. He's lost the jacket in the rolling maul, and he's scanning the floor for it, feeling exposed without it.

O'Malley sees his jacket, but it's behind William, out of reach for now. He keeps moving to his left, maintaining the circular dance that he's got going with William, hoping they'll soon have swapped positions and he'll have a chance to grab the jacket.

As they move, O'Malley sees Blue Shirt's knife on the ground.

He knows he won't have time to pick it up: William will be too quick to let that happen, and reaching down would leave O'Malley's back exposed. He doesn't like knives, anyway, has never used one on another man. There's something dishonest about them, and the idea of opening up another person's flesh makes O'Malley nauseous. He opts to take it out of the equation instead, kicking it so that it scuttles across the floor, ending up in the shadows under the Ranger.

William is stab, stab, stabbing forward, like a boxer throwing exploratory jabs, sending his brain information about the distance between the men, preparing for the strike that will land.

He switches gear, slashing a wide arc from right to left. O'Malley puts his arm up to protect his face, feels the light blow as the knife glances off him. No pain. That will come later. But there's blood, and it drips down his arm towards his elbow. O'Malley is thinking about the mess he'll have to clear up, but not for long, because William is slashing the knife back from left to right now, backhand.

O'Malley leans back, avoids the blade this time.

William has less control now that he's swinging his knife hand. When he was stabbing, lunging, the knife was always a threat, pointing towards O'Malley at all times. But now that he's switched to a slashing motion, O'Malley knows he's got an opportunity. William's arm is at full stretch, out to his right, and he's got to switch direction, like a golfer at the top of his swing.

It's a fraction of time and O'Malley seizes it, moving forward fast, putting his left hand on William's forearm, interrupting his swing. O'Malley grabs William's suit lapel with his right hand, pulling him forward, using his forehead to strike William full in the face. It's not a perfect hit, a bit lower than he aimed for, but it connects with devastating force anyway. William's nose flows freely, making his shirt look like a tablecloth at a bacchanal.

O'Malley doesn't pause to worry about the cleaning now, moving his right shoulder into William's right side, shifting the grip of his left hand as he moves. He puts his right arm over William's, rotating William's arm upwards and his body moves down towards the ground in response. It's a crude arm bar, but O'Malley's strength makes up for any lack in technique, and William lets the knife fall. O'Malley keeps up the pressure until he feels William's arm go slack, useless. But he's still a threat, O'Malley thinks, so he shifts position and punches him, a left hook that puts him to sleep.

O'Malley looks up to check on Blue Shirt. William's sidekick hasn't got back to his feet, but he's still conscious. Hoping William would take care of business, but now realising it's down to him, and he doesn't have his knife.

He looks at O'Malley, sighs, and gets to his feet, resignation across his face. He charges towards O'Malley, who just puts out his right fist and lets the guy run onto it.

Blue Shirt goes down, pride the only thing intact.

O'Malley surveys the scene. The threat has passed, for now. Both men will have headaches, and William might be down to one arm for a while, but O'Malley hasn't killed anyone. He checks out his own arm. The cut is shallow, and the bleeding just a trickle now. Nothing he can't patch up. He picks his jacket up, and wonders what to do about the two unconscious Chinese men in his basement. Then he hears three slow claps and realises he's not alone.

'Nice work, bro.'

He looks up and there's two more men standing at the bottom of the ramp that connects the car park with the street. They'd look threatening in their underwear, but they've chosen to wear their gang patches just to be sure no one mistook them for friends.

'Jimmy Tua wants a word,' the one who can use his words says.

O'Malley looks down at William and Blue Shirt, then up again at the two gangsters. Like, what makes you think I want to talk to Jimmy?

The patched guy is happy to play the silent game, too. He replies by waving his left hand at O'Malley. This time, it's a gun, not a knife.

# CHAPTER TWENTY-FIVE

O'Malley follows the patched men up the ramp, onto the street, decides there's no point pushing his luck against the gun. Couldn't, even if he wants to, because a knife fight does take it out of you.

'Put your jacket on, eh?' the talkative gangster instructs O'Malley. 'Don't want blood on my seats, bro.' By way of explanation.

O'Malley does what he's told, respects the other man's pride in his vehicle. Or his understanding of basic forensics.

The other gangster, the mute one, opens the passenger door, holds it for O'Malley, nodding his head for him to get in. It's like he's ordered a Corporate Cab and he's getting the premium service. Except the car in question is a Hilux that's seen worse days than O'Malley's Ford, and there's a month's worth of cheeseburger wrappers in the footwell. It's better than being hogtied in the back, though, and O'Malley tries to breathe, bring his heart rate down to sustainable levels. He's not optimistic about his future, but he wants to avoid a heart attack in a dirty Hilux. These guys are probably not trained in resuscitation.

O'Malley's hosts get into the car, so there's one alongside him in the driver's seat, the mute sitting behind him. He's got the handgun in case O'Malley gets any ideas. Which, right now, he doesn't.

O'Malley doesn't know what time it is, has lost track, but there are still plenty of people milling about outside, moving from bar to bar, chasing last orders. He *could* jump out and run for it, hope the cops get to him before his captors. But he doesn't know how serious these guys are, what their orders are. He might just end up as another gun-crime statistic. He decides to let fate play out, see where this goes. He might learn something, at least.

Like why everyone wants to kill him.

Whatever.

Go with the flow, find a way out down the track. O'Malley knows it's a weak strategy, but he's resigned to it, and he's very, very tired.

The driver puts some sounds on. West Coast rap, nineties vintage. Mood music. He turns to O'Malley.

'Thanks for being good about it, makes life easier, eh? I'm Manu. That's Chatbox in the back.' That makes O'Malley smile.

'O'Malley,' he replies, returning the courtesy.

'We know that, eh? We came to you, remember?'

Manu's pretty pleased with that witticism, and he's got a surprisingly high-pitched laugh that's infectious. The infection doesn't travel as far as the back seat, though, and Chatbox stays quiet, trying to shake his nickname.

'Don't suppose I can use my phone, text my girlfriend, tell her I'll be late for dinner?'

'Best you don't, eh?'

O'Malley nods, knowing it was a long shot. Manu doesn't ask for the phone, though, and, worst case, Claire's got that Life360 app installed on it, the one that lets you keep an eye on your kids' whereabouts. She'll know where to find the body, and where it's been.

They drive without further conversation, the music setting the scene. O'Malley gets a glimpse of Chatbox in the back seat, silently lip-synching 'Fuck wit Dre Day', word-perfect.

O'Malley expects a dark alley, or a field, or a boat ramp with easy access to the water. Instead, the route they take puts them on the Southern Motorway, taking the Mount Wellington exit, through back streets where commercial buildings and domestic houses sit cheek-by-jowl. They pull into a driveway that's long and dark, so

O'Malley's stress receptors kick in, putting him on high alert.

They get to the end of the driveway, and there's a bunch of cars parked up everywhere except in the actual spaces that are reserved for cars. It's a warehouse-cum-car shop, and it's busy.

Nothing discreet about this location, O'Malley thinks. By day, this is obviously a car repair shop, but now there's a boxing ring inside, complete with a makeshift bar, and plastic seats for spectators. Whatever fights took place are now over, but there's plenty of people still hanging around, drinking, smoking. It's a mixed crowd. Plenty of gang jackets, but civilians too — boxers, trainers, everyday joes. It's an unlikely place for a killing, so there's hope yet.

Manu parks up, blocking two or three other cars from going anywhere, but showing no signs of giving a shit.

'Let's go,' he says, getting out of the Hilux, and Chatbox doing the same.

O'Malley draws a deep breath, opens his door, and steps down from the cab, noticing that's he's already stiffened up, feeling the after-effects of his violent dance with William. There's nothing to be done but follow Manu to whatever awaits him, so that's what he does.

Inside, through to the far corner, up a metal staircase to the office that overlooks the ground floor. It's a location scout's dream: Scene One, crime boss's lair. Chatbox has obviously done his job, because he has already peeled off, joining his boys at the bar, so as O'Malley enters the office it's just Manu, him and, now, Jimmy Tua.

Jimmy's behind a desk, tapping away at a keyboard when they enter. He's letting the side down: no lines on the table, no strippers on the couch, just a big man doing office work.

'Fucking O'Malley,' Jimmy says, by way of greeting. Then to Manu: 'Any problems? Mess?'

'No problems at all, Jimmy. This fella's been sweet, eh? He was just taking care of business when we got there.'

'OK, then. We're good.'

It's Jimmy's signal to leave them to it, and Manu's quick on the uptake.

'OK, boss. Good to meet you, O'Malley.' He heads back downstairs, leaving O'Malley to ponder what was good about it.

Once the door's closed, Jimmy's straight into it.

'What the fuck have you stuck your nose into, Books?' It's what Jimmy called him all those years ago.

O'Malley lifts his hands in protest.

'Honestly, I really don't know, Jimmy. I was looking for a girl, thought it would be straightforward, then I saw your boys with Browning, and got the hard word. Back off, which I did. I'm not looking to cause you any problems.'

Jimmy Tua weighs this up. He carries himself well, and O'Malley knows all too well that Jimmy can decide someone's fate in an instant, but his face won't betray which path he's chosen. His forearms are resting on the table, covered in ink that seems to emphasise the muscle and sinew beneath. He's wearing a black t-shirt, emblazoned with a logo for a men's health charity: It's Good to Talk. Chatbox didn't get the memo. Jimmy's being true to his clothing, though, and responds to O'Malley's denials.

'You're not here because I'm worried about my business, Books. But you've really pissed someone off. I told Browning to leave you be, but when I spoke to him again today he said you were being taken care of.'

O'Malley runs through that in his head. Browning sent William? That doesn't make sense, and he's thrown by it. Jimmy mistakes the source of his confusion. Tells O'Malley why he's involved.

'I don't like being ignored, and I don't trust that Browning fella. He's another white dude who thinks he's the boss. I sent the boys out to keep an eye on you — help you out if you needed it. Sounds like you had it covered.'

'Appreciate it,' O'Malley says. But he's confused, and curious. 'I don't know why Browning would try to take me out. I thought it was all about this other thing. What's his business, Jimmy? Why are you doing business with him?'

'Still asking too many questions, eh, O'Malley? It's what gets you into trouble.' But he's smiling. 'What do you think?'

'Well, I guessed Browning is into something product-related,' is O'Malley's reckoning.

'Fuck you, O'Malley. Brown boys are involved so it's got to be drugs? That's what you think? You've got to have more faith in the brothers.'

Tua stands, which puts O'Malley on alert. It doesn't take much to flip his switch. But Jimmy makes no move towards O'Malley. He goes to a fridge in the corner, pulls out two cans of bourbon ready-mix, walks around to hand one to O'Malley. He gestures for O'Malley to stand, and walks to the window that looks down on the yard below.

'You know me from back in the day, O'Malley. I've done shit, no doubt. So have all the boys down there. Still do, but shifting a bit of weed is barely a crime anymore. White fellas trying to take that away from us anyway. I'm trying to change things, give these boys other options — like the car business. Takes time, though, so we're still a cash business for now. But we'll get there. You're not the only one who can turn things around: lot of those fellas down there would be good boys if life dealt them a decent hand.'

The road to Damascus starts in Auckland, O'Malley thinks. This is a different Jimmy Tua from the one he knows. Knew.

'Where's Browning fit, then?'

'The cash. He's an accountant. Reckons he's got a better way of turning street cash around. Arrogant motherfucker reckons him and his partners are going to be the Google of the crime world. Cleaning money, payment systems, logistics. Everything but the dirty work. He's trying to bring us on board.'

'Will you?'

'I don't trust the guy. He's cocky, thinks he's better than us. Financially, it makes sense — he's offering good rates, and it takes a bit of risk out — but my gut says no.'

'You know he's talking to others? Rebels, for example?'

'Don't surprise me. He wants to control it all, says it's the scale that makes it work. Told me to be smart, not worry about little rivalries. That's what he doesn't get. I don't let my boys touch meth, O'Malley. Don't trade it, don't use it. When I got out last time around, I saw what it had done. Fucks everyone up. Makes a brother stupid: once they're on the pipe, they'll rob their own mother. Costs us a lot of money, but it's a rule we agree on here, everyone knows the price if they break that rule. The Aussie boys, they don't give a fuck. Browning don't either.'

O'Malley takes a gamble, tells Jimmy about the van, the cops watching. Buxton wouldn't be pleased if he knew, but he's not playing this hand, and O'Malley needs to give Tua something. He's not going to keep talking for free.

'Figures. They'll have followed us — or the Rebels, or whoever. All that activity in one place, it's going to raise interest. Good to know, though, O'Malley. One more reason to steer clear. Might even be useful.' Jimmy's a pretty handy chess player, thinks three moves ahead. It's why he's the one standing in this office, above those he came up with. He turns to O'Malley.

'Maybe we can help each other out, O'Malley. Where do you fit in? Browning's not stupid enough, or brave enough, to be taking you off the board because of what you saw. Gotta be more than that. Spill.'

O'Malley gets Jimmy up to speed. The poker game, William, Danny, Big Tone and his lawyers. Leaves the minister out of it, for now. Jimmy whistles, impressed at how much trouble O'Malley's walked into in the space of a week.

'Ever thought of getting a proper job, O'Malley? Something to keep your mind working, stop you getting into trouble? I could use you around here — run the books on the car business, give me a break from this shit?' He points to the computer, a spreadsheet open in the screen.

'Thanks, but I like things as they are. Usually. I just need to fill in the gaps, work out exactly what's going on, then I can get back to my easy life. Tell me about the money: how does it work, the cleaning?'

'Ha. You always did like your studies, eh? OK, Books: Laundering 101. We'll use the Rebels as an example, because they, *allegedly*, are into some shit.'

Books. What O'Malley was called inside. Now Jimmy's his teacher. Funny old world.

Jimmy picks a pen up, draws as he speaks, enjoys sharing his knowledge with someone who will appreciate it and get it first time.

'First thing. Let's say you're selling P. Only idiots try to make it locally these days. It's all from Asia now, makes its way down through Myanmar, places like that, gets to Oz. Then it finds its way over here.'

Jimmy draws a map as he talks. The geography is spot-on.

'So it's made in China, but ends up sold here. Twenty bucks at a time, which when you shift a few kilos means a whole bunch of cash. Street cash — literally dirty, cos it's been stuffed in some P-head's pocket.'

Jimmy marks the street transactions down, a bunch of $ signs representing each sale.

'Whoever's sold it — let's say the Rebels — has two problems. First, they need to pay the guys who sent it. And they're in China. Second, they've got their profit, and they want to get that into the system. With me?'

O'Malley nods, there's nothing he doesn't know yet.

'So, let's pay for the product first.'

Jimmy's enjoying doing the telling. He marks a big cross where China sits on his map.

'You've got a massive organisation in China, and they want payment for goods sold. Sometimes, it's done with crypto — bitcoin. You can buy that on the street, too. Pay a premium for it and send the codes to China. That's one way. But it's too complicated for the Aussies, you get me?'

O'Malley's not surprised Jimmy is all over this stuff. He's CEO material in a leather jacket.

'So what's another way?'

'Right. So it's cheaper, and more old-school, to make payment *this* way. All those Chinese, live here, buying big houses, businesses? How do you think they pay for them?'

'They're rich, right? Bring the money with them.'

'Only fifty grand a year. That's all they can take out of China. Doesn't buy much of a house and doesn't get you a mortgage either. Mom and Pop want a house, they need to get their hands on local currency.'

This is all new to O'Malley. He focuses on the pictures Jimmy's drawing.

'So you've got middlemen. Remitters is what they're called. They're everywhere: all those offices downtown, full of them. Mom and Pop go to them. They get their money in cash, pay a commission for it. Don't think anything of it.'

He draws a couple of stick people, puts a $ sign above their heads.

'On the other side, your dealer provides the cash, through the middleman.'

Now there's a stickman with a gun, handing a bag of money to a stick middleman, who's handing it to Mom and Pop.

'The middleman gives Mom and Pop a bank account number in China, gets them to pay for the cash over there. The money never leaves China. The bank account belongs to the manufacturers … here.'

He's back to the cross in China, drawing a bank account alongside it. Draws an account for Mom and Pop, too, alongside it, an arrow running from that back to the cross.

'The drugs get paid for, Mom and Pop get cash. Then they can do what they want with it — buy and run a business, or get it into the system, buy that house. No one asks questions, because like you said, they're rich, they've brought the money with them.

'Now the dealer needs to get their own money clean. Bank staff aren't colour-blind. An Asian walks in with a big cash deposit, they don't look twice. They've got a cash culture, right? A brown man walks in with twenty grand in cash, alarms go off. So they need help smurfing that money. Need a crew of depositors who don't look like them. Or they need a bunch of people to sit in the casino, feed the machines, twenty bucks at a time. Take the hit on the rake, but once the cash has been through the machine, it comes out as winnings, and the casino will deposit that money for you.'

'And Browning? Where's he fit?'

'All of it. A one-stop shop. He's got partners. He reckons they've got the whole thing sewn up. Need your cash cleaned? Done. Need a payment sorted offshore? Done. Maybe you want to set up a business, use the cash to buy local product, export it to Oz? Sell the product and pay your brothers over there? Done. They're running mules, too. Browning says they've got teams all over the place; immigrants from all over. Come from anywhere they might be oppressed back home — Browning's crew help get them a visa, which doesn't come for free. They work it off in front of a slot machine or going to the bank every day. Some of them know it's not on the level, some don't. Either way, it's the price they pay.'

O'Malley thinks he's keeping up, but he has to run through the diagram a couple of times to be sure.

'Browning's got the bank accounts sorted, too. They'll find an international student who's heading home, or a tourist looking for some cash. They'll buy their bank account or pay them to set up a new one. Take their logins, cards off them, and send them on their way. It's smart, I'll say that for them. Clip the ticket on everything, but always at arm's length. They don't care what the money's for, or where it's coming from, but they'll keep it moving.'

O'Malley thought there were things in place to stop all this. Asks Jimmy about it.

'What about all the rules they've got set up? Don't the banks and the casino have to report all big cash transactions?'

'They've got to tick a box, is all. If there was only one or two people doing it, the cops would see it. But it's like catching fish with a rod. You'll get a couple but miss a hundred. The banks don't like saying no, so they fill the forms in, but take the cash. The casino cares even less. What are they going to do, watch every machine, trace every note? They make all their money from high-rollers, transfer their money in from overseas, no questions asked. It's how they make money. They're not making it by dealing cards to poker players like you, O'Malley.'

O'Malley doesn't know how Jimmy knows that about him, but lets it pass. Tonight, Jimmy is his guardian angel. He thinks about what Jimmy has told him, looks at the mess of boxes and arrows that sits on the table between them. Thinks how his two cases just became one.

'So, these partners of Browning's. You know who they are?' he asks Tua.

'Not until tonight. But sounds like you do. There's a lot to protect. Explains why you're so popular. Those lawyers you mentioned? Property, immigration, establishing companies? Put that together with Browning, sounds about right.'

Doesn't really explain why Big Tone's involved, though, O'Malley thinks. Or Robertson, the minister. The money mules need visas, sure, but they don't need a minister on the take to make that happen. Just a good lawyer who knows the loopholes, and they've got Howarth for that.

He's still missing something, and he's going to keep digging until he finds it.

Assuming Jimmy lets him.

# CHAPTER TWENTY-SIX

'So all that said, O'Malley, you're still in the shit,' Jimmy says, with a deep chuckle.

Jimmy is a man who has excelled in a brutal world, done enough to not only survive, but thrive. To do so has required a set of rules to live by, which he sticks to even now.

Never confuse fear with loyalty, keep information tight, and don't get involved in other people's business or respond to sob stories — everybody has one.

He has already broken the second rule, indulging O'Malley with a lesson in organised money-laundering, and now he's contemplating breaking the third, offering help to a man in need when he should be sending him on his way. But he's always had a soft spot for O'Malley. In part, because when he first met him, back when O'Malley was just a kid, he saw in the boy an instinctive understanding of rule number one.

O'Malley came into jail alone, a young, frightened kid. He was prime fodder for the bullies, who looked to raise their own status by preying on those weaker than themselves, and for the gangs, whose recruitment strategy was simply to appeal to man's survival instinct. There's safety in numbers, and if you haven't drifted towards gang life before you get to jail, there's a strong chance you'll leave converted.

O'Malley was immoveable.

He politely declined casual suggestions that he join Jimmy's boys, and when the predators determined he was unprotected and made a move to hurt him for status points, O'Malley was decisive in his response. A young Māori fella was the first to test him, and he was in and out of O'Malley's cell in less than a minute. He walked in, crawled out, and had a broken arm as a souvenir. O'Malley handled himself well, and over time built respect and even friendship across partisan lines. He became the one who got away, in Jimmy's eyes, the sort of man who would be an asset to have on his side, not a liability. But he didn't force the issue.

The main reason Jimmy considers helping O'Malley now, though, is because he owes him.

They were both in medium-security; O'Malley on account of his age, Jimmy there because, despite managerial misgivings, he was on the final leg of a stretch, and it made room for more pressing cases in max. The security designation reflected the constraints and attitudes of the institution rather than the inmates, though, and the occupants were still a threat to one another. There'd been tensions between Jimmy's crew and the Nomads, a gang with its roots in Wellington, but well represented in Pare. There had been a couple of casualties on both sides when someone decided to go for gold, take Jimmy out. Word spread pretty quick when something was going down, and those with common sense and no skin in the game made themselves scarce. O'Malley looked like he hadn't got the memo.

He was sitting in the yard, back against a concrete wall, nose in a book, which is how Jimmy always remembers him. Studying, trying to improve himself. Jimmy was on notice, and walked with a shadow, one of his more fearsome and trusted lieutenants, doing a couple of laps of the yard, talking shop. Jimmy let his guard down, he knows; should have been on high alert, but he got sloppy.

As he turned a corner, he didn't see the two Nomads behind him, with the shivs they'd fashioned from plastic pens and wire, melted together to form a deadly weapon. O'Malley saw them, though Jimmy is still convinced he didn't once look up from his book. But like a scene from a macabre pantomime, Jimmy hears

O'Malley shout 'Behind you!', soon enough for Jimmy to move fast, the shiv intended for his neck connecting with his shoulder instead. His walking buddy gets it in the head, the hard part of his skull neutralising the threat of his attacker's homemade knife. O'Malley's warning turned an ambush into a fair fight. Jimmy didn't lose those. If he hadn't turned around, though, he wouldn't be reflecting on it now.

O'Malley was a marked man with the Nomads then. Jimmy had a spell in isolation and a loss of privileges to contend with, but he got the word out, and wherever O'Malley went, Jimmy's guys went, too. There would be no reprisals on the Good Samaritan as far as Jimmy was concerned. Over time the threat faded as other issues took precedence, and Jimmy's attackers got transferred out, back to max. Beefs tended to stay personal, regardless of party politics. It came down to pride and respect, and shame. With the individuals removed, the groups let things lie.

So O'Malley needs help, Jimmy thinks. There might be an upside, too. Anything that interrupts business for the Aussie gangs is a win. O'Malley might just bring them all down before he gets killed, and there's benefit in that. What was it O'Malley told him back in the day, sharing what he'd learned from one of his books? There's no such thing as altruism.

'You're in the shit, and you need help. What can I do, O'Malley?'

'Appreciate it, Jimmy. I've got to assume they're going to come for me again. I need eyes in the back of my head.'

Jimmy thinks for a second. Works out what he can spare.

'I'll have Manny and Chatbox watch over you for a couple of days. Don't worry, they'll lose the jackets, won't ruin your street cred. You won't see them unless you need to.'

'Thanks, Jimmy.' Then a beat later: 'What time is it, by the way?'

'Coming up on one,' Jimmy responds.

'Mind if I use my phone, let my lady know I'm good, not to send out the cavalry?'

'Best you do. I don't like unexpected guests. Wait here; grab another drink if you want one, I'll be back in a few.'

Jimmy heads out of the office, goes looking for Manu and Chatbox. He needs to give them instructions, be clear on what he expects. They won't let him down. But Jimmy doesn't mistake that for loyalty.

O'Malley texts Claire. Keeps it brief. *I'm good but will be late. See you at yours*. Follows it up with his usual sign-off, so she knows it's him, not somebody who's got his phone.

Jimmy comes back in, Manu follows.

'The boys will take you back. If you need anything, just tell Manny.'

Manu smiles and raises his chin. Whatever you need, bro.

They head back to the Hilux, the gathering downstairs thinner now than when they arrived. They get back in the ute, taking the same seats as before, but Chatbox isn't training a gun on the passenger seat, which is progress as far as O'Malley's concerned.

'Where to, bro?' Manu asks.

'Back to the city. But not to mine. Head for the Nelson Street off-ramp.'

Manu nods. Chatbox is in the back, mouthing along to a track O'Malley's never heard before. Manu obviously covets his mate's nickname, because he's keen to talk.

'So you know the boss from back in the day?'

'I do,' O'Malley confirms.

'Must have been interesting times, eh?'

'They were.'

'Got any stories, bro?'

'I don't.'

Rule number two. Don't over-share. Manu gets it, knows he's on dangerous ground.

'Didn't mean any offence, you know?'

'None taken, Manu.'

'Thanks,' Manu replies, relieved.

O'Malley's phone rings. He looks to Manu, checking he's got permission to answer. The power's shifted since their first ride together, but he's making no assumptions. Manu tilts his head, giving him the nod. The number is withheld, so O'Malley wonders what's in store.

'O'Malley.'

'Yo, O'Malley. I've got what you asked for.' It's Milo.

O'Malley's hopeful, he's got a lot riding on getting something solid to back up his guesswork.

'What have you found?'

'Long version or short version?'

O'Malley glances at his companions. Chatbox has his mouth closed. Probably a natural listener.

'Make it the short version,' he decides.

'OK. Your boys have been busy. What you've got is a whole bunch of companies that are just paper and a bank account. A lot here. Some in the islands, too. Rarotonga, Fiji. I've drawn you a map — how they connect. I had to work a bit to get into the lawyers' records, but I rang them up. Their receptionist was really helpful.'

O'Malley's amused by that. Either there has been a change in personnel at Lomas and Howarth, or Milo's got better phone skills than O'Malley had face-to-face. But then, Milo was probably calling from the Department of Defence, or the Pentagon, or wherever would catch her off-guard and make her give him what he needed.

'So, after more hard work, and not a little skill, I got a good picture. There's money moving all over the place, here and abroad. Some legit businesses in there, too: food export, that sort of thing. I spent a bit more time on Lucky Country Construction — you were right to pick that one out. There's a ton of money going into that business. Hard to explain away all the funds that are flowing through it. That's where they're turning their own money legit.'

Enough to make Buxton take notice, pass it on to his mates in The Money Laundering Team. O'Malley's still got to link Tone to William, otherwise it's irrelevant. And Buxton's got to link William to Danny's murder. O'Malley's got faith, though. His case is shaping up.

'What about the other guy?' O'Malley's keen not to say the minister's name in company.

'The minister? Harder. I need more time, and his computer if you can get it.' Sure. That's likely.

'So nothing?'

'I didn't say nothing, did I? It's just not wrapped up in a bow. What I have got? Three payments, over eighteen months, exactly two million each time. They come into Morbius, then go out again within the hour. One and a half mill each time ends up with Lucky Country. The rest looks like it's going to a crypto wallet. My guess, your minister has the keys to that. But like I say, give me five minutes with his laptop, I'll tell you for sure.'

'That's good work.'

'I know that. I had to, you know, bend some rules to get it. But that won't show up. I've drawn you a few pictures, made it idiot-proof.'

'Thanks. I won't take that personally.'

'Don't. I meant anyone except me. I've got it all on a pen drive. Untraceable.'

'When can I get it?'

'Now. Where are you?' O'Malley works out they're about five minutes from downtown, gives him a location.

'Look for a white Hilux. But don't sneak up on us. Let me see you coming, otherwise it could end badly.' Thinking his companions would welcome a chance for some action.

Milo changes his voice, goes Cockney. 'All right, guv'nor. I'll be on me moped, no shooters with me, innit?' He enjoys this shit too much. O'Malley gets off the phone, turns to Manu. Who's ahead of the game.

'Corner of Fort Lane and Fort Street. Got it.'

The handover goes smoothly. Nobody gets hurt. The pen drive is in a paper bag: no prints, O'Malley thinks. He puts the bag in his jeans pocket, gives Manu another address. It's not quite two o'clock, but it feels like a lifetime since O'Malley left Claire at The Brandling. He's feeling like his luck is taking a turn for the better and is looking forward to updating his partner.

'Over here on the left. I'm going in that building there,' he says, pointing to Claire's apartment block. No point in giving the protection detail the slip. 'Meet you back at mine in the morning?'

'We'll be there. Want us to come in, get you to the door?' The offer is sincere, and O'Malley's strangely touched by Manu's concern.

'Nah, man, it's all good.'

'Whatever you say, boss. Tomorrow.'

Chatbox keeps his own counsel.

O'Malley rings the bell and Claire buzzes him in. He's hoping for a hug.

'What the fuck has happened to you?' is what he gets.

He's about to ask why, but he looks himself up and down, and sees what Claire sees. He looks like he's had a long night in an abattoir. His blood, William's blood, Blue Shirt's blood spatter his shirt and jeans. Some has soaked through the arm of his jacket, too. Claire's question seems reasonable. He starts to run her through his evening, stripping while he does so. Getting his arm out of the jacket makes him a little faint, but he's happy he's in better shape than the men he left behind in his car park.

Claire helps him out of his clothes without comment. She's looking at the mess in front of her, wondering whether it's too late to find herself a man with a boring day job, someone who waits up for *her* to come home, gets anxious when *she's* running late. Then she looks at O'Malley in his boxer shorts, and figures there's trade-offs in every relationship. She just hopes the current downsides are temporary, don't lead to permanent.

'Keep talking. I'm going to run you a bath,' she says, as she walks away from O'Malley, down the hall to the bathroom. He's just finished describing events in his car park, and she's hoping he's embellishing for effect. Then he's talking about guns, and she has to turn around, look at him to check he's not joking. She gets him in the tub, makes sure to give him a thorough examination, makes sure there's no other damage in places that might be important. Satisfied, she pulls the toilet lid down and sits on it to hear O'Malley finish his story.

'So we've got something we can use? On the pen drive?'

'I hope so, babe. I can't take much more of this.' He looks exhausted, but a damn sight better than he did when he walked through Claire's door.

'Do you want to look at it now? I can grab my laptop.'

'No. I want to forget about it all until tomorrow.' Claire watches O'Malley stand up to get out of the bath, hands him a towel, still appreciates what she sees, even if it's looking a little damaged right now.

'OK, soldier. Food or bed?'

'Food then bed, if you've got something quick.'

'We can bring breakfast forward,' she says, thinking of the bacon and eggs she had planned for tomorrow.

'Anything, babe.'

They walk back through. Claire heads straight for the fridge, pulls out what she needs. O'Malley's on the sofa. He's asleep before Claire cracks the first egg. She gives up on what she's doing and goes to fetch a blanket instead. She lays it gently over O'Malley and pulls a couple of cushions onto the floor beneath him. She's going to watch over him tonight, and he's not awake to put up a fight.

# CHAPTER TWENTY-SEVEN

O'Malley is up and about.

His body is sore, but he's not feeling it, because he feels he's close to the end now. He wants to get back to his place, check out what Milo has uncovered, give Buxton a call to finish what he's started.

Before someone has another crack at him.

Claire has set him a deadline. Figures he'll be safe while the sun's up, but is not taking any chances either.

One pm. Whatever he's got by one o'clock he takes to Buxton. Or she does.

O'Malley's spooked enough to agree without a fight.

They kiss, long and hard. In that kiss lies a bunch of feelings that could keep them talking for days. They're on a deadline, and the kiss tells them both more than words would ever convey.

'Let's do this,' O'Malley says.

'Go. Finish the puzzle. One o'clock, O'Malley. Then we lie low, get out of the way of this.'

O'Malley nods, likes the idea of finding a hotel room, hunkering down, letting time pass, giving Claire his undivided attention.

He's in his apartment now.

He's looking fairly respectable for a man who's eleven rounds through a championship fight. He's in the spare clothes he had stored at Claire's place, the bloody ones now doing somersaults in her laundry room. The pen drive is burning a hole in his pocket. It's either his salvation, or false hope. He's holding out for a few minutes, making coffee, tidying up, making this moment last. Like waiting to check a lottery ticket, or open exam results.

His phone disturbs the moment. It's charging, so he pulls the cord, answers. The number's withheld. Maybe Milo with a customer satisfaction survey.

'O'Malley.'

'You really should have left things alone.' The voice is familiar. Big Tone.

'Fuck off.' Since they're showing their hands.

'You didn't need to get involved, stick your nose in my business, O'Malley.'

'You didn't need to kill Danny.'

'I didn't. But you started digging anyway. Regardless, it's too late now.'

O'Malley doesn't respond. Figures Tone has something he wants to say, let him get on with it.

'What are you going to do with your last few minutes of freedom, O'Malley? Do you have a routine, some sort of ritual before you go inside?'

O'Malley's heart drops then, all the way to his shoes. He's being set up for something. He keeps the phone to his ear, but races from room to room, looking for whatever it is that Tone has put there to fit him up. Tone's enjoying the sounds of panic coming down the line.

'Violent men never really change, do they? All those courses they put you through before they let you back out in the world, they don't work. You've still got that sense of entitlement, haven't you? See the world as unfair, you can't help yourself. Then you look for someone else to blame. Classic cycle of behaviour. But facts are facts. It was only a matter of time before you went too far.'

O'Malley's looking for something else now. A weapon?

'See you later, O'Malley.' Then the connection is dead.

O'Malley forces himself to stop and think.

Downstairs. He runs out of his apartment, taking the stairs

three at a time. Gets to the car park to see it as he left it last night, minus the unconscious men. The concrete has some telltale signs of the struggle that took place, but otherwise it's empty.

His truck. There's something in the truck.

He unlocks it, checks the driver's side. Looks under the seats, in the console, finds nothing. Repeats the exercise from the other side. Nada. Goes to the back seats and draws a blank there, too. O'Malley works his way to the back of the truck and opens up the tray.

Finds William.

Wearing the clothes he had on when O'Malley saw him last, his DNA all over them.

Something's different from the last time they were together, though. William has two bullet holes in his once-white shirt. He's very much dead.

So am I, O'Malley thinks. No amount of talking is going to get me out of this. He has another look around, searching for the gun. He's not concerned about disturbing the body — there will be traces of O'Malley all over William's clothes. He pulls aside William's suit jacket, but there's nothing there. But there's a rag in the corner up past William's head. O'Malley knows it wasn't there before, and he guesses Tone has left the weapon to make the cops' lives easier.

The rag is from O'Malley's storage cupboard, which is ajar behind him. He's wondering what to do, whether he's got time to get his truck out of there, distance the body from his apartment building. Where's Manu when you need him?

It's too late, though, because he hears the car coming down the ramp, no siren, but red and blue flashes beginning to illuminate the walls around him. He's got time for one more check of William's jacket before he hears the cops issuing instructions.

'Step back from the vehicle. Now. Show us your hands.'

The cops have got guns out, which still isn't standard in this part of the world. They're well-informed, know what they're going to find.

O'Malley's thinking about Claire, and the hotel room that they're not going to share, and the times she's told him to leave this alone.

Manu and Chatbox are parked up on the street outside O'Malley's apartment building when they see the first cop car screaming towards them, lights flashing, no siren. Chatbox is up front now, and he's first to react. He taps Manu firmly on the arm, whispers 'Bro', and they silently decide whether to make a run for it or not. Someone's called the cops on them, two characters out of place in this part of town. Probably up to mischief. It's instinctive to assume they're the target for the police attention. Then the cop car turns down the ramp into O'Malley's basement, where they got to watch O'Malley handle the fellas with the knives a few hours earlier.

Soon enough, the first car is joined by another, and then a third. Chatbox is getting it all on his phone. He's had it running since he saw the first car approaching, because he knows they've done nothing wrong, today, and police harassment videos are popular on YouTube. They stick around, because if it's O'Malley the cops have come for, he might find a way out of the building, and he's going to need a ride. Manu calls Jimmy, who says to stick around, but fall back a little. It's a good thing they do, because where they were parked is soon taken up with more official vehicles. An ambulance comes and goes, and that's soon replaced by more fellas in suits, who are getting into white onesies.

Manu's nervous now. He's seen this scene unfold before, and when the onesies come out, it's because there's a crime scene. Where there's a crime scene, there's usually a body. If somebody got to O'Malley on their watch, Manu and Chatbox are in the shit. Big time. Jimmy was clear on that. Chatbox reads Manu's mind, which always unnerves Manu, but he's got different thoughts.

'Nah, man, we're sweet. Let's go see the boss.'

Manu knows he's not going to get any more out of him, so puts his faith in his partner, and turns the engine. He fucking hopes Chatbox knows what he's doing.

The next hour is all too familiar for O'Malley. He's cuffed, cautioned, transported, booked, swabbed and dumped in a cell. He realises how considerate the cops were back when he was a kid. This time around there's no finesse: the cops manhandle him, the cuffs are too tight, the cell door is slammed a little too fast. He's left to his own thoughts, while the cops work out the quickest way to get to a formal charge.

O'Malley can play the waiting game. He knows to get some rest where he can, not tire himself out when he can't control his situation. He lies down, closes his eyes. And sleeps. The cops don't leave him long. They pull him out and escort him to an interview room, introduce themselves.

Buxton is in the room, but he's not the lead. He's probably declared his knowledge of the suspect, and there's no room for sympathies to play out in this scenario. It's a doozy. O'Malley knows they're not going to be here for long. He's going to ask for a lawyer before he says anything. But he doesn't lead with that. He wants to buy himself some time, find out how they're reading the situation. They caution him again, get him to confirm out loud that he understands. Buxton's got a look of disgust on his face. Another disappointment in front of him. They introduce themselves for the tape.

The other guy is DI Roberts. He's got the look of a man who knows a slam dunk when he sees it. A little too gleeful. He's keen to show he's got it all worked out.

'You're in a spot of bother, son' is how he starts.

O'Malley dislikes him immediately. Roberts probably spends his evenings watching cop shows back-to-back, writing down lines he likes. Probably tries them out in the mirror. He's going to love O'Malley's version of events. He shares his first.

'William Zhang, found dead in the back of a Ford Ranger,

registered to you. You're present at the scene. Cause of death, to be confirmed, but the two bullets in his chest are a clue. Also found in the Ford Ranger — your Ranger — is a Kimber Desert Warrior handgun, which I'm sure we'll find is missing two rounds that we'll find in Mr Zhang. We'll wait for forensics, but early indications are that there are multiple blood samples at the scene, both on the victim's clothing and on the floor around the vehicle.

'Preliminary investigations have identified that you made a phone call to, and subsequently met with, Senior Sergeant Buxton, present, where you indicated that you were looking for Mr Zhang. You indicated that you suspected Mr Zhang of involvement in the death of a friend of yours, a Danny Cain.

'So, we can place you at the murder scene, connect you to the victim, and we've got a clear motive. And we haven't even got the forensics back. You know how this goes, O'Malley. Your record speaks to that. We'll welcome your co-operation, and we can all save ourselves a lot of time if you just tell us how it went down. Maybe there's extenuating circumstances you'd like to get on the record? That's reasons you might have—'

O'Malley interrupts. 'I know what extenuating means, Inspector. But I'll have a lawyer, please.'

Detective Inspector Roberts is irritated by this. Waste of fucking time, is what he's thinking.

'All in good time, O'Malley. Let's just have a chat first, you can tell us how we've got it all wrong.'

O'Malley looks up at the camera in the corner of the room and repeats himself.

'I'll have a lawyer, please.'

Roberts can't ignore it a second time. Goes through the formalities of concluding the conversation for the benefit of the tape. Turns it off.

'Suit yourself, O'Malley. You're fucked, and a brief will tell you the same. Plead out, and we'll make it clear in the file that you were co-operative.' Roberts leaves the room, leaving the door open for Buxton. Who turns towards O'Malley and shakes his head.

'Law unto yourself, O'Malley. You should have left it to me.' He walks out, still shaking his head.

Claire is showered, moisturised and fed. She calls in to uni, says she is unwell, will re-schedule the tutorial that she has later in the day. She wants to be with O'Malley today, and definitely isn't going to let him miss the deadline she's established. She doesn't want to crowd him, either. He's got the pen drive to work through, and he'll be quicker if he's not worrying about her. So she gives herself an hour before she plans to head over to his place. She's got something to do, anyway. Something is nagging at her, a distant bell ringing as O'Malley ran through the summary that Milo had given him. There's still a missing piece of the puzzle: how Robertson fits into the equation.

If Robertson is the reason all this started, there's got to be something that connects him, makes sense of everything. Something in her mind is saying she knows the answer, but it's not making itself known. Like when she's doing a crossword, and she knows the answer's an anagram, but she can't put the letters together. She gets her computer out, fires it up, starts learning more about the minister. He's had a long career, meaning there's plenty of news reports to go through, so she starts taking notes, sifting through the detail looking for whatever it is that's nagging at her subconscious.

She gets excited when she hits an article from three years back. She doesn't bother writing anything else down, just grabs her bag and heads out of the door. Claire wants to see O'Malley, tell him what she's found. So she's speed-walking as she turns the corner to O'Malley's street, and then she sees the commotion. And then she's running.

O'Malley's expecting a duty solicitor. Another over-worked, under-resourced lawyer who will be flustered when she arrives, and only half-attentive once she's here. Another way the system stacks against the accused. They're always too busy and, the way crime is, demand always trumps supply, so he's not surprised that he's left in his cell for an eternity. This time he doesn't sleep. He's trying to think of a way out.

Of course, he didn't actually kill William.

There's that.

But Roberts is right: there's a stack of evidence that adds up to the contrary. Again, the simplest answer is probably the right answer. What O'Malley's got to counter that simplicity amounts to a conspiracy theory. And what he's got to hand is just that — a theory. No proof. What he needs is a brief who can stop Roberts bulldozing him, slow him down, maybe let enough time pass for Buxton to let his anger subside so he can start listening to O'Malley. But for that to happen, he needs a brief who will listen to him first. Not a duty solicitor who will lay out the evidence against him and tell him to take a plea.

# CHAPTER TWENTY-EIGHT

Claire is fighting the urge to vomit.

O'Malley's apartment block is a swarm of police, forensics and passers-by who have stopped to watch. It's eleven-thirty, only ninety minutes to go to their deadline, and she's thinking she should have insisted they go straight to the police when they woke. Because now it's too late, somebody has got to O'Malley, and she can't imagine a world without him in it.

She pushes past a couple of cyclists who've stopped to take a look. She's never been a fan of men in Lycra, less so now as they seem to think that because they were here first, she can stand behind them. She makes it clear she's not to be fucked with, and gets through, only to be stopped again, this time by a uniform. The plod is giving nothing away, just says there's been an incident. Claire feels the panic taking over, her legs unreliable, that prickly hot sensation rising up her back and neck. Again, she thinks she might vomit, which would serve the cyclists right, because if she does there's no room to move and it's either them or the unhelpful policeman. Maybe both.

O'Malley has always told her you've got to give a little to get a little. The secret to getting people to talk. She sees what she guesses is a detective, from the way she carries herself and the trouser suit that's matched with shoes chosen for practicality rather than fashion. She pushes past the uniform, and grabs the arm of the detective, who's not impressed, but isn't an arsehole either. It gives Claire enough time to give a little.

'Hi, sorry, I live here with my boyfriend. What's going on, can I get to my apartment?'

'Not for a while, I'm afraid.'

'What's happened?'

'We've got a murder scene.'

Claire's eyes glaze over, and she feels herself hyperventilate. Now she's holding on to the policewoman just so she can stay standing. She manages to speak. Just.

'My … my boyfriend. I don't know where he is.'

'What's your boyfriend's name?'

Then, when Claire tells her: 'You'd better come with me.'

When O'Malley's cell door finally opens, the solicitor isn't what he's been expecting.

O'Malley looks up to see a striking woman, who looks early forties but could well be a decade older, dressed from head-to-toe from the boutique, not the high street. Her briefcase is leather, but looks soft enough to pet, and she's got piercing brown eyes that look down at O'Malley over a beak-like nose that gives her a natural air of authority. She scares him a little, which he reminds himself is good. She'll have Roberts shitting himself.

The lawyer introduces herself to O'Malley. Gabrielle Patterson, from Patterson, King & Black. So he's got a partner on his side. Literally, a partner in a private law firm.

Someone's looking out for me, O'Malley thinks.

He remembers the sting of jealousy he'd felt when Scott Cranshaw talked about having a good lawyer. Feels upbeat that he's joined that exclusive club. Feels elated when Ms Patterson turns to the policeman who has escorted her to the cell and reprimands him. Twice. Once for still being there, and then again because she doesn't expect to have to take a brief from her client in a goddamn cell. The cop scurries off to find them a more suitable room, and she turns to O'Malley with what passes for a smile. They've got a lot to cover, in a short space of time.

When they get moved to an interview room, Gabrielle makes it clear what will happen if the camera gets turned on by mistake. She gets the response she's looking for and gets down to business. O'Malley tells it all, doesn't leave anything out, trusts his counsel to work out the best way to play it. What he needs, most of all, is time. He needs to delay Roberts cutting to the chase, charging him with William's murder.

Claire recovered somewhat once she learned that O'Malley was the suspect, not the victim. It was something. She gave the policewoman a brief statement: when she last saw O'Malley, where, how he'd been acting. She played it straight, told the cop what she knew, but left Jimmy Tua out of it. If they had his phone, the cops would find that out eventually, but Claire wasn't going to be the one to tell them. If O'Malley was looking for a gun, it would be someone exactly like Jimmy Tua he would turn to. So she left it out.

Once she is finished with the policewoman, and discovers where O'Malley is being held, she tries to figure out what to do next. Standing outside O'Malley's apartment, beyond the crowd of onlookers, she is feeling helpless. Or maybe it's powerless. She needs to help O'Malley, although isn't sure she knows how. But what he probably needs most is a good lawyer. So she tries to work out how to find one. Calls someone she knows at the university, who puts her in touch with a law professor who's got a leaning that's staunchly anti-establishment. He puts her in touch with Gabrielle Patterson, who talks to Claire for four minutes before she says she'll help. This time Claire front-loads the conversation, and mention of ministerial shenanigans gets the desired effect. Patterson's desire to get a high-profile scalp turns a humdrum murder defence into a front-page opportunity, and she's not going to pass on that.

Senior Sergeant Keith Buxton is pissed off. O'Malley was one of the good ones. The one he always thought of when his colleagues suggested he was soft, that people don't change their spots, and he'd just end up disappointed when they let him down. O'Malley had turned his life around, come out of jail better than he'd gone in, and Buxton had him pegged as a rare success story. Now he's sitting opposite him wondering how he got it all so wrong.

Roberts is taking the lead, though in truth he's just repeating what he said earlier, this time for the lawyer's benefit. He's taking it more cautiously, though, because Ms Patterson comes with a reputation. Buxton wonders how O'Malley's got himself lawyered up so well. Guesses he saw this coming, wanted to give himself a chance to wriggle out of the hole he's dug for himself. Buxton's waiting to hear O'Malley's side of the story. He's going to puke in his mouth if he tries to argue self-defence.

O'Malley doesn't argue self-defence.

He says he didn't do it.

Spins a yarn that's long and complicated. Every time Roberts tries to bring it back to the car park, to the body in the truck, Ms Patterson stops him in his tracks, insists that her client tell it his way.

It's far-fetched, and Buxton wonders how O'Malley's got the stones to make up all this shit when they've got him bang to rights. He's taking his sweet time about it, too, either because he's trying to keep track of his own lies, or he's unaware of Ms Patterson's hourly rate. The best part of the afternoon goes by with O'Malley's time-wasting, his stories of shell companies and money-laundering, bent lawyers and accountants, none of which explains how William Zhang ended up dead in the back of O'Malley's truck.

What's nagging at Buxton, though, is that there are bits of O'Malley's story that ring true.

He'd followed up the lead when O'Malley gave him William's photograph. Got a match in the database. A name — and a flag. William Zhang was suspected of being a herder. A team leader, sending individuals out to deposit cash in third-party bank accounts. When a diligent bank teller got suspicious about a young man from Iran who was making his third deposit in as many days, they'd called the cops, and the Iranian student spilled his guts, pointed to William as the man giving him instructions. They had Zhang on a charge of laundering, but then they lost their star witness. Before Zhang's trial, Immigration got involved, found discrepancies in the mule's visa, and sent him home. They didn't think to consult with the police before they sent him packing, and Zhang's trial collapsed.

So, as O'Malley's telling his story, Buxton knows there's at least something in it. But then all good lies are based on truth, and O'Malley's smart enough to know that.

Maybe this doesn't even have anything to do with a poker game. Maybe O'Malley had a problem with Zhang that goes deeper than that. Visits Buxton to set up the bigger lie that he's telling now. Which makes it premeditated. And makes Buxton a participant in O'Malley's story. He feels his blood pressure rise and looks at O'Malley with fresh, angry eyes.

'You got any proof, O'Malley, or are you just going to sit here all day, spouting bullshit?'

Buxton's had enough. It's the first thing he's said since they all sat down, and even the lawyer looks surprised by the outburst.

'I'd remind you that the burden of proof lies with you, detective, not my client. He's simply telling you the truth. If you choose to ignore what Mr O'Malley is telling you, if you're blinkered and ignore other possible suspects, then we'll make that clear in court.'

So that's their game, Buxton thinks. Send us on a wild goose chase, wrap ourselves up in knots chasing rainbows. He's ready to call their bluff. He's turning to Roberts, ready to pull the pin, charge O'Malley. Roberts won't need persuading. He's already dreaming of propping up the bar, raising a pint to another case put to bed. Forensics will come through, back them up, and Buxton's ready to give them a chase-up as soon as he's out of here.

O'Malley speaks up then, responding to Buxton's question.

'Proof? No, I don't. But William might. When he was attacking me with a knife, he said he had insurance. Something about not going down on his own. Have you got anyone checking him out?'

It's a semi-bluff. William said nothing of the sort. But O'Malley knows there is proof that supports his story. It's sitting on a pen drive, which he slipped into William's jacket pocket as the police closed in. The paper bag that held the drive was sitting somewhere in the station, alongside O'Malley's keys, phone and wallet.

He'd hoped to delay his interrogation long enough for William's possessions to make it back to Roberts and Buxton from wherever his body was taken, but he can sense that he's running out of time. He needs to lead them by the nose. He isn't sure his hint has landed, but he can't be any more obvious. *Look at the fucking USB stick that's in William's pocket* would beg the question: how does O'Malley know it's there in the first place?

Ms Patterson knows where O'Malley is leading. Thinks it's a good time to take a break, allow her client to use the bathroom. Roberts knows better than to deny the request. Doesn't want to be accused of brow-beating the suspect. He could do with a leak himself. With any luck, they'll have preliminaries back, maybe have prints from the gun, wrap this up before the pubs get too quiet. He likes a crowd when he's celebrating.

When they get out of the interview room, Buxton heads back to his desk. He needs a cup of tea, and the stuff that's provided in the kitchen is offensive. He wants a decent Earl Grey, and he's got a stash of teabags in his drawer. He checks in with the team, asks if there's anything back from forensics. Cause of death, as expected, GSW. They're out of luck on the weapon. It's been wiped, and there's no sign of prints to connect O'Malley. His swabs are negative, too, so there's no telltale residue to show he's fired a gun recently.

Zhang's possessions are in an evidence bag, sitting on his desk.

There are only two items in there. A mobile phone and a USB stick. They've both been dusted, and the prints from the phone match Zhang. The stick didn't turn up any prints.

Roberts wanders back from the bathroom, adjusting himself demonstrably as he does so.

'What have we got?'

'Nada on the gun. Ditto on O'Malley's swabs.'

'Doesn't matter. We've got circumstantials from arse to elbow. We've got more than we need.'

'We've also got a witness who puts O'Malley elsewhere at the current time of death,' says a woman who has joined the conversation, somewhat unhelpfully in Buxton's opinion.

'Well, we've got both their phones. Get someone onto that, look at the location data, see when they're together. Pretty straightforward to disprove your witness's account.'

Roberts isn't letting a small detail derail the freight train he's got planned for O'Malley. He plays up to the reputation he knows he has earned as a no-nonsense, black-and-white copper, but the truth is Roberts is terrified of guns. Thinks anyone who uses a gun deserves the book thrown at them. He's seen the normalisation of his fellow officers being armed and thinks it can only result in an escalation on both sides: criminals arming themselves to protect against armed police, and vice versa. He doesn't want to be a policeman in a military state.

People like O'Malley, who can casually put a bullet in their fellow man, need to be put away without mercy. He'll charge the witness, too, if they've provided a false alibi.

Buxton has always been less decisive. The mention of a witness putting O'Malley elsewhere throws him. He's ready to drop O'Malley down a well, but he's also a stickler for the truth.

Facts are facts.

The gun has been wiped clean. O'Malley tested negative for residue.

There's a witness who says he was with her at the time of the shooting. That will be the girlfriend, no doubt, but he's met her and doesn't take her for a liar.

And O'Malley's got a story that's complicated but remained consistent whichever way they got him to tell it. Facts …

He picks up William's mobile, tries to access it, but gets asked for a passcode. That's going to take the techs days to get into, if they ever do. The tech companies are stubbornly unhelpful in that regard. So Buxton picks up the USB stick instead, and heads over to a laptop that's isolated from the police network. This is now standard procedure. The last poor schmuck who stuck an unknown stick into his computer brought the whole of Central Division into meltdown. The joker who had the stick in his pocket when he got nicked was a computer whizz, and the malware he carried with him found its way across the network, infecting half the station's machines with pig-related porn. So now there's a dedicated machine for USBs and whatever farmyard pornography they might hold.

He opens up the single folder that sits on the USB stick. What he sees is a beautifully structured set of sub-folders, alongside a single pdf, which he opens. It's a map, or a schematic, the sort an engineer would take pride in. Buxton has a quick look at it, and even a technologically challenged idiot like him can see what the files contain. He calls Roberts over. Knows he's going to be unhappy.

'Look at this. It was in Zhang's pocket.' Roberts takes a look, and he's soon got the look of a man chewing a turd. What he thinks he's looking at is a blueprint for organised crime. It doesn't prove a thing, but it does support the fairy-tale that he's been listening to all day. If it's real.

'Ah, fuck. Can a man not just have a pint?' is what he says. He takes another look, runs through the names that are identified in various boxes on the screen. He points to one, in particular.

'What the fuck is that? Are you serious, Buxton? We're going to walk into that shit-pond?'

Buxton takes a look, sees what Roberts sees.

'Erm, not us. I think we need someone from MLT to take a look, don't you?' MLT. The Money Laundering Team. Half of those guys never leave their desks. Roberts only calls on them when he can't get the printer to work. But yes, rather them than us, he thinks.

'Call them. Tell them there's a body decomposing as we speak, so they'd better cancel their plans tonight.' Then, as he thinks about it: 'Doesn't get O'Malley off the hook, though. He might be handing us a shit sandwich that gets a few white collars into trouble, but it doesn't give us our killer, does it?'

'No. Not that I can see. But it does sort of point to motive. Zhang's walking around killing people, drawing attention to this — whatever this is — and he's spooked enough to be carrying this in his pocket.' Roberts thinks on that.

'Maybe. Fucking tiny maybe. O'Malley was caught with the body in his own basement. He's been off playing private detective and forgets that in the real world you can't go shooting the bad guys.'

Buxton knows Roberts is probably right. But he's annoyed now that he's seeing O'Malley's point of view. Despite himself. Still, when it comes down to it, he doesn't think O'Malley's capable of shooting a man, and even if he is, he'd own it. He's a killer, but he's never been a liar. Which makes for a very confusing moral compass.

Buxton and Roberts come back into the interview room. They both look like the other one's farted.

'We're calling time for today,' Roberts announces. Then: 'You're not going anywhere, O'Malley. We're holding you until the morning.'

O'Malley's good with that. A cell in the station is as safe a place as any right now. His lawyer's not going to let it pass without challenge, though.

'If you haven't got enough to charge my client, I suggest you respect the law and release him now.' Which O'Malley thinks is a red rag to a bull. He'd have stayed quiet. But something's holding them back.

'Forensics is dragging the chain,' Roberts says. 'We'll get that back overnight, then have another wee get-together tomorrow morning. Which gives you,' looking at O'Malley, 'a few hours to decide whether you're sticking to your story, or whether there's another version of events you'd like us to consider.'

'Once the forensics are in, you lose that option, O'Malley.' Buxton, talking tough. But there's something in his voice that gives O'Malley hope. He's wavering.

'Very well. But I'm not happy about it, detectives. I'd like it noted that my client has co-operated fully with your inquiry. And I expect him to be in the same condition tomorrow as he's in now.'

Buxton and Roberts exchange a look, like, what are we, animals?

'Now, I'd like five minutes with my client. Alone.'

Which she gets. Then O'Malley heads off to the cells. He's looking forward to the door closing behind him, because what he really wants now is some sleep.

# CHAPTER TWENTY-NINE

The sun is going down when finally someone looking like the Gabrielle Patterson Claire has googled emerges from the station. Claire introduces herself and gets the good news and the bad news. He hasn't been charged, but they're keeping him overnight. Claire is almost relieved. Not even O'Malley can get himself into harm's way in a police station. She thanks Gabrielle, says she'll see her in the morning. Then doesn't know what to do. So she goes to work, to take her mind off things.

Manu and Chatbox are sitting in Jimmy's office. He wants to go over it again. Exactly what happened. Manu runs through it one more time. The drive into town, meeting the scooter guy, dropping O'Malley off. They did exactly what Jimmy asked, which was to keep an eye on O'Malley's place, be there if anyone else has a run at O'Malley. They watched the place all night, saw O'Malley come back, go in the door. Ten minutes later, there's cops everywhere. Waited until they saw O'Malley again, in the back of a police car. Called Jimmy. Came back to base.

'And you didn't see anything all night?'

'No,' Manu says, at the same time as Chatbox says 'Yes.'

Manu does a double-take, looking at Chatbox who's decided to join in.

'Oh, welcome to the conversation,' Jimmy says. 'What did you see?'

'Saw a guy drive into the car park. 'Bout five am. Came back out at' — Chatbox looks at his phone — 'five twenty-one am.'

Jimmy and Manu look at each other then, like, where do you start with this guy?

'Five twenty-one am exactly?' Jimmy asks. 'You know this how?'

'That's the time that the video says it was recorded.'

Really, where do you start?

'You've got a video of someone leaving the car park at five twenty-one am?'

'Yeah, boss. You told us to keep our eyes open.'

That he did, Jimmy thinks. Doesn't bother to ask Manu what he was doing at the time.

'Well, did you think I might want to see that video?'

'You've only just asked about it, boss. What happened during the night.'

Chatbox takes things very literally. He hands his phone over to Jimmy Tua. Who watches a ute emerge from the ramp that leads to O'Malley's car park. It's dark, but the street lighting is pretty good. He gets a decent view of the truck, gets most of the number plate. And the driver is easy to make out. Jimmy doesn't recognise him, but he's a white guy, big by the look of him. Reckons this is the dude who's been causing all the grief. He hands the phone back to Chatbox.

'Get the phone cleaned up. Take everything off it except that video. Can you do that? Leave nothing on it except the video. Then wipe the phone, get your prints off it.'

'Boss?'

'O'Malley needs that phone more than you do. But unless you want the cops knowing your business, the video is all they need. But it needs the time stamp, and I don't know if that'll be there if we just send the video. So we'll have to use the phone.'

Chatbox doesn't look very happy about it.

'What? You'll get another phone. I've no doubt O'Malley will buy you the best phone you can get.'

'It's not that, boss. Just my pigs. I've got loads of photos of the piglets that were born last week on this phone.'

Jimmy looks to the ceiling for support.

'Fuck's sake. Manu, sort it out. Send the fucking pigs somewhere before you clean the phone. Then bring it back to me.' Manu nods, wanting to get out of there before Jimmy asks why he didn't see the guy at O'Malley's place.

'And Manu? Don't fall asleep on the job again.'

Claire's shift has dragged. It's been a quiet night, and she's missing O'Malley. She's on edge, too. Gabrielle passed a message from O'Malley telling her she's safe; as long as he's in the frame for William, no one's going to come for her. But it nags in the back of her mind, that she's a loose end for Big Tone to deal with. So she fears the worst when a guy approaches her from the shadows as she's leaving The Brandling to head home.

'Claire?' the guy asks. He'd be threatening in daylight, but right now he's terrifying. She reaches into her bag, feeling for the pepper spray she keeps for moments just like this. The guy holds up his hands, indicates he's not here to cause trouble.

'My name's Jimmy. Does that mean anything to you?'

Claire nods.

'Cool. So, I'm not here to cause you harm, OK?'

Claire nods again. Jimmy reaches into his jacket pocket and pulls out a paper bag that's got Chatbox's phone in it. Hands it to Claire.

'Think this might help O'Malley. Can you get it to the cops?'

Claire nods once more. Realises she's becoming a one-trick pony.

'Yes, of course. Thank you?' She doesn't know why that's come out as a question, but her nerves have taken a beating in the last few days.

'No worries. You going home now?'

'Yes?' she replies, again a hint of a question mark slipping out.

'I'll walk with you. You can't be too careful this time of night.' There's no question in Jimmy's voice. So they walk, and they talk, about the bar business, the car business, and by the time they reach Claire's place they've moved on to politics and current events. Once he's sure Claire is home safe, he says goodnight and slips off into the darkness.

Claire doesn't sleep much that night.

O'Malley sleeps like a deaf dog. He's on his own, for a start. Once the door closes him into the cell, O'Malley faces no distractions, no threats, just time. He's got a week's worth of sleep to catch up on, and his body could do with an ice bath, but sleep is the next best thing. He's preparing for a day that could go either way. There's a strong chance that he'll be charged, which means he'll be spending many more nights locked up, but in cells less hospitable than this one. He'll find himself with company, too, which means he'll need his wits about him, as he retreats into survival mode once more. So he takes rest where he can get it, and he's no stranger to a thin mattress and a concrete bed. What will be, will be.

Gabrielle Patterson arrives at the police station promptly, bringing her own coffee, and one for her client, who she expects to be given access to immediately. Before the coffee gets cold.

The front desk staff shrink away from her hawk-like stare and make it happen. It's not long before they're back in an interview room, waiting for Roberts and Buxton to arrive. When they do, they are focused, getting straight back to where they left off.

'William Zhang was killed at approximately four am yesterday morning. Could you please tell us where you were at that time?'

Roberts still reckons O'Malley's in the frame, regardless of whatever conspiracies are getting the MLT all excited in another part of the station.

'I was asleep. At my girlfriend's place.'

'And your girlfriend, Claire Steadman, she can corroborate this?'

'Ms Steadman made a statement to one of your colleagues yesterday, so I think you already know the answer to that question,' Ms Patterson responds for O'Malley.

'And it is your assertion that you were with Ms Steadman all night, returning to your own apartment a little after eight am yesterday morning. That right?'

'Yes.'

'Where you happened upon Mr Zhang's body, which happened to be in your truck, which happened to be in a car park where you had recently been involved in an altercation with Mr Zhang and another unidentified male?'

'It was more than an altercation. It was a knife fight.'

'And it is this knife fight that accounts for the significant blood traces from both yourself and Mr Zhang?'

'My client isn't privy to your forensic discovery, detective, as you well know. Perhaps we can stick to questions he might reasonably know the answers to?'

Roberts is irritable, and she's not helping.

She decides to hurry things along. Reaches into her bag.

'Mr O'Malley has accounted for his whereabouts at the time you have determined the incident occurred. You have not provided any evidence to suggest you can confirm that the location of the crime was the same location in which Mr O'Malley discovered the body. Which suggests you've got some gaps in your timeline. Let me help you.'

Buxton and Roberts exchange a glance as Gabrielle hands them a plastic bag which contains Chatbox's phone. The phone that used to belong to Chatbox.

'This was provided to one of my team early this morning. It contains a video taken, according to the phone data, at five twenty-one yesterday morning. It shows a vehicle leaving the same location where Mr O'Malley discovered Mr Zhang's body. The driver appears to be Tony Jones, who my client has already implicated in a significant organised criminal enterprise that also involved the deceased, Mr Zhang.'

That gets a rise.

'Someone just happened to be taking a video outside a murder scene, featuring someone you want us to believe is involved in some big conspiracy, and whoever took the video just hands their phone over to you to give to us? Do you know how stupid that sounds?'

'Be that as it may, here we are. I'm duty-bound to share the video with you now that I am aware of it.'

'Even if what's on there is what you say, it could have been taken any time, manipulated, anything. Whose phone is it?'

'They didn't leave a name. Most unfortunate. You're right, of course — what can be done with video evidence these days,' she says, pointedly. 'But I'm sure you've got someone scouring local CCTV as we speak, looking for some inconsistency in my client's account. Perhaps you could widen that search, to look for the actual perpetrator? This video simply gives you a place to start.'

Roberts looks at the phone that sits on the table between them. Like it's toxic. But he gives a nod to Buxton anyway, who grabs the bag that holds the phone and steps out of the interview room. Roberts isn't done with the lawyer, though.

'We're going to need whoever took that video. "Anonymous" won't cut it.'

'We'll see what we can do on that front. Whatever we can do to help.'

O'Malley hopes that's a bluff. Thinks his ledger with Jimmy Tua is probably looking pretty bad already. But he senses that Roberts is fighting a losing battle. The facts are getting in the way of a good story.

They can't put him at the scene at the time of William's death.

They'll find O'Malley returning to his apartment when he said he did, and not before.

Unless Tone is very lucky, they'll find him, too, driving to and from O'Malley's place, shortly after William was killed.

It all fits the narrative of Tony Jones dumping the body, which might not be enough on its own to charge him, but is more than enough to put doubt into their minds about their current suspect. It will work wonders in O'Malley's defence if they decide to push ahead and pin William's death on him. A jury knows reasonable doubt when they see it.

Roberts knows how it goes when you waste the Crown's time and money. Yeah, Roberts is losing his grip on O'Malley. And the lawyer knows it, too.

'I'd remind you of my client's rights under the Bill of Rights, detective. You've been holding him for … nineteen hours and thirty minutes. It's getting more arbitrary by the minute.'

Roberts says nothing to that. He ends the interview and leaves the room.

They let O'Malley stew for another three hours.

They've focused all their attention on dotting the i's and crossing the t's on O'Malley's guilt. Now they've got to shift the focus of the investigation, and they've got their i's crossed and their t's dotted.

Buxton and Roberts are sitting in a conference room listening to their colleagues from MLT explain what the USB file is telling them.

It's a big deal.

The sort of bust that leads to promotions, and makes the good guys feel like they're making a dent. What Buxton and Roberts have stumbled on would usually take months of hard graft, but what they've found in William Zhang's pocket does all the hard work for them.

It's literally a fucking map.

All they've got to do is follow it.

Which isn't as easy as it sounds. Because they've got to follow rules. Which means warrants, multiple targets, and co-ordination. They've got to hit everyone at the same time, or close to it. Because giving the game away means time to destroy evidence.

The USB stick is great. But it's not the actual keys to the kingdom.

Not for a jury.

They need paperwork, emails, the stuff that people are familiar with, feel they can understand.

Roberts is trying to share his colleagues' excitement, but he's got a murder to solve. He's following what he's being told, and it's annoyingly consistent with the story O'Malley spun them the day before. But he's still not seeing why it would lead to murder.

'These are white-collar criminals, right? Accountants, lawyers, businessmen. Are they going to risk killing someone to protect themselves? What do these guys get if you catch them? Couple of years in min security? That's a lot different from a life sentence.'

'We're talking millions here, Jim,' says Powell from MLT. 'Tens of millions. A kid kills a pensioner for their next hit, you don't bat an eyelid. Just because these guys wear ties to work doesn't make them any different. Someone starts sniffing around their business, then Zhang's walking around with enough evidence in his pocket to cost these guys fifty mill? Yeah, it's worth killing for.'

'And if you can pin it on the guy who's doing the sniffing, so much the better,' Buxton adds, thinking he's got O'Malley all sorts of wrong.

'That, too,' Powell agrees.

Roberts considers what they're saying. Despite his rep, he's not immune to logic. He wants a result, so if O'Malley's not the guy, he wants the fucker who *is* responsible.

Besides, this is shaping up to be a big result. Nobody takes notice when they put away another wife-beater or street-dealer. But this is major crime. If anyone cares to look closely.

'All right. Well, I want to bring Jones in. See what he's got to say, check that vehicle out, see if Zhang's all over it.'

'Can you wait a few hours?' Powell asks. 'We need to sort a few warrants. We've got Lomas and Howarth, Browning, and Jones. Better to hit them all at once. Better still: hit Howarth first. He's a lawyer. We start talking about conspiracy to murder and he might roll on Jones. See the wind turning. Might make things easier with Jones.'

Roberts gets it, but he's worried about the delay on the truck. If there's anything connecting Zhang's body to Jones's vehicle, he doesn't want time or bleach to get in the way.

'OK, we'll locate Jones, put a car on him. But if he goes anywhere near a car wash, we're taking him, and you'll have to deal with it.'

Powell's good with that. They're standing up to get on with what they need to get on with, when Roberts remembers something from the file Buxton showed him.

'What about the other guy? Robertson. Where does he fit into all this?'

Powell makes a clicking sound with his cheek, says: 'We're not sure. He's taking money from them if the files stack up. For what, I'm not sure. We're going to have to take that one up the line before we go any further. Given, you know?'

Roberts knows. The higher they are, the less likely they are to fall.

The mood's different when they finally come back to O'Malley. Ms Patterson is about ready to have their badges, read them the riot act, start talking about egregious infringements of her client's human rights. But Roberts heads her off before she can get going.

'We have some new lines of enquiry to follow. Your client is free to go. For now.' He's keen to avoid an apology, so doubles down, adding: 'But you're still a suspect, O'Malley. Once we've had a chance to eliminate any other suspects, we'll be back to you.'

Ms Patterson is about to object vehemently, but Buxton steps in and immediately contradicts his colleague.

'What we're looking into, O'Malley, it's going to take us a bit of time to get our ducks in a row. It might be better if you don't advertise you're back on the street.'

O'Malley thinks about that.

He wants to bring the whole house down, but he's also got unfinished business of his own. He settles for a compromise.

'I don't mind if you're a little slow on my paperwork — makes no difference to me. But I've got somewhere I need to be. How's this: I'll stay away from all these guys, and you let me out the back way. I'll stay out of your hair.'

The cops have got no choice. They could charge him with something, hold him longer, but Gabrielle Patterson won't let that slide, and wrongful arrest is expensive.

So they let O'Malley out, through the back door, and hope he doesn't fuck things up.

# CHAPTER THIRTY

Loto Tupuola is angry.

He's angry with his daughter, who is growing up too quickly for his liking, and is going to be in a world of trouble when she finally comes home.

He's angry with his son, who is getting too big for his boots and has no respect for his father. He hopes the lesson he's taught him gives him time to work out who's boss.

He's angry with the world he lives in, a world that is stacked against him and doesn't provide enough opportunity for him, a good family man, just trying to raise a family.

And he's currently really seriously angry with Roy O'Malley. This guy's meant to be the best. He promised he would find Sefina, but it's been almost a week now, and he's done nothing. He hasn't even answered his phone — Loto's been calling for a day now, and O'Malley can't even show him the respect of answering the damn phone.

Well, Loto Tupuola has had enough of the run-around. He's going to find O'Malley and tell him just what he thinks of the guy. Grant must have rocks in his head to think O'Malley was the guy Loto needed. He couldn't find his own prick in the bathtub. Come to think of it, Grant deserves a piece of his mind, too.

Loto Tupuola sets off to give it to him.

It's one of those beautiful March days that suggest summer will never end. The humidity that makes Auckland uncomfortable has gone, but the sun is still fierce, and there's no wind to take the heat out of it. O'Malley stands next to Claire's VW and lets himself feel that heat, taking deep breaths of the air that he could swear tastes different today. Fresher. More oxygenated. He's only been locked up for twenty-four hours, but he's got the same sense of renewed freedom that he got nearly a decade before, stepping back out into the world. He's not out of the woods entirely. Yet. But he knows the cops don't have enough to charge him, and don't really think he pulled the trigger on William Zhang.

Claire's happy just to have him in her sights, breathing. She leaves him to whatever silent ritual he is performing, because she doesn't want to break the silence, and she doesn't want to start their new life together with an argument. Because she knows O'Malley too well, and, whatever he's told the cops, he's going to want to see this through personally. So she's going to wait for him to call their next move. Before she argues against it.

When O'Malley finally speaks, he utters three words that Claire doesn't think she's ever heard him say before, would never have bet on him ever saying.

'Let's go shopping.'

Claire's never had O'Malley down as a retail therapy sort of guy. But she likes that he has surprised her. She was expecting *Let's find Tony*. But it throws her, so she remains silent. O'Malley fills the void.

'Come on, let's go shopping. Out of the city. Let's drive over to St Luke's. I doubt we'll run into trouble on that side of town.'

So they get into Claire's car, O'Malley taking his time to lower his body down into the passenger seat. He's had the best sleep he can remember, but his body is screaming in submission, begging to be left alone for a few days to regroup after all that it's been through. Claire sees him struggle and leans across to help him with the seat belt.

'It's like taking my granddad out for a drive,' she says, laughing. 'Let that be a lesson to you.'

'Yeah, yeah,' O'Malley replies, 'always listen to Claire. I know.'

But he's glad of the help because he really doesn't think he'd have been able to do it on his own. He's thirty-one years old and feels twice that.

'So what are we shopping for, O'Malley?' Waiting for the sting in the tail. Again, he surprises her.

'Clothes. We both deserve some new clothes, the week we've had. We can't very well check into a hotel with me smelling of the cells, and I promised you a night to ourselves, remember?'

'I do,' she says, smiling. Go, O'Malley.

'It's probably best we don't go home for a day or so, let Buxton wrap things up.'

It's either the sleep, or the sobering interrogation, but this is an all-new, sensible O'Malley sitting in Claire's car. She likes it. So she doesn't break the spell, and they set off to do something they've never done before together: shopping for clothes like a regular, ordinary, domesticated couple.

It's quite the shopping trip. O'Malley's got some new jeans, but smart ones, dark denim, which Claire thinks look great with the dress shirt she's persuaded him to buy. He wanted three black t-shirts, but she's got him in a dark blue shirt patterned with small palm trees. He concedes that it looks good on him. And the long sleeves cover the forearms that in their current state make him look like an aggressive self-harmer. Claire's gone to town herself, and she's found a little black dress that is trim at the waist and flares at the hem. It would look silly without a new pair of shoes to go with it, though, so she gets those, too. She's enjoying the role of kept woman, more so when she sees that O'Malley's a little uncomfortable as the shop assistant wraps the lingerie that goes with the dress. Claire makes it quicker than she could have done, because O'Malley's a fish out of water, and she wants to get him to a hotel before he changes his mind.

O'Malley's got one last thing to buy, and he pulls Claire across the mall, heading for JB Hifi.

'If you're buying a PlayStation for our night in a hotel, I'm divorcing you,' she says.

'Nope. No PlayStation. We need a phone — for Chatbox. Whichever one's got the best camera at the moment.' He wants to settle all his debts before they get old. Claire's filled him on what Jimmy told her about Chatbox and his videos and his pig pix. They buy the best phone available and agree to drop it off with Jimmy before they go to the hotel.

They put all their new purchases in the back of the VW and repeat the exercise of getting O'Malley safely belted up.

'So, where to? Jimmy's? I'll need you to direct me.'

'No, Jimmy's second. First, I just want to pop my head in and check the kids are behaving themselves at Grant's. That OK?'

'I guess so. But quick, O'Malley, OK? You've spent enough time looking out for other people for one week.'

They head to Grant's.

When O'Malley and Claire pull up outside Grant's house they see Loto Tupuola standing on the doorstep, gesticulating wildly, and giving Grant every piece of his mind. O'Malley takes a deep breath, because while he's had plenty of sleep, he's tired of men like Loto.

Grant's got both arms out, his hands resting on the frame of his doorway, blocking the entrance and making it clear that Loto's not coming in. When he sees O'Malley walking up the path towards the house, he holds a hand up, like he's got this. But Loto's blowing hot air and he's not showing any signs of cooling down.

Then Sefina shows her face over Grant's shoulder. *Now* Loto's got something to shout about. So much for the mild and timid man that O'Malley offered help to. Now he's trying to reach past Grant, to grab his daughter like she's his property. O'Malley figures it's time to draw his attention away from the house.

'Mr Tupuola? I think it's time we had a word.'

Loto turns and sees that it's the so-called detective who promised he'd find his daughter. The one who doesn't answer his phone and didn't find his daughter. Now he's not sure where to direct his anger, so he shares it liberally with them all.

'Fucking O'Malley! I asked you to find Sefina, and you've done nothing. And now I find her here, with Grant. What the fuck is going on? Sefina, get out here now! We're going home.'

O'Malley's really very tired of Loto Tupuola.

'Sefina's not going home with you, Loto. You asked me to check that Sefina was safe. Now she is. Will be. So she's staying here, and you're going home.'

Loto doesn't know what's going on. *His* daughter. Will do what *he* says.

'I'll call the cops on all of you,' he says. 'Sefina does what I say, and the law will back me up, too.'

'Well, you're welcome to call the cops, Loto. Please do. Maybe we'll ask them to a chat with Sefina, maybe visit your boy, too. I spoke to Scott Cranshaw, Loto. You lost your rights when you chased your first daughter to her death.'

'Fuck you. That boy's a liar, and she's no better,' he says, throwing an arm in Sefina's direction. 'This is my business, not yours, not Grant's.'

He's getting louder, and more sure of his ground. It's going to get physical pretty soon.

Which it does.

Claire walks past O'Malley and up to Loto Tupuola, and slaps him hard, a full right palm planting itself on his cheek, with follow-through. He's too shocked to respond, but Grant and O'Malley are both prepared if he tries to retaliate. They both know now that he's comfortable hitting a woman. But Claire's tired of Loto, too, and she's only just met him. She stares him down and asks him a question.

'Have you heard of Jimmy Tua, Mr Tupuola?'

'What? What the fuck? Yes, I've heard of him.'

'Well, he hasn't heard of you yet. But he will. If you don't go home now, if you ever come back here, if you try to contact Sefina, he will hear about you. And Jimmy's got some pretty strong views on parenting, Loto. Think of him as Sefina's new godfather. He's very protective.'

Loto processes the threat. Recognises it's real. And starts crying, playing the wounded father routine that worked so well first time around with O'Malley. But no one is buying it. He's muttering all manner of things, but he's walking slowly backwards as he does so. Away from the house, and away from Sefina.

O'Malley's standing with his mouth open. His chick is really something.

Claire gives him a wink and says hello to Grant as she steps past him into the house. As if nothing's happened.

# CHAPTER THIRTY-ONE

The kids are all right. For now. O'Malley takes Grant to one side, tells him to keep an eye on Jesse the next couple of days because he's probably going to get some bad news about his father before too long. He's going to need looking after. Grant's cool with that. O'Malley wants to get going, but Sefina's taken a shine to Claire, and they're chatting like BFFs. He reckons Sefina could do with someone older she can actually look up to, so he lets them talk for a while. Enjoys just sitting in the kitchen, drinking tea, hearing the sounds of a house that's full of life and free of conflict.

They head off once Claire's promised Sefina they will hang out at the weekend. She's as soft as O'Malley when given the opportunity.

'To Jimmy?' Claire asks.

'Yep, to Jimmy. Whom you seem to know very well, all of a sudden?'

'What? Oh, yeah, he and I go way back,' she responds.

And when they get to Jimmy's car yard/HQ, she gives the gang boss a long hug to prove the point. O'Malley rolls with it, because he's not surprised by anything anymore.

O'Malley and Jimmy half-shake, half-hug, and talk about where things are at. Jimmy seems satisfied. O'Malley makes a point of asking Jimmy to pass his thanks on to Manu, and goes one better with Chatbox, giving Jimmy the phone that he's bought for him and had gift-wrapped.

'That, you've got to give to him yourself,' Jimmy says, and

hollers out for Chatbox, who emerges from a back room, speed-walking to his boss.

'Hey, I wanted you to have this,' O'Malley says. He hands the box to Chatbox, who looks at the wrapping, and the bow that's been placed around the box, and hesitates to take it, like it's going to explode in his hands.

'Go on, take it. I owe you. It's got a good camera on it. Hear you like taking pictures.'

Chatbox takes the gift and slowly unwraps it. He looks stunned, and his head and shoulders start nodding repeatedly, like he's picking up a beat, ready to join a song. When he looks up, his eyes are glassy, and he finally speaks.

'Thanks, O'Malley. Thanks, bro.' He looks to Jimmy Tua, wondering if it's alright to leave, and when he gets permission he goes back to wherever he came from, still nodding away to himself.

O'Malley looks to Jimmy, his eyebrows asking what that was about.

'That boy's never received a birthday card, never mind a present. You blew his mind, is all.'

O'Malley thinks about that for a second.

'So, we good?' he asks Jimmy.

'We're good, O'Malley. We're good. Don't be a stranger. You're always welcome — when Claire's with you.'

O'Malley thinks about that for a second, too. They really are best buddies.

As they walk back to the car, O'Malley and Claire hear someone singing from the back room. Chatbox, finding his voice.

'OK, O'Malley. Where to? Which hotel are you treating me to?'

O'Malley looks across to her, doesn't answer straight away. Claire joins the dots.

'Oh, come on, O'Malley. Really? A busman's holiday?'

He's taking her to the casino hotel, of all places.

'I know, I know, but here's why. First, there's more security there, and cameras, than anywhere in the city. We're not safe yet. And there's no way anyone can make a move on us there. Second, I know a guy who knows a guy. They've got rooms they keep aside for the high-rollers they bring in from overseas. Tonight, we're the high-rollers, baby. A proper suite, bath that looks out over the city, Champagne on arrival, the works.'

'OK, you might have persuaded me. What's the third reason?'

'How do you know there's a third reason?'

'There's always three. Whenever you try to argue with me, there's always three reasons. One logical, one emotional, and the real reason. So, what's the real reason?'

'Those are the real reasons. But also, I guess, it's where all this shit started. It seems like the right place to be when it all ends.'

Claire nods, sees why he thinks that.

The suite is spectacular. There's a large lounge overlooking the city, and sea views reminding you which city you're in, the absence of smog a real drawcard for the international traveller. Two bedrooms peel off the lounge. Both have en suites. The master bathroom really does have a tub that overlooks the city. It's one of those sleek, white, ultra-modern baths that appear to have no plumbing, and the taps sit in the middle, leaving both ends free, an open invitation to share a bath with a friend. The décor is all dark wood, with subtle accents of colour, soft furnishings and padded headboards completing the look. The lighting is moody and warm, however much you play with the settings. It's demanding that sins be committed, like someone's going to be offended if you don't live out at least some of your fantasies while you're here.

Claire's misgivings about the hotel's location disappear. This, she could get used to. She's got the bathwater running before O'Malley's even closed the door. Claire throws herself backwards onto the bed, spreads herself out, starfish, like a little girl who's got her own room for the first time.

'This is more like it, O'Malley. Tell the cops to take as long as they want — I'm happy here for as long as it takes.'

'I'm glad you like it, madam,' he says, transferring the clothes they've bought into the wardrobe. 'Would madam like a glass of Champagne with her bath?'

'*Madam* would like a glass of Champagne by the bath, and a tall, dark, handsome man *in* the bath. Can that be arranged?'

'I will see what we can do, madam.' But he's already out of his clothes, such is the service when high-rollers come to town.

They spend the afternoon reacquainting themselves with one another, because that's what a man needs when he first gets out of jail. One bath and two showers later, they're getting pretty hungry. Scratch that. Claire's getting pretty hungry. O'Malley's happy to keep doing what they've been doing. But he could probably stretch to some room service. He says as much.

'Nope. Not good enough. Don't you want me to wear the dress you bought me? You'll need to take me downstairs, wine and dine me, and then maybe I'll be persuaded to come back to your suite. Deal?'

Deal. But first O'Malley wants to check that the coast is clear. Buxton and his mates have had plenty of time to start sweeping up. He puts the call in while Claire's finishing up. He needs the distraction, or she's never getting that dress on.

O'Malley gets Claire up to speed as they take the private elevator down from the suite. They've picked Howarth up, and, with warrants in hand, they're all over the lawyers' offices. They got to Browning even quicker, because they already had a van-load of cops parked at the end of his driveway. There's a bit of bickering going on behind the scenes, because the surveillance crew were convinced they had a significant drug operation in their sights, and they're a bit sniffy now they know it's just a bit of money moving about. Lomas, the other lawyer, is on a flight back from the Cook Islands, where he seems to have spent a lot of time in the past year, so he's getting a lift back into town when he lands.

'And Tony?' Claire asks, as they walk across the gaming floor of the casino.

'No sign of him. Roberts is doing his nut because he wants him for William's murder, and the forensics will be going stale.'

'So where does that leave us?'

'Safe here. If we stay here, under all these cameras, we're fine.'

He points to the glass domes that scatter the ceiling every five metres or so. They're there to protect the chips, watch for cheating, or to catch out a light-fingered dealer, but they'll do just as well offering Claire and O'Malley protection for the night.

'All right, then. Wanna teach me how to play blackjack?' Claire's moving towards the tables that line the centre of the cavernous room.

'I thought you wanted dinner?'

'Oh, I do. But it'll taste so much better if we win it.' She's got that mischievous look in her eye that tells O'Malley she's out to play. He's happy to go along for the ride.

As they walk towards the blackjack tables, O'Malley pulls up suddenly and grabs Claire's arm.

'Hold on, baby.'

'What is it?'

'There.'

He points to the middle of the pit, where Big Tone is walking bold as brass, king of the fucking hill, like he doesn't have a care in the world. He's obviously not up to speed on what's been happening in the real world, beyond the fake embrace and false hope that the casino takes so much care to cultivate. He's ambling towards the rear of the casino, not showing any signs that he's worried about being seen.

'Hold on,' O'Malley says to Claire, and he gets his phone out to call Buxton.

'No news, O'Malley.'

'You didn't look very hard,' O'Malley responds.

'What do you mean?'

'I mean I'm standing in the casino and I'm looking straight at Tony Jones.'

'Fuck's sake. I mean, that's good, but — oh, whatever. Now listen very carefully, O'Malley, we'll be there in ten minutes, max. Do not, whatever you do, go near him. Do you understand me?'

But O'Malley hangs up then. He couldn't do what he was told even if he wanted to. Because Claire has already gone ahead and picked up Tone's trail, and she's in step with him now, making it impossible for O'Malley to call her back without alerting Tone to his tail.

Tone's heading for the lifts at the rear of the casino, and Claire is right there with him as he waits for the next available elevator to take him down to the car park below. Tone looks to his right and sees the pretty woman standing next to him, giving her a smile. Claire smiles right back, no hint of fear or concern for Tone to pick up on. She's really quite something. The lift arrives, and, after standing to one side to allow an old couple to exit, Tony allows Claire to enter first, then follows her in. O'Malley's got no choice but to follow, waiting until the doors begin to close before slipping into the lift and joining the party.

Inside the lift they are not alone; there are three unsuspecting punters calling it a day and heading to their cars down below in the bowels of the building. Tony's on one side of the lift, O'Malley on the other. Claire is standing at the rear of the lift, behind the strangers, as if ready to referee this unusual showdown.

O'Malley raises his chin in recognition, opening the conversation.

'You winning, Tone?'

Tony takes his time answering. He's considering the question that has probably been asked innocently inside this lift a thousand times.

'I think I am' is his answer.

There's a natural pause as the lift stops at Level Two and the other passengers get out, blissfully unaware of the changing temperature they leave behind. Now it's just O'Malley, Claire and Big Tone, but the lift feels full, with little room to move for any of the occupants.

'Hmmm,' O'Malley says, doing some calculating of his own. 'I think you may be over-valuing your hand.'

Tony looks at Claire now, who's staring straight ahead, looking nervous just like any woman would when she's stuck in a confined space with two big men who appear to be reaching a disagreement. He obviously thinks she's going to be out of there as soon as she gets the chance, so when he responds to O'Malley he ditches the metaphors and gets straight to the point.

'Well, you're here, I guess, so that's not a good sign. But what have you got, really, O'Malley? A bit of guesswork? Nothing solid, that's for sure.'

'Hmmm. Maybe. But I think William had some sort of insurance on him when he … Well, you know what happened to William.'

'Bullshit. William didn't know anything.' But he's starting to look rattled. Claire's staring at her toes now, her faux anxiety now all too real.

'What I didn't get was why Danny had to go.' O'Malley's pushing for Tony to spill, but his opponent isn't giving anything more away, and a silence consumes the small space. Claire fills the vacuum.

'I've got a theory on that, if I may?' Claire joining the conversation takes Tony by surprise, and he adjusts his posture, standing tall and no longer leaning against the elevator wall. O'Malley mirrors him, also readying himself for action.

'What's your theory?' O'Malley asks Claire, staring straight ahead at Big Tone.

'Well, we know that Danny saw something he shouldn't have in the Parnell casino. *Your* Parnell casino, Tony. I'm sure it won't take the police long to connect the address to you. Anyway, Danny saw something. But we didn't know what. But then O'Malley visited your lawyer, who panicked. So suddenly there you are having a heated little lunch with the lawyer and Patrick Robertson, who happens to be our Minister for Immigration.'

Tony is shifting from foot to foot now. Claire's batting a perfect game so far.

'But there could be plenty of reasons for that. I'm sure you've got a few. But O'Malley remembers seeing a Crown car in the alley behind your house the night of the game. So — and join in if I get anything wrong — this is what I reckon.

'I think you got Robertson on the hook for something. You compromised him somehow. Dirty pictures, something like that? Anyway, once you've got him on the hook, you start paying him, too, so he can't claim blackmail down the track. So — and this is just a theory — he likes them young and Asian? And Danny took the wrong door when he went for a smoke. So he walks in on Robertson, balls deep, pardon my French. William, or you, panic, and decide to spare the minister's blushes. Warm?'

Tony's keeping a strong poker face, but his weak eye is starting to twitch a little.

'Why? Why would I want to have a minister on the payroll? That makes no sense.'

'Yeah, we thought that, too. You've already got a lawyer on the team, so you can push through all the visas you need to service your little empire. But it's not the little guys who make the big bucks, is it? It's a shame for you that Bobby Q was at the game with Danny and O'Malley.'

'What's Bobby Q got to do with it?' Tony asks, but everything in his slow delivery says he knows the answer.

'I did a bit of digging. Bobby had his own, quite public, battles for a visa. He got citizenship when everyone knew he was wanted back in China. He got the visa, even though he'd been red-flagged by Interpol. I didn't really think that stuff happened, but it turns out it really does. So, despite being a wanted man, despite senior officials saying he should be denied citizenship, he gets it anyway.

Because your mate Patrick Robertson signs it off.'

Claire's happy to tag-team with O'Malley and lets him take over.

'So what Danny walked in on wasn't just a mate of yours in a compromising position. You've worked out how to make real money. What did you charge Bobby Q? Five million, something like that? And Bobby's not the only one, is he? You're selling safe harbour to the highest bidders.'

Tony's definitely heard enough now, and the lift doors open to Level Six of the parking lot, the end of the line for the elevator, and possibly for Big Tone, too. He's got a decision to make, and the odds of out-running O'Malley don't look good. But when he does move, it's with surprising pace. Still inside the lift, he places his right foot in the path of the doors, ensuring they don't close, and swiftly grabs Claire with his left hand, pulling her in close. In his right, he's holding a utility knife, and, before O'Malley has a chance to move, the blade is hovering over the side of Claire's neck, worryingly close to her carotid.

'Here's what's going to happen,' Tone says, with the confidence of a man who's got someone's life in their hands. 'You are going back up in this lift,' he says to O'Malley, before turning his head towards Claire, his voice almost down to a whisper in her ear, 'while we go to my car. Maybe I'll take you with me, or maybe I'll leave you behind. But one thing's for certain, O'Malley, if you come anywhere near us, her blood will be on your hands.'

O'Malley is working through the permutations and realises he's got little choice but to comply. His mind is racing, but his body is taking a few beats to catch up, and even as he knows Tone has the upper hand, he takes a step towards him, testing the waters. Tony sees the move and emphasises his deadly seriousness, pressing the blade of his knife into Claire's neck just enough to draw blood. Claire flinches away from the blade, but Tone moves his hand accordingly, and the pressure of the knife remains constant. O'Malley shows willing and retreats, holding his hands up in front of him in surrender.

'It's OK, O'Malley. We've got no choice. Do as he says — I'll be fine.' Claire's voice is much calmer than O'Malley expects, and reminds him that she's no damsel in distress. She's stood beside him every step of the way in his quest for the truth, formed bonds with gangsters, and slapped sense into domineering fathers. She'll do everything she can to avoid the harm that Big Tone threatens now. He steps back into the lift, acquiescing to the man's demands.

'OK, Tone, you win. But know this, if you hurt her, you will die. I promise you that. The only hope you've got is if she is left unharmed.'

'Sure, whatever, O'Malley. Thanks for the heads-up.' Tony steps out of the lift, pulling Claire with him, and walking backwards towards the doors that connect the lobby to the parking bays beyond. He pauses, waiting for O'Malley to fulfil his part of the bargain. O'Malley steps forward to press the button for Level Five, desperately hoping to minimise the time spent separated from Claire. As he presses the button he tries to communicate with Claire, using his eyes to will her to stay safe. Then the doors close in, and he's on his own, with the worst-case scenario consuming his thoughts.

Once the doors have closed and Tony's sure the lift is actually moving, he tries to pick up the pace, turning Claire around so that they are walking forwards, through the doors into the parking structure. Claire's smart enough to know that struggling at this point could be fatal: Tony's only objective is escape, and he could dump her now and move more quickly on his own. But she's also the only insurance he's got, and he's showing no signs of giving that up just yet. So she keeps pace with him, but tries to slow him down by talking. In her experience, a lot of men seem to struggle doing two things at once, so she throws the dice and questions his logic.

'What exactly are you hoping to achieve here, Tony? It's like you're throwing good money after bad.' To Claire's surprise, he bites, hubris forcing him to respond to the challenge, prove his strategy is the right one.

'What are you talking about? It's a bit late to be questioning my approach, don't you think? O'Malley's out of the picture, and soon enough I'll be out of here.'

'Yeah, but to what end? You're just making it worse for yourself. This place is full of cameras, and now you're adding kidnapping, and whatever else this is, to whatever other charges you're already facing. It's like you don't know when to fold.' Her final words land as intended, and Tony tenses up as his skills are called in to question.

'You talk too much. I might help you out in that regard if you can't stop yourself. Anyway, what this is, is just a little domestic — no big deal. I've got some loose ends to attend to, so I'm leaving while I can. Now get a move on.' With that, Tony pulls Claire more firmly, which causes her to lose her footing, one of her high heels giving up on her, and she stumbles to the ground, which slows them down just enough for O'Malley to spot them and move swiftly to the bottom of the inclined bay that they are now halfway up.

O'Malley has been in some spots before, but his sense of helplessness as the lift doors closed on him was profound, the stress causing sharp pains in his lower back. His worst fears were realised when he reached Level Five and it was clear that the lift had instructions to continue travelling upwards once the doors closed in on him again. He stuck his leg between the doors and exited the lift, with no option but to wait for another lift to descend and get him back to Level Six. He couldn't take the risk of trying to change levels on foot — the construction of the car park was a bewildering combination of downward inclines coupled with flat stretches that were likely to lead you further away from your planned destination. The wait for another lift felt like another year of jail time, but when it did arrive, O'Malley jumped inside and pressed the button for Level Six a dozen times, willing the doors to close and his journey to pick up speed.

When he got back to Level Six he was alert to any sound that would send him in the right direction. He had three paths to choose from: left, which led to a flat stretch of parking bays the length of the building; right, which mirrored the left-hand side; or the central path, which was the stretch of parking that inclined upwards towards the exits many levels above. He couldn't see Tone or Claire from where he stood, but then he heard a faint noise of movement that sounded like it was coming from above. He raced to the bottom of the ramp in the middle, and saw Claire on the ground, Tony Jones towering above her.

'Get away from her, Tone!' O'Malley shouts, hoping to provide enough distraction to give Claire the opportunity to scramble away from the man above her holding a knife. Tony looks down at O'Malley at the bottom of the ramp, and looks back up the ramp towards his car, gauging the relative distances and his chances of escape. It's obviously not stacking up in his favour, because he grabs Claire roughly by the arm and pulls her to her feet, closing his forearm around her chest, and placing the knife blade once more against her neck.

'Stay where you are, O'Malley. Two more minutes and I'm out of here. Shame for your girlfriend to get hurt now.' He starts walking backwards slowly, keeping a firm grip on Claire as he does so. O'Malley ignores the command, and begins walking up the ramp, trying to close the distance between them. In that, at least, he is successful, because Tony is being hampered by Claire's inconsistent footwear; she's got one bare foot and a high-heeled shoe still enclosing the other. Keeping up with Tony is difficult, so he pretty much has to carry her. When he sees O'Malley pursuing them, Big Tone decides to signal his intent, and quickly swipes the blade across Claire's ear lobe, causing an immediate flow of blood to fall down onto her shoulder and the dress that is only hours old. Claire doesn't give Tony the satisfaction of screaming, but mutters something short and appropriate that O'Malley can't hear.

'I warned you, O'Malley. Any closer and I'll make it count.'

They are nearing the middle of the ramp now, so O'Malley figures that Tone's car must be close. There's an intersection a metre or so behind Tone that connects ramps and levels in the car park, and if the car were on the other side he figures Tone would have used a different lift exit. O'Malley's wondering what to do, Claire's immediate safety his only concern. He's running out of ideas. So he discovers faith in the power of prayer when Buxton quietly appears on the ramp above Big Tone, flanked by four uniformed officers who all look like they mean business. Two already have tasers drawn as Buxton seizes control of the situation.

'Police!' Buxton shouts, getting Tony's attention and causing him to turn towards the newcomers. 'Let her go and drop the weapon.'

Claire, who up to this point has been the model of restraint, decides enough is enough. She does two things at once, both of which take Big Tone by surprise. She drives her remaining heel hard into the top of Tony's left foot, while sinking her teeth into the forearm that holds her in Tone's hostile embrace. All of which elicits a howl from Big Tone and is enough for his grip on Claire to weaken. Claire falls to the ground, putting space between her body and the weapon that Tony Jones has in his hand, and providing the policemen behind her with a window of opportunity. The cop to Buxton's right wastes no time discharging his taser into Big Tone's back. Electricity courses through his nervous system and Tone seizes up, crumpling to the ground.

O'Malley is running from the moment Claire lifts her heel above Tone's foot, and now he's put himself between Claire and Big Tone, acting as a shield in case Tone gets a second wind. The taser could incapacitate a man twice Tone's size, but O'Malley's taking no chances. When he sees Tone weakly look up from his foetal position, O'Malley instinctively closes his fist and punches him, just once, and puts him to sleep.

Big Tone is down, and out for the count.

# CHAPTER THIRTY-TWO

Buxton's got a few choice words for O'Malley, but they are for show more than anything. He's got Tony Jones in custody, so there's not much to be gained from arguing about how it went down. Big Tone's getting a cursory check-up from the medics that arrive on-scene, but they are more concerned with ensuring that Claire's injuries are only superficial. They clean the graze on her neck and patch her ear up, and suggest she go to the hospital, just to be sure, but she waves them away. She's got enough adrenalin working through her veins to keep her going for a week. Despite O'Malley's attempts to persuade her otherwise, she insists they make a night of it, which involves a quick change out of her bloody clothes and her first foray into O'Malley's natural habitat.

Claire figures that escaping relatively unscathed from a knife-wielding murderer means her luck is in, and she decides to try her hand at blackjack. She turns a hundred bucks into four hundred, which she reckons is more than enough to treat O'Malley to dinner. It doesn't go quite as far as she thought it would in the expensive Japanese restaurant down on Federal Street. But it's a celebration, and spending winnings is sweeter than spending hard-earned cash, so she's happy as she pays the outsize bill.

But they don't stay out for long. They have two beds, two baths and three ottomans to keep them occupied upstairs. And when they finally exhaust one another, they share the king-size bed in the master bedroom. O'Malley wakes in the morning in exactly the same position that he fell asleep in. With Claire resting her head in his armpit, her legs wrapped over his. He had no dreams in the night.

Buxton leaves it until a respectable time in the morning to call O'Malley, giving him a heads-up. No one is going anywhere anytime soon. SOCO, or CSI, or whatever they call themselves these days, have had a long and successful night. Big Tone might well be a borderline genius in moving money, but he let himself down when it came to moving William. Even this early, they have plenty to tie Tone to William's death, and they've tracked his movements pretty much all the way back to the original crime scene.

It wasn't hard to work out where William had been shot. Because when the police raided Browning's farm, they found another body in the barn, which Browning hadn't got around to dealing with. Buxton's guess is that this is the other guy who attacked O'Malley, but he'll need O'Malley to confirm that when he can make himself available.

Paul Howarth has been incredibly helpful. He isn't having any part of a murder. He's claiming ignorance on everything. Sure, he's set up some companies, and helped his client move monies around, but that's what lawyers are for. Lomas isn't being any more revealing. But they have both been quick to offer assistance to MLT in identifying all of Tony's companies, and showing how they all link back to Tony Jones. Including, of course, a house that doubled as a casino, in the old part of Parnell.

No one is making much of Patrick Robertson's involvement, and when Big Tone tries to offer a trade, it doesn't get any takers. Even Buxton knows to quit while he is ahead. Taking down a minister will have to wait for another day. Gabrielle Patterson accepts this outcome, too, even if it conflicts with her reasons for taking O'Malley's case. No doubt considering that dirt on a government minister might come in useful down the track for a lawyer looking for leverage.

Claire and O'Malley eventually check out of their high-roller suite. Claire insists he drag her kicking and screaming. O'Malley's sad to leave, too, because he's not an idiot — but he can't help wondering how much dirty money has passed through that room. How much is flowing through the casino at that very moment, as they descend in the lift, back to reality. But it's not his problem. He settles for what he's achieved, which is to uncover the truth, or most of it. Danny's death has been solved, and if Big Tone gets convicted then O'Malley will call it closure.

O'Malley broke his own rule that night in the suite. He took a risk and let himself sleep alongside Claire. And it turns out everything was just fine when he woke in the morning. So Claire persuades him to try it again the next night. And for three nights after that. And the world doesn't end, and O'Malley sleeps, undisturbed. Better than he can remember ever sleeping. Which means Claire has been right about that, too.

So, as he sits on his balcony, on another glorious March day in Auckland, he thinks that he's pretty much got this whole life thing sorted. Claire's sitting alongside him, resting her feet on O'Malley's knees, and she's chuckling to herself as she reads the front page of the *Herald*, which O'Malley has already read, so he knows what's making her laugh. The government are in damage control. It seems there's been a security breach, and a minister's files have been stolen and published online. The government is trying to claim the moral high ground, outraged by the crime, but they're also trying to manage what's in those files. It's manna from heaven for the scandal-hungry press. The minister, it seems, has some unusual expense claims on his official credit card. Hotel porn is the main headline.

'Ha. Who pays for hotel porn anymore, anyways?' Claire asks. Along with everyone else in the country. 'It's not a good look, though. Porn, escorts, using the Crown car for visits to brothels. He's fucked, isn't he?' She's loving every minute of it.

O'Malley's enjoying it, too. Because he knows that if someone's got into Robertson's files — someone talented, like Milo, for example — then they've probably found those bitcoin codes, too.

And Robertson is probably wondering where his money has gone. What's he going to do? Complain that he's been robbed? No. He'll keep his mouth shut, as he sits on the backbenches in disgrace and reflects that at least he's not in jail.

So, yeah, O'Malley, thinks, life's pretty good right now. Sitting here, watching the boats go back and forth beneath a cloudless sky, with Claire using him as a footstool.

Claire and O'Malley. The detectives.

* * *